Passion's DUTY

ROMANCE AND THE AMERICAN RANGER, BOOK ONE

LIZZIE JENKS

eBook ISBN 978-1-960402-02-8
Print ISBN 978-1-960402-03-5

Wheel Horse Press
685 Watervliet Shaker Rd., #461
Latham, NY 12110-9998

Book Cover by Emily's World of Design
Editing by Lucky Author

First edition 2025

LizzieJenks.com

ACKNOWLEDGEMENTS

A huge thank you to the readers who have picked up this book and my previous book. You are the reason I write. And an especially big thank you to readers who have left reviews. Those are key to people finding books they will love, and they are more precious than gold to authors. Thank you from the bottom of my heart!

This book could not have been written without the constant feedback and encouragement of my writing group. So, thank you to the lovely ladies of the FLFLS, and to Andrée Cusson, for her trademark brilliant beta-read of the entire manuscript.

A big thank you also to Bryn and Gill Donovan, of Lucky Author, for their quick, professional, and ever-so-helpful editing and proofreading services. And to Emily, from Emily's World of Design, for her gorgeous cover design work.

And finally, thank you to my family, both two-legged and four-legged, for their patience and support. Love you!

Chapter 1

THE MOHAWK VALLEY, NEW YORK COLONY, FORTY MILES WEST OF ALBANY, APRIL, 1755

James Carroll stopped under the dense canopy of trees before a bend in the trail and cocked his head to listen. Squirrels chattered above him, and birds sang and argued. No sign that anything had disturbed the vast forest surrounding them.

Bloody hell.

He glanced over his shoulder and gestured to David to follow him around the bend. Neither friend swung his musket off his shoulder as they stepped silently along the deer path. Unfortunately, nothing indicated the need.

James slapped at a mosquito. They were worse than the midges he grew up with in Ireland. And bigger. Normally, they swarmed David, but apparently, there was too much competition for his flesh today.

James killed another one. He could have smeared bear grease on his skin to keep them at bay, but that stank, and it was impossible to wash off his shirt, breechcloth, and wool leggings.

David's voice came quietly from behind him. "Kill a few more, please."

James just grunted. He wasn't hunting mosquitoes. Mosquitoes were not going to earn him any rank in William Johnson's household. With most of Johnson's top men off with Johnson himself in Virginia, James was in charge of protecting his patron's holdings, and this was exactly the sort of opportunity he had hired on for.

They were trying to track and gain intelligence about any raiding parties or scouts trying to spy on Johnson's compound. That assumed the French wouldn't send a larger force to attack while Johnson was away. They weren't at war, but General Braddock was in the colonies with a large force and was raising an even larger one. The French weren't daft. They knew what that meant and were presumably doing the same.

David muttered something in Mohawk. James didn't catch the words, not that he would have understood many of them.

As they walked, James scoured the ground in front of him, looking for any signs of recent human passage.

David silently bumped his arm and then gestured for him to stop.

James cocked his head, and David pointed to a downed tree. James studied it, pulse picking up.

"Sit so I can eat something and get the stone out of my moccasin," David said, his voice barely audible.

James released his breath. What a gobshite. "You're worse than Okwaho." David's cousin could eat more than any man James had met.

David sat himself on the log, adjusting his shirt tail and breechcloth to make sure the coarse bark didn't scratch his ballocks.

James grasped the front of his own damp hunting shirt and peeled it away from his skin. He repeated the motion several times to get some air moving to cool his torso. April weather was odd here. One day it could snow a foot, and the next it could get fiercely hot, like today. He adjusted his own breechcloth and sat on the log. Then he retied the strips that held his leggings to his belt and flicked a mosquito off the bare skin of his thigh. At least he didn't stink of bear.

David pulled some dried meat out of a pouch hanging from his tumpline and handed a piece to James.

James raised the stiff venison to his mouth and gnawed off a small chunk. "How did you survive to adulthood with all your teeth eating this stuff?"

David's face softened, his expression almost wistful. "I missed it when I was at school eating English food."

James shifted on the log and looked away. There was no point in being jealous of David's education.

David gave James's arm a hearty slap. "How did you survive to adulthood with any teeth at all, eating nothing?"

James had at least managed to keep all of his teeth, which was more than anyone in his family back in Ireland could say. Abject poverty didn't lend itself to a pleasing smile.

He yanked off another piece of meat, chewed it hard, and swallowed, scanning the woods again. The most that he and David could do was track any French they found and report back to Johnson on their movements. It would be stupid to engage a larger party, unless they got very lucky and one of the French wandered off to take a piss or something. Then they could bring back a captive, question him, and get a better sense of what the French intended.

But all James saw was some wolf shit.

David pulled a pamphlet from his pack and started to read as he ate, but then he waved it at James. "Tanaghrisson may have been rash to kill the Frenchman, but that Virginian was making your people look foolish. He talked like a big war chief, but wouldn't fight the French until Tanaghrisson led him to them." David looked at James, his brows low and serious. "You British need to do better if you expect the Kanienka-haka to stay allied with you."

James ground his teeth. He wasn't British, and David damned well knew it.

He didn't sound Irish anymore, though. In fact, he just sounded like a New York provincial. And being accepted by the British was the only way for a poor Irishman to make his way. William Johnson had done it. Johnson's uncle had, too—Johnson's uncle was an admiral in the British navy, for the love of God. If they could, he could. Even if they had started out with more coin in their pockets, they were as Irish as he was.

And David was right. The Virginia militia had blundered in letting Tanaghrisson kill the Frenchman. That had moved the French and English much closer to war. But war made opportunities for men like James.

The sun glinted through the thick blanket of leaves above them.

David shoved the pages at James. "That Virginia colonel is incompetent."

James smacked the pamphlet away. He wasn't about to struggle through trying to read the damned thing in front of David.

David glared at James. "You need to read up or you'll be stumbling in the dark."

James gave him a friendly side hug that turned into a headlock. "Why do I need to read up on it when I have you to drone on about it until my ears bleed?" Then he released David's head. "We need to move out."

David stood and slung his musket over his shoulder, then James did the same, careful not to catch his long queue under the strap. No need to yank his own scalp off when plenty of French and Abenaki were itching to do it for him.

He listened to the woods before moving.

David eyed the wolf shit. "Sucks eggs to be a slow squirrel." He gestured at an undigested clump of gray fur in the middle of the pile.

It did, indeed.

The birds and the faster squirrels still chattered. The critters in the woods were an excellent warning system if you knew to listen, and they had obviously not detected any threatening movements from either wolf or human. After years of hunting and trapping with Leo Ten Eyck, he and David had learned to avoid disturbing them as they went, but most people couldn't. On the one hand, no French roaming the woods around Johnson's manor was good. On the other hand, it meant another day with no way to catch one and find out what they were up to. Capturing a lone Frenchman they could question before Johnson returned from General Braddock's conference in Virginia would be ideal.

James scanned the area one last time, then gestured for David to follow him. They walked, searching for signs of the French, until the sun got noticeably closer to the horizon than the sky's midpoint.

They rounded another bend in the trail, and James halted. David almost bumped into him from behind. Rotten eggs. James's heart kicked at his sternum, and he scanned the ground for the inevitable copperhead nest that came with that smell out here. David sniffed, then followed his lead, inspecting the ground under the surrounding thickets.

James spotted it a few feet off the trail and pointed. David nodded. They left the trail in the opposite direction, giving the nest a respectfully wide berth. James gave it twice as much space as David. There might not have been snakes in Ireland, but James had learned quickly to avoid the evil creatures in his new home along the Mohawk River.

Snakes were the one thing that made him question his ten-year-old self's decision to leave the only home he had ever known and indenture himself for a chance at a future.

He shuddered his shoulders to relieve the tension there. Seventeen years in the colonies and he still couldn't abide the slithering devils.

They returned to the trail and continued to scan the ground and the trees. The French wouldn't be up in the trees, but the creatures who could warn them of a French approach would be. Leo Ten Eyck was the most skilled woodsman in the valley and he had taught James how to track dangerous prey. And the French were dangerous. Far more dangerous than the British in the woods.

The Abenaki, too, were no friends of either the British or the Mohawk, so neither he nor David wanted to be surprised by them.

They came to a small creek and, without a word, he and David spread apart and studied the bank for signs of passage. James spotted a scuff on the moss.

Were they walking into an ambush?

He leaned in and inspected the mark carefully, and then the surrounding soft earth. There weren't many rocks anyone could have walked on to hide their tracks. Cloven deer prints by the water were the only indicators of anyone stopping for a drink.

James straightened and stretched his back.

"The sun's getting low," said David.

"You just want to get back because the post from Albany may have brought the papers."

David shrugged. His appetite for information was insatiable, and they weren't finding any out here today. On James's orders, the next patrol would leave the blockhouse behind the manor house soon, so they wouldn't have a gap in their surveillance to let the French sneak through.

James gave a last look around.

Crack!

The sound of a gunshot echoed through the woods. James's heart slammed against his ribs. What the hell? He and David swung their muskets from their shoulders as the birds fell silent.

There was no good reason for any Englishman to fire a musket in these woods right now. Any *English* man.

James turned and ran silently toward the sound of the shot, not having to look back to know David was right behind him.

Chapter 2

"**D**amn!" Faith Richmond's father cursed his aim.

She looked around at the forest. "Perhaps we should make our way back to the carriage?" Maybe now that he had missed the deer he'd been stalking, he would stop dawdling and they could get to Fort Hunter—the fort nearest their new lands—before dark. Lovely as it would be to explore these wild woods, they had limited time to accomplish what they were here for. It had already been two days since they left Albany.

Her father looked dashing in his red lobsterback coat with all the trimmings of his rank as colonel, but it didn't exactly blend in to the scenery, so it had kept him from being able to stalk the deer closely enough to get a clear shot. He gazed longingly at the path the animal had taken when he fired at it. "Maybe I winged it."

He had not. "The light is starting to fade," she said, taking his arm and trying to lead him back toward the road. He wouldn't budge.

"If Caleb were here, he would help me track it," he said.

Of course, Caleb would help him track it. He was her father's lieutenant, and he worshipped his commanding officer, though that was only part of why her father had his heart set on marrying her off to him.

Her father still gazed after the deer, as if it were an antlered siren singing to him.

He'd insisted on stopping to hunt on their way to seeing the lands he had just purchased—with yet more money borrowed from Caleb's family. But they needed to hurry if they were to take stock of the land and get back to Albany before General Braddock wrapped up his conference in Virginia.

It wasn't worth reminding her father that he had ordered Caleb to remain in Albany. It was the only way they would get news of Braddock's conference the instant it arrived.

Right now, they were on someone else's land, and that someone might not appreciate it. She glanced around and tried again to get him moving.

He patted her on the hand. "Fear not, my girl. I will protect you in the woods."

Something screeched behind her, and she spun. A large black crow glared at them with its dark eyes and aimed its long, stout beak in their direction. She watched it until it stopped glaring and went on about its crow-ish business. Its feathers glinted like obsidian in the sunlight. Faith's pulse returned to normal.

She looked up at the sun. There was no way they would reach the safety of Fort Hunter tonight. From there, it was still ten more miles to reach the land her father had not been able to resist purchasing. He was convinced the income from it would quickly cover the purchase price and that buying it was his duty to her to secure her future when he was gone. He meant well.

The air blew across her cheeks, and she briefly closed her eyelids to let the breeze caress them. But lingering wasn't wise. Or safe.

"I should have brought Caleb instead of you," her father said. "I've put you in danger."

"Come, father, I am fine, and we need to get back on the road." She gave him a big smile. "Do you think you will start a mill or hire the new land out?"

He would no doubt like tenants, so he could fancy himself lord of the manor, but that didn't seem likely to work with so much open land available.

"Maybe when you and Caleb are married, he will give you a brace of pistols to keep you safe in the wilderness," he said. "I will discuss it with him."

She said nothing. The thought of depending on Caleb for her safety—or anything—made her shudder. But her father was good to Caleb. Good with all young soldiers, really. He understood what they needed in order to mature, and he made it happen. Unfortunately, while marrying her off to Caleb might be good for Caleb, and for the Richmond family coffers, it would condemn her to a life of tedium. Managing their investments would have to suffice for excitement. But if she couldn't talk her father out of the idea, she would do her duty. He was trying to secure his own future, too.

"Come," said her father. "You are right. We must head back to the carriage. I know this must be frightening for you."

The trees breathed around her. Trees in London didn't do that. This wild edge of the empire stirred her blood. But they did need to get moving.

She took his arm, and he placed his hand over hers.

"Don't worry, there will likely not be any Mohicans about at this time of day." He eyed the underbrush as they walked, picking up speed.

This wasn't Mohican territory, according to her reading. It was Mohawk territory. And it was Mohawk land they had purchased. But her father rarely bothered to differentiate between a Yorkshireman and a Scot, so he wasn't likely to condescend to learn which native groups lived where.

"I am sure they have better things to occupy themselves with on a lovely spring evening than to wander the woods looking for English officers." She gave his arm a squeeze and kept them walking.

The Mohawk were loosely allied to the British, but if she and her father were trespassing on their land, this might not be the best moment to meet them. Poaching in someone else's woods was not an ideal introduction, and she preferred to make a better first impression with their new neighbors. Good neighbors would be good business.

Her dress caught in the underbrush, and she stooped to free it so the creamy white fabric didn't tear.

Her father tutted. "Skirts are not suited to the woods."

"Would you rather I had worn breeches?" She smiled at him, to soften the words, but she shouldn't have said them.

His brows lowered, and his face grew stern. "This is no place for you."

Her chest tightened again. He *would* prefer she wore breeches, because she was supposed to have been a son. It was her greatest failure of family duty, and nothing she had done in the twenty-four years since her birth had made up for it. "I am fine." She pulled the last bramble from her skirt and started marching forward.

"I should never have brought you from London."

"Nonsense. Who would keep your house here?" She was all he had. Her father had to acknowledge he needed her as hostess, if nothing else. Her mother, for all that she would have preferred to stay quietly at home, would never have let him come on campaign without her to tend to him while she was alive.

He looked into her face and finally smiled. "You are a dutiful girl." He patted her hand. Then he looked around the woods, and the corners of his mouth turned down.

Birds sang, and there were no sounds of humans.

"I don't know that I trust the Mohicans not to jump us if they see you."

She shouldn't have let him go tearing off after the deer. Now his agitation was contagious.

They turned back in the direction of the road, skirted around a large boulder, then stopped dead.

Her breath caught at the back of her throat as time slowed, and her father made a choking sound next to her and fumbled his musket. She forced her hands to stay at her sides so she looked as nonthreatening as possible.

Her heart banged so hard it might bruise her breastbone. They were fools to have left the road.

And now they were going to pay for it.

On either side of their path stood a Mohawk man, musket cocked and aimed directly at their hearts.

Chapter 3

S *on of a Bishop's wet-nurse.*

James glanced at David, whose eyes were narrowed as he aimed his musket at the chest of the brainless British officer. Clearly your standard purchased commission, not one of the rare few who rose to his rank through merit, walking straight into them like that.

And clearly not French. They had spotted a flash of light-colored fabric through the trees and hoped. But the man's full British dress uniform gave away his nationality, as did the foolishness of bringing a woman in a gown the same color white of a French army uniform into the untracked woods with him. What in the hell were they doing here?

The officer swung his musket from one of them to the other.

James slowly lowered his own weapon. He had better placate the man. "We apologize if we startled you. We have been patrolling, searching for French raiding parties."

The elegant young woman, recovering herself faster than the officer, flashed a brilliant smile at them. She was stunning, with chestnut hair and bright blue eyes. And totally out of place in this setting.

Then the officer's shoulders squared, his musket lowered, and his chin rose. "I thought you were Mohican. Not Irish." The man jutted his chin toward David. "Is this one Irish, too, or Mohican?"

James's jaw tightened. Apparently, he still sounded Irish to an Englishman. And the fool thought David was Irish, too?

"Kanienkehaka," David corrected him, not lowering his musket. And not in a mood, apparently, to simply say "Mohawk," the word they would have recognized. Really, who could blame him?

James gestured to him to lower the musket, and David hesitated just a moment longer before he complied.

The woman's eyes darted from himself to David and back again. She glanced at their loincloths and the gap between those and their leggings that ended above the knee, and her fair skin fired red.

James's skin fired hot in response. And not from embarrassment. He could feel her eyes on his skin as if she had touched him.

David scratched his leg under the edge of his loincloth, exposing more male thigh flesh than the woman had likely ever seen. James swiveled his musket slightly so the butt end knocked against David's shin.

"What brings you to the Mohawk Valley, sir?" James said. A lone British officer roaming the area, even without dragging a woman with him, made no sense.

"Are you here with Braddock?" David asked.

The officer straightened, and his nostrils flared. The arrogant ass was probably just out sightseeing before the war began in earnest.

The woman still smiled, and a few coppery wisps of her hair escaped its pins, making her look more alive than the typical sitting-room ornament.

"Can we help you find your way somewhere? The woods are perhaps not the most fitting place for your...daughter?" James asked.

The officer narrowed his eyes, clearly no happier to be addressed by an Irishman than by a Mohawk.

Before the man could speak, the woman jumped in. "Thank you very much, sir. We are traveling by carriage to Fort Hunter, but we got out to admire the woods and the wildlife, and I am afraid we wandered rather farther than we had intended. I believe that is the way back to the road?" She raised her delicate hand and pointed unerringly in the right direction.

The officer's musket was presumably the weapon they had heard. Admiring the wildlife, indeed.

"You've strayed a ways," James said.

"Scout," said the officer, "take us to the road in haste, if you would. I wish to get my daughter out of danger."

James almost laughed at being called a scout, but David did not. Before David could voice his obnoxiously articulate thoughts on this, James headed him off. "Sir, we are not attached to the army." An officer would run in Johnson's circles, and he and David represented Johnson's household, so he'd best leave a good impression. Johnson was his ladder up, and by God, he would rise.

He forced himself to give the officer the small bow he no doubt expected. "James Carroll at your service, and this is David White."

David snorted.

"We are very pleased to meet you both." She was beaming at them. That was the only word for it. "This is my father, Colonel Ebenezer Richmond, and I am Faith Richmond."

James's muscles released a little of their tension. For all that she was an Englishwoman of obvious breeding, she behaved decently enough. Most highborn ladies didn't around him or David. He gave her a nod.

"How did your friend here come by a Christian name?" the colonel asked.

Faith's full lips pursed as she no doubt tried to find words to take the edge off her father's rude ones.

"In the customary manner," David said, before James could answer for him. "My parents gave it to me when I was baptized. I would tell you all about it, but since I was but a few days old at the time, I cannot remember over much of the day." He gave a smile that made James tense his shoulders. David got formal when he was in a mood. "You may call me by my Mohawk name if you have a taste for the exotic. Tawit."

Oblivious to the edge of mockery in David's tone, or just desperate to keep her father from speaking, Miss Richmond dove into the trap. "May I ask, what does Tawit mean?"

David leaned in like he was sharing a great secret. "It is Mohawk for...David."

The colonel turned a dark shade of red, but his daughter laughed heartily. "I deserved that, Mr. White. Please forgive my rudeness."

David's laugh lightened, and his shoulders visibly relaxed. "So you see, they came by my name no differently than you, presumably, came by the name Faith for your daughter."

Miss Richmond stiffened visibly, and her face braced as if against pain. An odd reaction, even if David was being an ass. Then she caught James watching and pasted on a smile. "And how did you find your way to this valley from Ireland, Mr. Carroll?" she asked.

He looked away. "The same as most Irishmen."

Enough with airing personal histories. She wouldn't find his as amusing as David's.

He stepped out ahead of the party and gestured for them to follow. David fell behind to watch their rear. James could feel the lady's eyes on his back.

The Richmonds had not been careful and could have drawn the attention of any French skulking in the area. An officer would be a prime target, and what a bunch of rough French rangers from the Canadian woods would do with a beautiful English lady made his gut churn.

Something rustled to the left, and he swung his musket off his shoulder and stepped in front of Miss Richmond. Then black and white fur flashed in the undergrowth.

He jumped backward and dragged her with him, his arm wrapped around her waist. She looked at him with wide eyes. He stared for a moment at her red lips, slightly open.

Her breath wisped across his face.

David cocked his musket somewhere to their left. Then he gasped and flew backward, dragging the Colonel with him, unbalancing him, so the colonel stumbled into James.

James yanked his hand from Miss Richmond like it had been scalded.

"Is that a badger?" asked the colonel, blustering, but poised to run like a jackrabbit.

"No," said David.

"Is it dangerous?" asked Miss Richmond.

It took James a moment to regain his equilibrium. "Not exactly."

Then he turned and continued leading them back toward the road, his brain too addled to explain the defenses of a skunk. Yet another animal he had been blissfully unaware of before arriving in North America.

Time to return these two to the world they actually belonged in. They had already been enough of a distraction.

A half mile later, he gestured ahead of them. "The road is just here."

They rounded a large clump of scrubby undergrowth, thick from the sunlight the road clearing provided, and stepped out onto the rutted dirt. Not a furlong back down the road stood an open carriage with a pair of chestnuts standing in the traces, their check reins undone and their ears being fondled by the coachman.

"Driver!" the colonel bellowed.

The man jumped and spun. Seeing their party, he buckled the horse's check reins, swung himself up on the box, and urged the horses to a brisk walk.

James let his eyes stray to Faith Richmond, who looked away and blushed. She was pretty, but he had no time for a woman, even if his loins were questioning that after holding her close, however briefly. Her blush was giving his cock ideas it had no business having.

"Mr. Carroll," she said. No Englishman called him "mister," and this woman was the last person he would expect to use that title for him. Yet here she was doing it twice in one evening. Perhaps she just didn't know what else to call him. "We have purchased land along the Schoharie, and I am curious as to your opinion of the best use for land in this region."

Shit. He and David exchanged a look.

"Don't worry," she said. "We have purchased it from a reputable broker. We would not have land that was not legally titled."

James stared at her. The only reputable brokers of Mohawk land were Mohawk, and somehow these two didn't seem the type to consider that.

"That is none of their concern, my dear." The colonel squared his shoulders and stepped closer to his daughter.

James resisted the urge to roll his eyes. They were no threat to her. Did the colonel really think they were suddenly going to abduct her after leading them out of the woods to their driver? What a blighted fool. They would leave David's uncle, Hendrick, to deal with the land issue.

James shook his head slightly and turned to watch the driver approach. They were an odd pair, father and daughter. He was a colonel and used to command, but she was clearly the diplomat. He glanced back at her. She had cocked her head, apparently studying him, and she blushed pink again at being caught doing it. The skin on his own neck burned in the unseasonable spring heat. She didn't belong out here.

The carriage arrived, and the driver reined the horses to a halt.

"We thank you for your service to us," she said, her blue eyes glinting in the setting sunlight.

The driver set the brake, climbed down from the box, and lit the lanterns at the front of the carriage. It would be dark soon enough.

James reached for Miss Richmond to help her up into the carriage. A feminine scent reached his nostrils. Roses? She smiled down at him, and he couldn't help smiling back. Her hand was soft as velvet against his own, and he wanted to run his fingers over it, savoring the sensation. But his own work-calloused hand must feel like grit to her.

He let go as soon as her second foot touched the carriage floor.

The colonel brushed past him and climbed in next to her, blocking James's view, and James took the hint. No staring at the colonel's daughter.

He wasn't about to lose his focus over a highborn English lady who thought he and David were exotic amusements. He couldn't afford to, even if he wanted to. Which he didn't.

As soon as the driver was back on the box, he picked up the reins and clucked to his horses. Rested from their wait, the horses pulled away at an orderly trot.

The carriage receded around the next bend.

"That family is claiming to have bought land on the Schoharie, but my people have not sold your people any land there recently," David said.

"Don't call them my people."

David raised an eyebrow at him.

He punched David on the arm. "You practically waved your giblets at her in the woods."

"I was merely scratching a mosquito bite, as anyone would." David pursed his lips. "A little bare skin and everyone gets in a dither. The British are odd."

That they were. And arrogant.

He wasn't British, but he was damned well going to make them accept him. He had sacrificed too much to allow any other result.

Chapter 4

Faith sat silently next to her father in the carriage as they bumped along the high road that was really more of a rutted track at this point.

The sky was dark now, so she couldn't see any of the woods to her right or the river to her left. She just heard them and imagined she felt their physical presence. The only things visible were the horses and the ever-changing small patch of road that was illuminated by the carriage lamps. The horses' rumps rhythmically tilted back and forth with each stride as they walked briskly down the road, undaunted by the darkness. The driver had slowed them from their trot when the jolting of the carriage over the ruts had gotten so bad her father's trunk had almost fallen out.

Her mind wouldn't let go of their encounter with James Carroll and David White. "Why would an Irishman be dressed as a Mohawk?" His soft d's and hard th's still marked his speech, even if he otherwise sounded like the rest of the provincial men they had met in New York.

Her father grunted. "Why does an Irishman do anything?"

"Presumably for the same reasons an Englishman does things."

"An Irishman is hardly an Englishman. They are here to manure the continent and make it fertile for their betters. Much more like a Mohican than an Englishman."

She let it go. She was not an admirer of Richard Hakluyt and his theories, but her father would be horrified if he knew she had read them.

James Carroll's clothing had been rather provocative, but presumably served some purpose. Beyond displaying well-muscled legs she should not have been looking at. Her cheeks grew warm and her belly did an unsettling flip.

Both men had been perfectly polite, apart from aiming their muskets at them, and presumably they had good reason for that, too. Indeed, if they were expecting French raiding parties, it was a lucky stroke they hadn't fired on them.

This was not Hyde Park, to be sure. Her skin shivered despite the hot spring evening.

She watched the horses' rumps again. Their tails swung left and then right in unison, like two fly switches, which she supposed they were.

What had James Carroll meant when he said he came to the valley the way most Irishmen did? His look had gotten stormy, so she hadn't questioned him further. He was stern, but was that his natural state, or had something she said caused it?

She mulled those questions while the horses walked on for an hour, then the driver pulled them to a halt.

He turned on the box. "Sir, I feel like we should have reached the ferry by now. Are you certain of the distance?"

Her father bristled next to her, so she jumped in. "We did check with multiple people about the distance to the junction of the Schoharie. It should be off to the south."

"You live here," her father said to the driver. "How do you not know your way?"

"Beg pardon." The driver lifted his chin just a fraction. "I live in Albany. I have never had reason to venture further west than Schenectady. I did mention that."

Her father leaned toward the driver. "What sort of man never ventures beyond the next town?"

The driver was a small, fastidious man—Dutch, as best Faith could tell by his clothes and name. He paused before answering. "This is Mohawk land. They have no need of my services, and I no need of theirs." He gestured around to the dark surrounding them. "No one beyond William Johnson's home has money enough to pay for any services at all, and Colonel Johnson lives east of where the Schoharie branches off."

"Are you telling me you hired yourself to us under false pretenses?" her father asked.

The driver straightened and threw his chest out. "Most certainly not. You said you had accurate directions, and I said I could drive you the distance." He faced forward and gestured at the vast darkness again. "I have driven you the distance, but your directions seem to be in error."

Her father huffed a breath. "My directions were accurate."

Faith had double-checked his directions, but the driver was right. He had driven them the distance, and they had yet to come to a ferry to cross the Mohawk River and turn south along the Schoharie Creek.

An owl screeched in the distance. Was it the only thing hunting out there? They should never have tarried to go after the blasted deer.

"You have given us exceptional service, and we thank you for it," she said. "Is there any chance we have missed our turnoff in the dark?"

The driver turned back to face her, his posture softening just a fraction. "There have been no turnoffs at all to the south. There is only one very wide river."

It was too dark to see the river, but its powerful current whispered ominously in the dark.

The driver asked, "Are you sure there is a ferry?"

"Of course there is a ferry," her father said. "How else would people get across the river? There should be a bridge if this were a more civilized area."

Faith's stomach dropped a degree. They had simply assumed there would be a ferry near the fort. Was it possible there wasn't?

The driver rubbed his chin. "Well, not many people do cross the river past Schenectady. The high road is on this side."

One of the horses stomped its foot, and its harness hardware jingled in the quiet. The road was empty and dark, and it occurred to her just how conspicuous they were, with their carriage lanterns the only lights for miles. Anyone tracking them could simply stroll through the woods next to them, and she would be none the wiser.

Their encounter with James Carroll had jangled her nerves.

She asked, "There are people who live on that side, are there not?"

"Mohawks and Palatine Germans, mostly."

She waited. He didn't seem to think that needed further explanation.

"How do the Mohawks and Palatines cross the river?" her father asked.

The man looked like he was talking to a child. "The Mohawks cross by canoe, and the Germans probably cross at Canajoharie. It's not as if they can afford fancy coaches, so some might swim, for all I know."

So there was a crossing, even if it was not right at the junction. She breathed a little easier. "Then perhaps we, too, should cross at...Canajoharie?"

"Canajoharie might be twenty miles beyond the Schoharie and is the Upper Mohawk Castle."

Twenty miles? If nothing else, her bladder would not last that long. But what came out of her mouth was, "The Mohawks have castles?"

"Is this really relevant, daughter?"

Probably not. But the driver answered. "That is what their larger palisaded villages are called. Canajoharie is where Hendrick lives."

Oh. They really had bungled this. Even she had heard of the Mohawk chief, Hendrick, back in Albany. Somehow the idea of ferrying across the river and into his castle unannounced and in the middle of the night didn't seem the wisest course of action.

"I am not afraid of the Mohawks," her father said. "They are allied to us, are they not?"

"When it serves," the driver said.

Her father lurched forward. "What do you mean 'when it serves'?"

What *did* he mean by that? David White and James Carroll seemed perfectly at ease with each other. He must be mistaken.

"Father, the driver is not at fault." It was dark and not time to be visiting vacant woodland anyhow, and that delay lay squarely at her father's feet. "We need to find a place to stop for the night." She turned to the driver. "Where would you suggest?"

"This isn't exactly the sort of area that has inns at regular intervals," he said.

Her father was now leaning back in his seat, arms crossed, like a petulant child. "Obviously not."

"Are we safe on the road here?" she asked.

"It's not likely that either a bear or a wolf would attack a carriage with multiple people in it."

Not likely, but not impossible. "And the French?"

The driver glanced from one side of the road to the other. "There have been stories of French raiding parties in the area. Mostly Canadian irregulars and Abenaki." His close-drawn brows suggested it was just occurring to this man from the fortified town of Albany that he was not behind those fortifications right now, as they stood arguing in the dark, pinned between the river and the equally daunting wilderness.

Mr. Carroll and Mr. White knew where they were and how to navigate and protect themselves here in this rough country, and she and her father had not thought to ask for guidance once they were back at the road. That had been unwise. She would have felt safer with them here right now.

But they had to have come from somewhere. "How far would you guess to the next settlement?" she asked the driver.

He puffed out his cheeks as he considered. "I believe the next settlement after the Schoharie is Stone Arabia."

"Stone what?" said her father.

"I didn't name the place. The Palatines are poor, but not too hostile, from what I hear."

Well, that wasn't inspiring, but they couldn't stay and argue all night. And no matter how urgent her bladder's needs, she was not about to climb out of the carriage and squat in the bushes. Heaven only knew what might bite her, even if no one could see her.

She turned to her father. "Shall we seek a Palatine roof for the night?"

Chapter 5

James led the way back through the woods. David followed silently. Saints be praised that David wasn't giving him a headache parsing the politics of their encounter.

Obnoxious Englishmen were hardly a novelty for either of them. And this one was a fool to boot, since he brought his daughter out into these woods after the blasted Virginia militia had killed a French diplomat. A diplomat who happened to be a French officer's little brother. And then that French officer had sent the Virginia militia squealing back to Williamsburg with its tail between its legs. Bloody stupid.

The French were angry, and they were coming. And if almost a hundred years of past actions were any sign, they were coming stealthily through these woods and would strike without warning.

Butcher and run.

What made rich people like that colonel think more money equaled more brains when they disproved it almost every day?

"General Braddock's entire reason for being here is to lead an army against the French. If that colonel came over with Braddock's forces, it makes no sense that he is wandering alone out here in our country, unless he is truly as brainless and self-serving as his story implies," David said, voice pitched low so as not to be heard by any lurking French.

So much for the blessed silence.

"My experience of British officers is that they are self-serving and brainless as a rule." He stopped, and David stopped behind him. The night creatures of the woods chattered undisturbed. He walked on.

The sun had sunk below the horizon, but the moon was already up. With no lights to ruin their night vision, they could make their way in this familiar territory of Johnson's holdings with no trouble.

David snorted a quiet laugh out his nose. "Do you think they have discovered there isn't a ferry stout enough for their carriage to cross at Fort Hunter?"

James smiled and kept walking. "I should think they may have come upon that realization by now."

"Well, I am sure they will enjoy sleeping in a German barn somewhere between here and Stone Arabia."

It was better not to picture Faith Richmond sleeping anywhere if he wanted to walk comfortably. She was quick-witted and pretty. A distracting combination.

The birds and squirrels and other creatures continued their nighttime songs and squabbles. At least the onset of darkness had cooled the air a bit.

"I hope he didn't pay too much money for the land he thinks he purchased," David said as they continued down the trail, his voice so low it was almost a growl.

Yet another bloody Englishman had been fooled into thinking he had purchased Mohawk land. Or substitute Onondaga, Seneca, Delaware, Shawnee—the list went on. The bastards who "sold" them the land got wealthy and caused wars because the English didn't think "buyer beware" applied to them. They paid some idiot money so by God they could take that land. So what if the snake selling them the land had no legal title to it?

They walked on in the dark, then the regular nighttime chatter of the woods went quiet and they stopped.

Nothing.

James's pulse quickened.

They both stepped wordlessly off the trail and crouched behind a downed tree and listened. Absolute silence. Normally, the woods were a noisy place at night, but not even a frog croaked.

They held their breath to listen, and then a faint rumble came from the left. They both swung their muskets off their shoulders and checked their flints.

The sound grew louder. Running feet—many of them.

James strained his eyes in the dark until shapes began to form coming down the trail. His limbs tensed. David shifted beside him to get a better view without giving their own position away.

The shapes got closer, and then James's knotted shoulders loosened. He exhaled softly.

Deer. Probably eight or ten of them. They were in a full-on run, not stopping to check behind themselves. And they were heading right down the trail toward where he and David crouched. His finger itched on the trigger of his musket. That was a lot of meat on the hoof.

David's finger twitched, too, and James shook his head. Not that David would be fool enough to fire.

The deer pounded the ground with their hooves, and the vibrations rose through James's feet and legs as they approached. His heartbeat matched their thundering rhythm. They swept past and created a wind that lifted leaves up off the ground and whipped them around. Eleven of them, and they passed so closely that James could have reached out and tapped them with his musket.

They swept on, and after a few moments, disappeared into the darkness and trees.

James's heart thumped eagerly in his chest. They waited. Something had spooked the deer. They didn't run like that out of joy and to exercise their legs.

The leaves quieted, and the silence settled back over them.

Then a large shape coalesced down the trail. It was moving, but at a lumbering pace.

David shifted behind James. He sniffed the air. They both shrank lower behind the tree, neither fool enough to make a sound.

Bear. Its stink preceded it.

His pulse picked up its pace. Was the beast the only danger out there?

He exchanged a glance with David. If they stood and waved and shouted, and fired their muskets, it would likely take a different route. Under other circumstances, they would already be doing that. Staying quiet until a bear was too close was a mistake most people didn't get a chance to repeat.

But if they made a ruckus and scared it off, then anyone else out here would hear them, too. And while the bear might be frightened of them, the French would not.

James ran his finger along the edge of his trigger. The beast upended logs and searched for food as it made its way along. It was lean, and a lean bear was a dangerous bear.

The surrounding trees were easily climbable, but if they climbed one, and if the French found them treed, they couldn't escape without a fight.

David shifted next to him, getting in a better position for quick action.

It was close enough now they could hear it snorting and grunting as it searched for supper.

He looked at David, who looked back at him. Decision time.

The bear stopped and stood on its hind legs like a man.

James would have sworn it was looking directly at them. Then it turned its head, sniffing like it had a caught a scent.

It shuffled off on a different path, and he took a normal breath for the first time in several minutes. Thank goodness the breeze had been in their favor.

David flicked a mosquito off his arm without making the slightest sound. They let the bear move on at its own pace until it was well out of sight and hearing. James drew in a slow breath and let it out with a sigh.

He was about to stand when something caught his eye over David's shoulder.

"Well, this has been a fruitful day," David muttered. "Bear, skunk, snakes, English...." He trailed off when James pointed.

A small patch of something white a couple hundred yards off. Had it been there before? He signaled David to circle around to the right, and he, crouching as low as he could, circled left.

As they closed in on it, no human shape materialized, nor did the patch move.

Birch bark. But there weren't any birch trees nearby.

David came up and carefully freed the bark from where it was wedged between two branches, while James scanned the woods for movement and kept his musket ready to cover David.

Someone had to have put it there. None of their own men would have done it without informing them.

David peered at it, but it must have been too dark to see if there were any marks on it, because David shrugged and tucked it into a pouch he carried on his belt.

James scoured the ground in the moonlight. Close to another tree was a dark spot on the ground, and he knelt to sniff.

Gor! Someone had taken a piss there. He stood back up.

But a couple feet away, there was something else. Corn? It was too dark out to identify it, so he scooped it up and put it in his own pouch to inspect it, along with the birch bark, in the light back at the blockhouse.

His pulse danced. If it was parched corn, that meant raiders. He steadied his breathing and held up his pouch toward David. "You were saying?" he whispered.

He and David circled around the area looking for anything else, but everything seemed in order, so much as they could tell by moonlight. A frog croaked. Then another. The general rumblings of the night woods slowly resumed. He motioned to David, who shrugged and waved his hand in the direction of Johnson's compound.

It was time to get back. He nodded to David and then returned to the trail, scanning the undergrowth as they went. They stopped a few more times on the way back to listen, but the din of the night continued steady on.

When they reached the blockhouse, two other men had long since headed out for their own watch. James set his musket against the wall, went to the hearth, and pulled the grains from his pouch. David leaned in over his shoulder.

Definitely parched, ground corn. Canadians or Abenaki, most likely.

"Let me see the bark," James said.

David pulled it from his pouch and handed it to him. They both leaned in toward the light of the fire to get a better look.

There were faint marks on it, but he couldn't decipher them. It certainly could be writing, but he couldn't make out any of the words.

"Do you read French?" James asked.

David shook his head. "Sorry, just English and Latin."

Of course David read Latin. Schooling did strange things to people. And not useful things.

But bark didn't just float on the wind. Someone left it there, and it wasn't any of them.

Chapter 6

The next afternoon, James and David sat on the front steps of the main house. They wore loincloths and woolen leggings again, in case they needed to head back into the woods on short notice. It was still too hot for breeches under the leggings.

With Johnson not yet returned from Virginia, and after finding signs of the French in the area, James had stepped up their guard. This was his first time in charge, and he wasn't going to muck it up.

He had sent out two pairs of men to patrol the woods, and since he and David had to clean their weapons anyway, he decided they could do it where they could keep an eye on the river traffic past the house.

"Do you think the French really have a map of the grounds and out-buildings?" David asked.

"I would if I were them." James grabbed his musket and popped out the flint to clean the lock. "You worried the map shows you napping under a bush?"

David snorted out a laugh. "That would solve our map problem, because then all the French women would fight over it, and it would be torn to shreds."

"You are such an arrogant ass."

David was unmarried and showed no signs of wanting to change that status. That was pretty common among young Mohawk men in times of war. Warriors tended to remain celibate to keep their focus, but James suspected there was more to it for David. Eventually, Hendrick would have words with him about that, and David would probably find himself a good political match. Good luck to her competing with politics for his attention.

James grabbed his oilcloth and rubbed it around the flintlock.

David did likewise.

Hoof beats sounded up the road. James looked up, and there was a pair of matched chestnuts trotting toward them. "Jesus, Mary, and Holy Saint Joseph."

"You need to learn to swear like an Anglican if you want to move up in the British Empire. I shall compose some lessons for you. First...oh shit." David stopped talking.

"I learned that one in Ireland. Teaching is not your calling."

They both stood as the carriage pulled off the road, through the iron gate, and into the palisaded courtyard of the house.

Bother and damn. Colonel Richmond and his lovely daughter climbed down. Both moved a little stiffly, and the colonel's face was all puckered like he ate a sour cherry.

Miss Richmond looked around, clearly taking in the big fieldstone building. No doubt her sunny expression of appreciation would shift when she saw the gun loops in the rear wall. A lavish English-style manor it might be, but out here, a stone house was never just a house.

He had better go bow and scrape, since he represented Johnson.

"Greetings," he called out.

"There's no ferry," the colonel said.

"But there is," said David, before James could placate the colonel, "if you can rouse the soldiers at Fort Hunter to bring their skiff and they haven't wandered off hunting. The lower castle is right there, and it is their land you purchased, so they could have sent someone to guide you to it. I had assumed that was your plan. Was it not?"

He could kick David in the shin to shut him up, but the colonel deserved it. So he just poked David gently with his ramrod. "I trust some kindly Germans offered you a roof for the night?"

The colonel grunted.

"They did, and we are very appreciative," Miss Richmond said. "Had we realized we had driven right past Colonel Johnson's manor in the dark, we would have turned around and saved them the trouble."

She didn't seem to mean that as a dig at them. Instead, she smiled openly, like she was genuinely concerned to have put a poor family out of their beds for a night. She was a most curious Englishwoman.

"Is Colonel Johnson at home?" she asked.

He should alert the household that someone of quality had arrived so they could be catered to in a manner fitting their station.

He looked at David.

"Oh, do let me," said David, bounding up the steps to find whoever was serving as housekeeper. Johnson and housekeepers were a complicated matter.

James turned back to her. "None of the family is at home, as the colonel is in Virginia."

This colonel's head snapped up at the mention of Virginia. The British military had too many damned colonels.

"Why is he there?" Colonel Richmond asked.

"Because General Braddock summoned him," James said. "Perhaps you would know more of that?"

The colonel harrumphed, apparently not liking that Johnson had been included in the conference and he had not.

"How lovely," said the daughter. "We did not know Colonel Johnson knew General Braddock." She took her father's arm and led him to the short stone staircase that led to the manor's front door, which opened to reveal David giving a sweeping bow, gesturing them in and generally doing his best impression of an English butler.

The half-wit was going to get them sacked.

"Please tell the housekeeper we need a proper meal." The colonel seemed to have forgotten that David was not actually a butler, but David played along. "And we will need someone to arrange for us to get to the other side of this damned river."

"Of course, sir." David even threw in a hand to his forelock. The colonel didn't seem to notice that it was a jest and not in earnest, and he took the gesture as his due.

Miss Richmond dipped her head and covered her mouth briefly with a handkerchief. David gave her a wink as she passed him, and James stiffened. Enough.

He hustled up the four steps and elbowed David as he passed him. Then he turned and handed him their muskets. "Go buttle, butler." He kept his voice low, so the Richmonds didn't hear.

He turned to the father and daughter and led them to the left, into the front room favored by the colonel who owned the house. Hopefully, it would quiet this colonel, too.

David reappeared, carrying a tea service. James almost spat out his own tongue. Louisa, the cook, must have sent him in with it.

Miss Richmond turned, skirt swirling, and took the tray from him. "Allow me, Mr. White."

The bastard winked at her again as she set the service down on the table and began to pour as if she were the lady of the house. He did not need David or any of the other men distracted by Faith Richmond with the French crawling around the woods and war begging to break out.

He needed to get rid of them.

But he took the tiny cup she handed him and nodded solemnly. He wasn't such an ass as to be rude to her.

Her back to her father, she gave him a warm smile, and he tried to remember how to sip his tea properly.

Why the hell she was being so...friendly? Any other woman and he would think she was angling for some activity her father wouldn't approve, but that was obviously not the case here. She wasn't that sort, and he certainly wasn't her sort.

And he didn't have a sort because he couldn't afford that sort of complication. He couldn't even afford to replace his missing shoe-buckle.

"We need powder and shot," said Colonel Richmond.

James focused back on the officer, where his focus belonged.

"I assume Colonel Johnson has a large magazine, out here in the wilderness, surrounded by—"

"Father, please," the daughter interrupted. "Let us drink our tea first. Then we can make our arrangements."

At least she understood her audience better than her father did.

She turned to James. "We just want to be sure we are provisioned before we cross the river. We hadn't realized how much wildlife is about."

James caught David's eye, and David closed his mouth before any words came out. For all David's faults, he was smart enough to know when to take a hint and shut up. On good days.

Louisa came in with some koekjes on a plate. She put them on the table, looked around to make sure everyone had enough, then bustled off. Most of Johnson's staff was at his house in Albany right now, but Louisa could single-handedly run the place if she had to, and she could always call on her many Palatine cousins to help in a pinch. Frontier women were forces of nature.

Miss Richmond reached for one of the small biscuit-sized cakes. "These look lovely. What are they?"

"Koekjes," James answered.

She cocked her head.

"Cook-ye" he said more slowly. "They are Dutch."

She lifted the koekje, and his eyes locked on her lips as they closed around it. Her eyelids fell, and she made an appreciative sound that should not be made in mixed company.

James tried to pretend he hadn't heard it. He looked at her father, as that remained the safest place to look.

"These are divine." She held the plate to her father. "You must try one." Her father refused her offer, and she turned back to James. "This is the most delightful thing I have ever eaten."

The chair-back dug into his shoulder. And if he focused on that instead of the sensual noises she made as she took another bite, he might survive.

The colonel said, "While you are eating tea cakes, we should be getting across the river." He stood, done with niceties, apparently. Thank God. "As these...gentlemen have reminded us, there are international tensions afoot that General Braddock is orchestrating our response to, so we mustn't be dawdling about here. We need to go check on our new holdings while we have time, so we are ready to serve in case another provincial goes haring off, and the war begins in earnest."

"Find some shot and powder for the colonel, and procure a ferry and a guide. Now," James said to David.

Hooves pounded in the courtyard, and someone yelled.

In half a breath, James was on his feet, knife drawn. He stepped in front of Miss Richmond and motioned David to the side of the door.

A loose horse trotted past the window. What the hell had happened to its rider? Dammit, they shouldn't have left their muskets in the front hall. No time to think on that now.

Then the front door slammed open, and James tightened his grip on his knife.

Chapter 7

Faith's heart almost jumped into her throat as James shoved her behind him. Her skin was on fire where his hand still rested against her hip. His broad shoulders almost blocked her view of the doorway.

Footsteps sounded through the hall to the sitting room, and James and David both tensed, muscles coiled to spring on the intruders.

Then someone knocked politely and stuck his head in the door. The man paled in the face of their hosts' drawn knives.

She let out a gusty breath. *Caleb.* Not a raiding party.

James still held her behind him, and David covered Caleb from the side. They looked ready to fillet him if he so much as twitched. And James's protectiveness should not be sending a thrill of pleasure throughout her body. Caleb didn't deserve filleting, much as it would solve her largest problem. She waited, silent.

Caleb blinked and looked from one of them to the other, and then to her father, who barked "Stand down!" at James and David.

They both ignored him. Caleb wasn't doing anything to stand down from, so he just straightened his uniform coat.

Her heart returned to its accustomed place in her chest, and she moved out from behind James before any one of the men in the room did something foolish. Her hip still smoldered where James's hand had grabbed it, but she needed to diffuse the tension in the room.

She cleared her throat. "This is Lieutenant Caleb Adams, my father's aide. I'm sure he didn't intend to cause alarm."

David and James slowly lowered their knives, but they kept their eyes on Caleb, like he might be more dangerous than he appeared.

"Don't stand there gawping, my boy," her father said. "They aren't really savages, I assure you."

James and David both visibly stiffened, which her father didn't seem to notice.

"Everyone, let us all sit, shall we?" she said. "Caleb, you look winded. Have you come all the way from Albany today?" That would have been a very long ride, indeed.

Caleb glanced over to make sure her father was seated before looking for an empty chair and parking himself in it.

David stood by the door, and James moved near the front window, where he was silhouetted, but no doubt had a lovely, well-lit view of everyone else. Neither appeared inclined to sit, and James openly looked Caleb up and down, like he was assessing a horse and finding it wanting.

Well, if they wouldn't play host, she would.

She went to the tea service and turned to Caleb, whose cheeks hadn't yet regained their color. "Can I pour you some tea, Caleb? It will revive you, and you must try these lovely..." she turned to James, "kookyes?"

James's lips turned up just a tiny fraction on one side. He inclined his head toward her in assent. She suspected she didn't get it right, but he wasn't going to correct her. She was so used to being publicly corrected by her father that she wasn't sure what to think about James's restraint.

She poured Caleb a cup of tea, handed it to him with one hand, and offered the plate of koekjes with the other. He declined the koekje, just like her father had. What was wrong with them that they would refuse to try something new and so utterly delectable?

"What brings you to track me down with such haste, young man, and how did you find us?" Her father might have patted Caleb on the head like a spaniel if he were sitting closer.

Caleb looked up like he had momentarily forgotten the errand that had brought him all the way from Albany in such great haste. "I saw the carriage I had hired for you and turned in here."

Everyone watched him expectantly. That was not the important half of the question.

"Oh! News from General Braddock, sir."

Her father straightened in the chair as if the general had entered the room himself, and the other two men, for all they looked nonchalant, were listening so intently their ears would fall off soon.

Caleb took another gulp of tea. "He's announced his plans, and you are to prepare to march to Fort Niagara under Governor Shirley, who is now General Shirley, sir."

James and David traded glances but said nothing.

Her father's mouth worked like he was trying to form words for a moment before he found his voice. "I'm to serve under a provincial governor?" This was a blow, she knew. He had so hoped to serve directly under Braddock.

Caleb's brows rose. He never quite grasped which postings held more status than others. "Yes, General Braddock will lead a force against the French to push them out of the Ohio country, and they will march to the Mon...Mononogla River."

David pursed his lips. "Assuming you mean the Monongahela, that would make sense. The French have built a fort where it joins the Allegheny."

Caleb looked at David, and his eyes widened. He had apparently just realized that while James was only dressed like a Mohawk, David really was a Mohawk.

But then he continued. "Yes, that is the name. Thank you...sir." He turned back to her father, whose jaw was set, and the muscles in his temple rippled in agitation. Her father always thought he was the only "sir" in the room.

"Where is this Fort Niagara?" she asked. "Is it near the falls I have heard of?"

James's brows drew together, and his eyes studied her. "You are well versed in the geography of the area."

Her father huffed, like he had just been insulted by James pointing out that she, his daughter, was well versed in something inappropriate for a woman. She kept her face from reacting. He was happy enough about it when it got him out of jam.

"Yes," James said, "it is somewhat near the falls, though it is a long march." He turned to Caleb now. "How does this all coordinate?"

"Well, sir, I didn't hear the whole of it, because I was sent to fetch the Colonel." He gestured to her father. "But it sounds like Braddock plans to swing north after driving the French out of the Ohio country and then join Governor, I mean General, Shirley, and then they will push toward Montreal."

"Lieutenant," her father said, and Caleb's head snapped back to him. "What troops will I be commanding under General Shirley?" He almost choked on Shirley's name.

"Oh, I think Shirley is getting provincial militia."

Her father's eyes grew wide, and the red from his face was spreading down his neck, but he wouldn't take his frustration out on Caleb.

Caleb shifted in his seat. "I think Indian scouts, too, sir."

Faith stood to draw everyone's attention away from her father while he collected himself. "Caleb, I should have introduced our hosts earlier. Where are my manners?" She walked across the room to David. "This is David White. He is a Mohawk, and he and his family and connections likely know far more of the area you will be heading into than anyone else. You will be very lucky to have Mohawk men with you."

David gave Caleb a slight nod. Faith glanced over at James.

"And this is James Carroll," she said. "Are you with the militia, Mr. Carroll?"

"I am currently retained by Colonel Johnson." He turned to Caleb. "Have you any word of which militias will go west with Shirley?"

Caleb stared for a moment. "How many different ones are there?"

James kept a straight face, but she was fairly certain David snorted over by the door.

"Each colony has its own," said James.

"Oh, yes, of course. That makes good sense." Caleb seemed to feel on firmer ground now. But then he turned to her father, who was scowling. Caleb was discussing Braddock's plans with James and David instead of his commanding officer. "I am to bring you back to Albany with all due haste, sir, because Shirley wants to start gathering supplies and forming up and training the militia. He is apparently very pleased to have you assigned to him, with your reputation for being able to train new troops."

She turned and beamed at her father, who responded with a slight nod of his head. His color returned to a healthier shade with the compliment. Bless Caleb for worshiping him.

But the sun was already lowering outside the window. "Well," she said to them all, "we cannot leave for Albany this afternoon, as it is too late in the day. Shall we dine and get some rest so that we can leave at first light?"

James looked to David, who shrugged, and then turned back to them. "Yes, that does seem the reasonable course." He wasn't smiling, and then he said to David, "Tell Louisa that there will be five of us to eat dinner as quickly as she can pull it together."

David didn't try to hide his grin as he nodded and left the room.

Did this house even have staff? She hadn't seen any but the woman who brought the delightful cakes. But of course it did. This was a large manor and its owner was a wealthy officer and trader. Someone had said he might be the wealthiest man in the colony.

Not two minutes later, David returned. "We shall dine in half an hour. Would anyone like to freshen up before then?"

This time, it was grumpy James who snorted. Was he laughing? His mouth was drawn back into a tight line, and the muscles along his temples flexed. If he had laughed, the mirth had died. He didn't appear happy they were staying.

That made sense, since they were obviously an inconvenience. She wouldn't think about the constriction in her chest. Instead, she forced a smile.

"What can we do to lessen the burden on the staff, since we have sprung ourselves on them with no notice?" she asked.

"Nonsense," her father said from his chair. "I am sure Johnson keeps a capable staff that knows how to handle visitors of status, even if he is Irish and lives in the howling wilderness."

Caleb nodded, then looked at her and stopped. Perhaps he realized her father had just been incredibly rude, not only to their absent host, but to James, who was right in front of them.

James looked like his jaw had locked shut, and David was chuckling to himself. Dinner was going to be an adventure, but she had handled worse.

A maid stepped into the room. She couldn't have been more than fifteen or sixteen years old. "May I show you to a bedchamber to rest, miss?"

Faith looked around the room. With luck, if she was just gone long enough to wash her face and take care of necessities, they wouldn't start brawling before she returned. "Thank you. I would love to just wash up a bit."

She followed the girl out into the center hall to the stairs, and her shoulders relaxed a little as she left all the male posturing behind. The ceilings in the house were high and airy, and the staircase was rather more elegant than she expected this far west of Albany. She ran her hand along the curved end of the railing, and the wood was smooth and almost soft beneath her fingers. Then she ascended the wide steps. It was a long climb to the upper floor, and she was breathing deeply by the time she reached it.

The maid directed her to a bedchamber at the front of the house, explaining it was the colonel's sister's chamber, but she was at the colonel's house in Albany. Then she showed her the wash basin and left her to her toilette.

She filled the basin from the pitcher next to it. Then she leaned over, cupped her hands together to collect the water, and plunged her face into the cleansing liquid.

It ran through her fingers and dripped off the tip of her nose. She repeated the motion twice more, then rubbed her wet hands to the edges of her face and down her neck. The water in the bowl was now the color of road dust. Lovely.

She ran her hands over her hair. It felt like the simple knot had survived the day more or less intact, but since she had a mirror and comb available to her, she should take advantage of the opportunity.

She turned to the glass.

Well, at least there were no twigs in her hair, like there had been last night. She removed her hairpins, quickly combed out her hair, then pinned it back up. It wasn't like she could make up for a first impression, and a second one, by trying to create a few curls. She made a face at herself in the glass. She shouldn't care what sort of impression her appearance made on the men downstairs.

Her cheeks were freckling a bit from traveling in the sun. It was a small price to pay, even if her father would add it to his tally of reasons she should not be allowed to leave their townhouse in London. But she was here. And her father might not admit it, but he needed her. He hadn't been himself since her mother had died, and it pained Faith to see him so lost.

She listened for sounds from downstairs.

No raised voices—just a gentle murmur of civil conversation. Thank goodness. Perhaps her father would learn something from the men that would help with the land they had purchased so they could actually make it profitable. They weren't likely to get there themselves now that her father had his orders, which meant she was going to have to sort it all out from Albany while he was heading to Fort Niagara. That was the only way they would be able to repay the loan.

She needed to look at a map again to get her bearings. New York Province seemed bigger than all of England, and the scale of it kept catching her out.

A thump sounded downstairs.

She turned to the door and hurried back down the staircase.

James appeared at the foot of the stairs. What had happened?

He lifted his eyes to her, and when she descended the final step, he paused, then raised his arm somewhat awkwardly for her to take. "May I show you to dinner?"

Whatever she had expected, it wasn't that. The incongruities of the location and people here kept putting her slightly off balance. "Thank you, Mr. Carroll." His brow lowered slightly, like he was considering something, but he said nothing. She gave him a polite curtsy and took his arm. It was firmly muscled under her hand, which shouldn't have surprised her. She forced her fingers to remain relaxed and still. It wasn't like she wasn't accustomed to virile young men, with her father being an army officer, but this one kept surprising her. Or at least, her reactions to him did.

"No one got hurt while you were upstairs," he said.

She looked up, and surely she was not mistaken. His eyes, at least, were smiling. Her insides gave a brief flutter. Perhaps he wasn't quite as stern as she had initially judged him.

"And the thump I heard?"

"Just a chair."

A chair didn't go thump by itself.

Male laughter reached them where they stood. James frowned and hurried her through the front hall.

"Surely laughter is a good sign?"

He didn't answer, but raised voices spilled out of the dining room. They stopped in the doorway.

"Braddock thinks the sound of cannon will be enough to scare off France's Abenaki allies?" David asked, eyes wide in apparent disbelief. "Does he have plans beyond this?"

Her father harrumphed. "Of course he does."

James's arm tensed beneath her hand.

Caleb looked back and forth between her father and David. He had probably never seen anyone challenge his commanding officer. "Sir, I believe he plans to make a grand show of force."

James anchored her in the doorway. He was being rather controlling, but she wanted to hear what came next, too, in case someone decided it wasn't an appropriate discussion to have in front of a lady once she joined them at the table.

Her father nodded at Caleb, which seemed to give Caleb the permission he needed to continue. "And I believe that is much of the plan for General Shirley, heading to Fort Niagara, as well."

James breathed quickly out of his nose. Not quite a snort, but close. Then he led her to her seat, held her chair for her, and sat down next to her. Caleb stood, but apparently realized too late that he should have been the one escorting her to dinner, and he sat back down.

To say that neither James nor David looked impressed with Braddock's plans would understate the case based on their scowls.

She said to James, "I am curious why you and Mr. White seem skeptical." They perhaps didn't know military matters as Braddock did, but they knew the area and its inhabitants.

The woman who had brought the koekjes earlier and the young maid entered the room, laden with platters.

"Let's eat," James replied and gestured to the women and their overflowing trays of food. He hadn't answered her question. No doubt, he agreed with her father that her interest in such things was unseemly.

Everyone began arranging their napkins and scooting their chairs closer to the table, and the staff bustled about serving them roasted fowl. At least the food had diverted the others' attention from the escalating debate.

The scent of crisp chicken skin set her belly rumbling in anticipation. The family that had housed them last night had been kind and generous to the extent they could, but that had meant bread and butter, and even that the family could probably not spare easily. She had left a half-shilling behind in their room when they had refused payment for their hospitality, despite her father's insistence that a penny would do.

Her stomach launched a louder, rumbling growl.

James looked her way, apparently not willing to pretend he hadn't heard. She let one shoulder rise in a slight shrug. She was hungry, and the food smelled good. Surely ladies could be permitted hunger as well as men. Of course, if her father had heard it, he would have been appalled.

James took the platter of chicken and forked an extra piece onto her plate and gave her a slight nod. She snuck a glance at Caleb, and he was ignoring her. She glanced back at James and gave him a quick smile. He held her gaze for a moment. Then his cheeks started to pink, and he dove into his own dinner.

Everyone ate in silence for a few moments. The roasted chicken tasted even better than it had smelled. It quickly took the edge off her hunger so she could speak intelligently again.

"Mr. Carroll, I am most interested in your thoughts on the region and its people. What can you tell us of manufacture in this area?" she asked.

"The manufactures are my duty, Faith," her father said.

She had turned around her father's household finances before, when he had begun to neglect them after her mother's death, and she would find a way to make his latest flight of fancy pay for itself. But that would be easier if her father let her ask questions. She twisted her napkin in her hands, but didn't press further. He didn't respond well to that in public.

David leaned across his dinner toward Caleb, who reflexively drew back. "When does Braddock plan to line up allies for his campaign?" David asked. "I've not heard of any emissaries in the region."

"You wouldn't have heard of the General's doings," her father said.

"Yes," James said, "he would have." Everyone's heads turned to look at him. "If David hasn't heard of anyone out among the Iroquois, Delaware, or Shawnee, there hasn't been any concerted effort there."

David had a friend willing to stand up to her father to defend him. And he, no doubt, would stand up for James if the circumstance arose. No one had done that for her since her mother died, not that she needed anyone to defend her.

She glanced at her father. The empty feeling in the pit of her belly returned. She ate another bite of the chicken James had made sure she had enough of. That helped ease the emptiness.

Her father turned on James, shoulders back and chest out. "Do you really think his majesty's armed forces need permission to defeat the French?"

"They need help, and they won't get it by tromping through other people's lands without asking first."

Other people's lands. She stopped chewing. Her father always spoke of English land and French land. Never anyone else's. It only now occurred to her what an incomplete picture that was. And that others might defend what was theirs.

A commotion erupted in the courtyard, and voices began shouting. James and David both reached for their knives for the second time in as many hours. Her stomach lurched, and her appetite vanished. This colony was far more unsettled than she had anticipated.

"Do people just burst in here at every hour?" Her father slammed his napkin down on the table.

"Father."

He needed to stop distracting James and David, since they obviously understood the possible dangers best and were arming themselves.

James was on his feet motioning David to the door, but James, as before, didn't leave her side.

She held her breath and grabbed a knife from the table.

Pounding footsteps echoed in the hall, then a blond man exploded through the doorway like the hounds of hell were after him.

Chapter 8

"Jaap, what are you on about?" James asked, setting his knife back on the table as his pulse pounded in his ears. Jaap liked dramatic entrances, but this one was unnecessary, considering the circumstances. He was lucky Johnson hadn't witnessed it, or he might get his wages docked.

Jaap looked from him to David, to the others, and back to James. "I have news."

"I had rather got that impression."

Jaap huffed out a breath. Or he might still have been out of breath from his hard ride.

James turned to their guests. The colonel looked irritated, and his aide looked confused. Miss Richmond's cheeks were in high color, and she was setting down her knife, as if she had followed their lead and armed herself. At least *she* had had a sensible reaction.

"This," he waved toward Jaap, "is Jaap Ten Eyck. He is also connected to Johnson's household."

He turned to Jaap, who gave a bow like a player after a grand performance. Gobshite. "Jaap, these are Colonel Ebenezer Richmond, his daughter, Miss Faith Richmond, and his lieutenant, Caleb Adams." He should get a medal for remembering the dim lieutenant's name.

Jaap's eyes fixed on Colonel Richmond. "Have you got your orders, sir?"

Richmond stiffened. "What would you know of my orders?"

Jaap made sure he had everyone's attention before he answered. "Braddock has appointed Johnson a Major General of provincial militia and he is to lead a campaign against Crown Point."

The colonel made a choking sound, and Caleb pounded him on the back. "Are you all right, sir?"

The colonel sucked in a few breaths. "Johnson is a general?"

Miss Richmond reached across the table and squeezed his hand. "Of provincial militia, father."

If the man said one word about being outranked by an Irishman, James would pound him, and consequences be damned.

Jaap seemed to tire of the attention being on the colonel. He cleared his throat. "And Governor Shirley is also appointed general, and is to lead an attack on Fort Niagara. You, sir, I believe, are to serve under him."

Jaap pulled out a chair and sat on it backwards, his legs straddling the ladder back like he was in the blockhouse instead of the dining room of the manor house. "Both campaigns are to start from Albany, so the entire city is humming. Men are already signing up for the militia, even though they don't know the pay yet."

Miss Richmond leaned in. "How will the army get to Fort Niagara?"

"The road west, daughter," the colonel said. "You needn't worry yourself about such things."

She smiled and turned back to Jaap. "Does the road run the full length of the river?"

Jaap looked at David and James as if to ask if she was serious. James gave him a tilted nod. The colonel had apparently not learned from his adventures in navigating the country yesterday if he thought the road ran that far. This was the western edge of the empire, and they were lucky when they had deer paths to follow.

"It ends at German Flats." Jaap looked around at the blank looks on their guests' faces. "A ways past Canajoharie, but on this side, obviously."

"I didn't mean literately the road." The colonel stabbed his fork into a piece of roast chicken. "Rivers are roads for an army." The man was an ignorant fool and would have assumed there was a road if his daughter hadn't asked.

"The army will have to do a lot of paddling and then portage from the Great Carry. Once they get through Wood Creek, they go down Lake Oneida to the Onondaga River, then they will get a respite at Fort Oswego. Of course, they are only halfway there at that point and still have to press on along the edge of Lake Ontario by boat to Fort Niagara." Jaap's eyes glinted merrily. He was clearly getting a thrill out of dashing the colonel's hopes.

"Oswego is a mess," said David. "The troops out there haven't had enough support to keep the place maintained."

"Who does Johnson get to go to Crown Point?" James had been part of a scouting party Johnson had sent there last summer, and that was not going to be an easy assignment.

"He gets militia from New York, Connecticut, Rhode Island, New Jersey, and Massachusetts, and he is supposed to raise as many warriors as he can, and not just from the Mohawks, but all the Iroquois and their client nations."

The colonel looked back and forth like he was watching a tennis match and did not approve of the skill of the players. His daughter tracked their every expression.

"What are his odds, David?" James asked. The Iroquois were technically neutral, and they acted on agreed foreign policy, but he hadn't quite sorted out the internal politics of it all.

David considered this for a moment. "Everyone is still angry about the Albany traders—"

"Wait," said Jaap, and everyone looked back at him. "Johnson was also appointed the sole superintendent of Indian affairs for the Northern District. Sole. No more Albany traders. They all have to go through him."

The colonel grunted like they were talking of irrelevant matters, but Miss Richmond leaned in again, listening and clearly trying to understand the importance of this news.

"That does change the picture," David said. He spun his fork in his fingers.

"How do Indian affairs affect military affairs?" the colonel asked, like the ass that he was. "How many cannons does Shirley get? I need to plan transport. Cannons will make all the difference."

James turned to Jaap, who looked bewildered. "Braddock is apparently under the impression that the big boom of cannons will be enough to make the French allies abandon them on the spot."

Jaap guffawed and almost fell backward out of his seat.

"I don't see why you find that so amusing," the colonel said.

"They seem to believe that cannon will not have the intended effect, father, and they do know the inhabitants of the area." Miss Richmond looked thoughtful.

James had never met a woman so curious about military affairs. Her curiosity looked like the only thing that might save her father's hide, since he clearly saw no need to ask relevant questions.

"They do not know British military might." The colonel stood, his napkin falling to the floor. Caleb stood up next to him.

The colonel turned on him. "Why did you not tell us all this? Is Johnson being named a general, and to command an entire campaign, not newsworthy?"

Caleb opened and closed his mouth a few times like a fish on a line. "I...I learned your orders and came to get you."

"You didn't think letting me know I am to be outranked by an Irish provincial important for me to know?"

James bristled, and his pulse quickened, but the poor lieutenant paled, so he bit his tongue. He wouldn't blame the lieutenant if he had kept the news to himself rather than be the one to deliver it. Or perhaps it just hadn't occurred to him to mention it. Initiative did not seem to be one of his strengths, if he had any at all.

"At least Shirley is an English gentleman," the colonel said, consoling himself.

"Why don't we all finish our dinner," Miss Richmond said. She turned to Jaap. "You must be famished after your hard ride."

"His dramatic entrance," David said. "If he rode that hard, your man"—he gestured at the lieutenant—"would have not have beaten him here by hours."

James turned on Jaap. "Yes, what did take you so long?"

Jaap snapped his head back. "I couldn't very well ride from Albany to here without stopping to check in on my oma."

David looked sharply at Jaap, obviously wanting to ask the same question James did. Jaap's grandmother was the best baker in New York, and she never sent Jaap off without some of her delectable creations to share. The sounds Faith Richmond had made eating the koekjes Louisa had baked were nothing compared to the ones she would make if she tried Oma Ten Eyck's. She would come completely undone.

And he did not need to think about what that would sound like right now. Or look like.

"Daughter, we need to make ready to leave at first light," the colonel said, already halfway to the hall.

"Of course, Father." She turned to Caleb. "Would you be so kind as to help Father while I finish my dinner?"

The lieutenant drew his brows down for a moment, as though he was about to tell her she was who her father had asked for. Then he looked at the colonel's retreating back and said, "Of course," and followed the colonel from the room like an obedient puppy.

Miss Richmond watched them go. "So cannon aren't what is called for?" she asked once her father was out of earshot.

"Does he think we haven't heard them before?" David asked. "That seasoned warriors will run like rabbits from a loud noise?"

"It sounds unlikely when you put it that way." She pursed her pretty lips.

The colonel was lucky. She might not technically be his aide, but she served the role more effectively than the lieutenant did.

She said, "Since we must leave first thing tomorrow, please forgive me for taking what might be my only opportunity to ask a few questions about the area. I need to turn a profit from our holdings quickly while we are still here to oversee it personally."

And she was also his man of business, it seemed. Her lips softened into a warm smile. Woman of business.

Her breasts pressed against the low neckline of her gown. Definitely woman.

Jaap's brows puckered, confused by her question.

"Her father has apparently purchased land along the Schoharie," James said.

Jaap looked to David. "From who? You all haven't sold any tracts, have you?"

David shook his head but kept his mouth shut.

Jaap, never one to stand on ceremony, asked, "Who did you buy it from?"

She appeared unaffected by his directness. "We purchased it through a broker, but I assure you we have all the proper paperwork. My father would like to clear it for tenant farms, but I would like to have your opinion on the viability of a lumber mill. There seems to be no shortage of lumber, and the river seems quite suited for shipping it to Albany and from there, down the Hudson."

All three of them stared at her.

"Is that not viable? Would a grist mill be better suited in this area?" She treated them as if they were having a serious business conversation with her...instead of staring at a pretty woman who was asking very intelligent questions none of them had answers for.

"I think your father is waiting for you to help him prepare to leave for Albany in the morning. And I am afraid we need to plan for General Johnson's return," James said.

She straightened. Then she set her napkin beside her plate. "Yes, of course." Then she stood and marched from the room.

Chapter 9

Faith left the dining room. James had practically thrown her out, which probably meant he thought her questions inappropriate. Heaven forbid anyone answer her inquiries, and of course they would no doubt say women didn't understand business or war and completely miss the irony. She was asking questions to understand it better.

He wasn't the first man to think she was interested in things that were only for men, and she'd been foolish to think she might have discovered a logical man who would talk to her like a competent adult just because his reaction to her stomach growling had been to give her more food.

The front door opened and Caleb backed through it, trying to drag a trunk by one handle because that was the only way for one person to move it.

"Let me help you." She went to grab the handle on the opposite end.

"No, no," he said, eyes wide. "Your father wouldn't approve."

That was likely true. "But I can't let you do this yourself. Shall I get one of the men to help?"

Caleb went pale. "Please don't."

Maybe this campaign would allow him to prove himself to her father. Happily for him, her father wasn't nearly as attuned to Caleb's faults as to her own.

She studied him. He was trim and tidy, and at one point she had thought him handsome. Not that she had technically consented to marry him, but that was irrelevant as far as her father was concerned. He saw himself as doing his duty to them both by arranging their future.

"Where did my father go?"

Caleb pointed to the ceiling. "He went to find shot and powder."

"Upstairs?" Who kept shot and powder in their home when they had outbuildings and a blockhouse?

"They said there's a couple of two-pounders in the attics. And they have musket balls up there too, for defense."

"He has cannon in his attic?" Cannon in a blockhouse she had seen, but in the attic of a manor house? This was indeed the wilderness.

Caleb nodded. "They even have gun loops all along the back of the house on this level."

"Through the actual wall?" That should have made her feel protected and safe. But Johnson's feeling the need for them did not.

"You don't believe me?" Caleb took her arm and pulled her toward the back of the house like a little boy wanting to show off a secret treasure. "I'll show you."

There they were. This was not new construction for the coming war, either. They looked like an original part of the house.

This was something she would have to factor in as she figured out how to keep her father from bankrupting them with his new purchase. No doubt Johnson's position in the military made him a bit of a target, but her father had a position, too. Not that he would live there. Still, she needed to better understand this so she could plan accordingly, or they could have their financial future wiped out in one raid.

"The two-pounders are in the attic?"

Caleb nodded again, like he was pleased that for once he knew something she didn't already know. He really hated how much she understood that he did not.

"I'll go help my father with the shot and powder." She left Caleb to wrestle with the trunk, turned for the stairs, and went up.

At the top of the stairs to the second the floor was a second staircase. It was quite civilized for access to the attics. She grabbed a candle from a side table in the hall and climbed that next flight of stairs, then ducked her head a little as she stepped off the top step into the large room. She wasn't tall enough to need to duck, but after the high ceilings of the two lower floors, the beam over the door felt low.

Once in the attic proper, she held her candle high to look around. "Father?"

No answer. He must have gotten sidetracked back in his bedchamber. He had certainly been handed quite a bit to digest today.

She took her candle toward the windows at the front of the house, and her jaw dropped open. She couldn't manage to close it.

Holy Moses. Indoors, the two-pounders looked considerably more intimidating than such small cannon usually looked. She stepped toward the windows, careful not to disturb anything. Some of the household clearly slept up here, even though it was all one large room.

The guns had some sort of contraption that attached them to the frame of the house. That must be to keep them from scooting backward when they fired. So clever. The windows were large enough that a few men could lay down some significant fire with muskets as well.

She ran her hand over the guns. The metal was cool beneath her fingertips. Had she been the son her father had expected, she might have relished a military life, being part of a band of brothers, like Henry V.

Powder and shot.

There were kegs along the wall to her left. She turned, careful with the candle. Three horns lay lined up neatly along the wall to her right. She picked them up but looked around for some pre-wrapped cartridges. It had been a while since her father had had to measure his own powder.

Perhaps on the other side of the attic. She set the horns by the stairs and went to look.

Wooden crates were stacked all along the wall. She brought her candle close to them. The first was labelled *Blankets*, and the second, *Beads and Lace.* Johnson was a trader first and foremost. That was how he had made his fortune. She had read up on him since she was trying to help her father do the same.

She straightened and kept searching. A stout ladder led to yet another level.

Maybe that was where the men with muskets defended the house, and the cartridges, or at least some loose shot, would be up there. There might be room for gun loops on either end of the house at the roof peaks to defend it from east and west.

The ladder rungs were broad, but she would still need both hands to climb. Her skin prickled. All the defenses were tricking her imagination into thinking there was imminent danger, which was ridiculous. Any raiding parties would come from outside, not from the attics. She was not about to turn coward now.

She set her candle on the nearest crate. With luck, it would still cast enough light to help find any shot. There was a moon, and if there were a few more windows up there, she should be able to spot what she was looking for. If she couldn't, she would go back and get Caleb or her father.

Since no one was about, she hiked her skirt and petticoat up and tucked them in at her waist to make climbing easier. At least the next level wasn't too high. Time to get on with it.

She grabbed the rung in front of her and started climbing. Her body cast strange shadows on the ladder, with the candle directly behind her. They shifted as she moved and kept catching her eye as she rose higher. Light tricks usually fascinated her, but with all the talk of war and raiding parties, she focused on the rungs instead.

Her head rose above the rough boards that made up the floor of this top level of the attics.

She looked up, and a huge shape loomed above her.

Her heart took off in a sprint and she jerked her hands up to fend off whatever the shadow was, but the movement unbalanced her. She flailed for the ladder, but the shadow moved, and she missed her hold.

Her pulse pounded so loud she couldn't hear if she cried out, and she kept trying to grab hold of anything, but only found air.

She was plummeting backward to the floor as the dark shape hovered above her.

Then sharp pain.

Then nothing.

Chapter 10

James grabbed the mold from the shelf where it sat to let the lead cool and harden, and he dumped the shot into a canvas bag. He would dump his own cartridges in if it would speed the Richmonds on their way.

If the colonel hadn't gone poaching, he wouldn't need more powder and shot.

James stuffed some wadding in with the shot, then shoved the top of the bag in his belt and left the outbuilding for another behind it. Luckily, the evenings this far into spring were long, so there was just enough lingering light that he didn't need to risk lighting a lantern as he grabbed a horn of powder to add to the colonel's defense against "wildlife." He had enough on his hands without blowing up their powder stores and himself with it. He slung the horn's strap over his shoulder and carefully latched the door behind himself.

People moved past the glowing windows in the house. Their agitation carried all the way out here. Presumably the colonel was stirring everyone up, and Miss Richmond had not yet reappeared from her chamber to smooth his way. She had probably saved her father from public humiliation more times than anyone could count, though he likely didn't realize it.

James headed up the front steps to the house and almost ran into Jaap, coming out.

Jaap grinned. "The colonel has misplaced his most valuable asset, apparently."

"And what is that?"

"Miss Richmond."

How absurd. She couldn't really be lost. The damned house wasn't that big.

Jaap swept his arm toward the door, gesturing for him to enter.

"Where is she?" the colonel barked at his aide, who blinked a few times before he answered.

"I thought she had retired for the night after she went upstairs to find you," said the lieutenant.

James shook his head and entered the front hall. "Is there a problem?"

The colonel turned on him. "Someone has absconded with my daughter."

"She is not in her bedchamber," Jaap said. He had probably volunteered to peek his head in to see if she was undressed.

The colonel looked like he might damage Jaap, and Jaap leaned casually against the door, utterly unconcerned. Someday, an irate father would dismember him, and with good reason.

James asked the colonel, "Did anyone send her on an errand?" She was no doubt getting something done that these two hadn't even remembered needed doing.

The lieutenant shuffled his feet. "The last I saw her, she was going to help the colonel find shot and powder."

"I was in my bedchamber, Lieutenant. Then I sent this man"—he waved toward James without looking at him—"to get powder and shot."

James's head ached. How on earth could she have gone missing in the space of an evening? "She wasn't in the powder magazine, so apparently that is not where she went."

"Oh, I thought it was in the attic," said Caleb, the idiot lieutenant.

Great—he sent her after the powder and shot they kept to defend the house in an emergency.

James shook his head. "I will go look in the attic."

He climbed the stairs quickly and breathed easier once he had reached the second floor. If she was up there, she was probably hiding from the chaos, and that would just prove her good sense.

There was no candle in the hall. Well, he didn't need one to climb the stairs, so he started climbing. He should be getting ready for Johnson's return, not worrying about missing houseguests. Even if they were unusually pretty and smart.

He reached the attic. It was dark, because there was no real reason she would be up here.

"Miss Richmond?"

Silence, as he predicted. He turned to go, and his foot bumped into something. He reached down and his hand landed on a powder horn. No, two...three powder horns. Who the hell would have left all three of the horns they had up here right by the stairs? He was going to rip the head off whoever was responsible. Or Johnson would rip his head off, and he wasn't going to let that happen.

His skin prickled. Something was off.

"Miss Richmond?" he called again, louder.

It smelled funny up here. Like something had burnt. He inhaled deeper. The attics couldn't be smoldering. There hadn't been any lightning for weeks. He stepped into the large room and turned his head slowly, sniffing in each direction like a hound.

He walked toward the windows at the front of the house, then turned toward the ladder to the upper level.

His foot hit something, and it rolled away, echoing in the otherwise silent expanse. The smell was stronger here, and that could have been a candlestick that rolled. He felt around with the toe of his shoe. He should have taken the time to grab a lantern, dammit.

His toe hit something large and soft, and he reached a hand down. His fingers brushed against something far too human-sized. His pulse leapt and started throbbing in his ears.

"Jaap," he bellowed, without moving from the spot. "Bring a lantern. Now!"

His voice bounced through the cavernous room that ran the entire length of the house. He ran his hand along what had to be a torso and there was movement. A slight up and down. A chest, breathing. What the hell had happened? And who was it?

He ran his hands upward over...breasts. *Shit.*

It was Faith Richmond. It had to be.

She deserved better than to have him groping her as she lay unconscious, but he needed to know she wasn't slipping away.

She was breathing, so he ran his hands up her neck to the base of her head. Nothing felt out of place in any dangerous way. His thumb traced her warm cheek. Then he felt down her shoulders to her arms and his left hand brushed the floor. It was sticky.

Sweet Jesus, she was bleeding. His hands shook now as he felt around, trying to find the wound. She was utterly unresponsive.

"Jaap!" he bellowed at the top of his lungs.

He ran his hands down each leg. Hot blood met his fingers. Right thigh.

Footsteps pounded up the stairs, and about damned time. He bunched up her skirts and pressed them against her leg.

Light began to glow into the room as the lantern approached. "Watch the horns by the top of the stairs."

Jaap charged through the doorway, shoving the horns aside with his foot so no one in the train behind him stepped on them.

"Unhand her!" the colonel shouted from behind Jaap.

With the light, the pool of blood she lay in wasn't as large as the one his mind had conjured, but it was still too big, and it was expanding. He wadded her skirts more tightly under her leg and shifted his free hand under her shoulders. Then he pulled her in to his chest and heaved himself to his feet. Her head lolled against his neck. His chest constricted and his arms tightened around her until her heart bumped gently against his chest with each beat. It reverberated through his body.

He looked at Jaap. "Bedchamber."

Jaap nodded and lifted the lantern so it shone over James's shoulder and he could see his way to the stairs. The colonel and lieutenant stared.

He practically ran down the steps and into the bedchamber that had been assigned to her. A fire burned low in the hearth despite the warm temperature, and candles burned in the sconces on the wall.

David charged through the door. "What happened?"

"Get Sarah Philipse."

David nodded without a word and pounded back down the stairs. The front door banged shut.

James lay Miss Richmond down on the bed, careful to place her so she had a pillow under her head, and rolled her to one side. Blood soaked into the counterpane, and he pressed his hands more tightly against the open wound.

The colonel shoved his way to the side of the bed. "She needs a doctor, not a midwife."

"Sarah is not a midwife—she is a seamstress. If we wait for a doctor to stitch this, she might bleed out."

She was so pale. Her skin cooled under his hand.

No, no, no. He chafed her good leg with his free hand, trying to infuse some warmth in it, then he grabbed the counterpane and wrapped her torso with it, tucking it around her as tightly as he could with one hand. How long had she been up there? He shivered despite the warm night.

The colonel sputtered behind him. "I will not have a common seamstress mangling my daughter's leg."

James shifted to get a better angle to press against the gash, his hip shoving the colonel out of the way. Sarah was Faith's best hope. "She has stitched more wounds than either doctor in Albany, and does a far more tidy job of it." His eyes swung to Faith and her closed ones. Her clever mind was shuttered and silent.

"Who would General Johnson call?" Her father was wringing his hands and looking from him to Faith, and back again.

"He would be the first to call for Sarah if he were here," said James.

"Very well." The colonel still looked dubious. The lieutenant just gawked at Faith and turned slightly green. Had he never seen anyone wounded before? Another purchased commission, apparently.

The parlor maid rushed through the door with a sheet in her hand. James grabbed it—and stopped. But there was nothing for it. He set the sheet down and pulled her skirt up to expose the wound, careful to expose as little of the rest of her as he could. Then he wound the sheet tightly around her leg.

They waited. The sound of the ticking case clock in the front hall echoed up to the bedchamber. James pressed his hands on the wound as it slowly bled through the sheet. He shifted his body to block everyone else's view of her thigh. He could at least do that for her.

Then the front door banged open, and two sets of footsteps thundered up the stairs.

David popped through the door, with Sarah right behind. James's muscles went slack. *Thank God.*

The colonel gaped like he'd never a seen a free Black woman before.

James said, "She is going to save your daughter. Now that she is here, everyone else, get out."

Sarah went straight to inspecting Faith. "James, you stay. I need an extra set of hands."

"He will not," the colonel said. "He has had his hands on her quite enough."

Sarah leveled her gaze at him. "He is the only one of you all I trust not to vomit while I work."

The lieutenant swayed ominously on his feet. The colonel steadied him and looked back at Faith.

Sarah's face softened a fraction. "You tend to him, and I will take care of your daughter."

The colonel finally nodded. He took the lieutenant's arm and looped it over his own shoulders. "Come, my boy. Let's get you downstairs and find you a stiff drink." Then he led him out the door.

"Jaap," she said. "Set the lantern on the table and make sure those men stay downstairs and out of my way."

Jaap gave James a little grimace and headed downstairs.

"You, too, David. Jaap will find an excuse to leave them on their own." David followed in Jaap's wake, jaw set. Sarah had been able to anticipate their actions since before any of them could grow chin whiskers.

She ran her hands along Faith's limbs, much as James had, but she inspected Faith's eyes and ran her hands along her ribs, too. "Nothing seems to be broken. Let's carefully roll her over on her stomach."

James kept pressure on the wound as they rolled her gently. Sarah tsked when she saw the back of Faith's head. Her hair was singed. That must have been what he had smelled. Thank God her head must have snuffed the candle quickly.

Sarah's finger ran gently through Faith's hair, and she muttered to herself. Then she arranged the pillow so that Faith could breathe easily on her stomach and unwound the sheet.

She arranged James's hands on either side of the wound, which appeared as much a puncture as a slice. Faith must have hit the corner of a crate, and it gouged her flesh like a wooden spike. Sarah ripped the already torn stocking and pulled it away.

She surveyed the wound, grabbed her needle and some silk thread, and began stitching. He had seen her work before, on himself as well as others, but her sure hand still impressed him. And reassured him. His muscles ached from holding the same position for so long, but he didn't shift his grip.

Then she was done. She doused a rag in a bowl of water on the washstand and cleaned the blood from around the wound, leaving behind an angry red patch crisscrossed with neat brownish-yellow stitches. They looked out of place against the pale pink skin surrounding the area.

Sarah went to work probing Faith's head and cleaning a little dried blood from the spot that had taken the brunt of her fall.

James couldn't help with that. He took Faith's hand and stroked it.

Chapter 11

Faith was floating, but wrapped in safety. Warmth enveloped her, and a reassuring heartbeat thudded somewhere near her ear.

Then she was alone. She called out.

Something touched her cheek, and she leaned into its warmth. Someone murmured something she couldn't understand. A low, gentle sound that vibrated through her and lit her on fire.

Finally, she opened her eyes. The room was light. Full light.

Oh no.

Her heart banged against her ribs, and her head throbbed in time with it. She had made them late, and her father was going to be furious.

She sat up, and the world lurched. She grabbed the bedpost to steady herself.

"Hold on," said a female voice. The maid?

She turned to look, and the world tilted, and this time her stomach turned inside out and emptied itself into a wooden bucket that appeared in front of her just in time.

She heaved for an age until her stomach and throat hurt as much as the rest of her, then she collapsed back on the bed.

Her eyes didn't really want to open again.

She could have sworn James had been there. Then her cheeks burned. Leave it to her dreams to conjure an image of safety and comfort that was pure fantasy. There was nothing safe about the flesh and blood James Carroll. Fantasies were not for her.

And she really needed to get up now. She would not slow their return to Albany. Her father and Caleb had orders.

Her head hurt. Her back hurt. Her right leg hurt. Her right arm hurt. Her tailbone hurt.

She wiggled her toes. They were fine.

She wiggled her fingers. Same result. She could do this.

Everything after climbing the stairs to the attics and finding the powder horns was hazy, but she must have fallen.

How unforgivably stupid. She needed to make it right, or at least as right as she could, having delayed them from their planned departure at first light.

With great care, she rolled to her side.

"Don't sit up," said the female voice from earlier.

"I have to." Her own voice sounded drunk.

"I'll get you a chamber pot."

"No. I have to get up." She had to get dressed and ready to go.

"You will not get up, and that is the end of that discussion. But since you are on your side now, would you like to try a little water?"

The thought made her stomach churn. A full day's carriage ride was going to be a trial. "I need to see my father. I've made him late."

The woman came into view in front of her. She had much darker skin than even David had, and her black, tightly curled hair was pulled back in a tidy knot. She ran a cool hand over Faith's forehead.

The woman sat on the edge of the bed, which rocked ominously. Faith bit her lips, refusing to lose whatever might be left in her stomach, which couldn't really be much, anyway.

"You aren't making anyone late." The woman sounded kind. Not in a coddling way, rather more of a no-nonsense way. "Your father left three days ago."

James sat on the front step, alongside Jaap and David. He was taking advantage of the light from a sunny day to clean and repair all the spare muskets he had dug out from the crates in the outbuildings. They were going to need every one of them if they were heading to Crown Point, and James wasn't going to wait for Johnson to have to tell him.

"Poor woman must have seen the smoked beef hanging in the attics," Jaap said. "Can't blame her. I nearly pissed myself the first time I climbed up there. Looks like a bear coming at you in the shadows."

James needed Jaap to focus on the job at hand, not on Faith Richmond, lying in a bed upstairs, unprotected by her asinine father, who had taken mere moments to decide to leave her behind rather than delay his own return. Fine. That wasn't an entirely fair assessment. The colonel had orders, and he probably hadn't been supposed to leave Albany in the first place. At least he had paid Sarah for her continuing services before he left.

"Too bad she is unconscious." David shoved a ramrod down the muzzle of the musket he was working on. "She's not half bad company."

James grunted and got back to work on the firing mechanism in his hand. If Johnson left soon after the express got his orders to Jaap, he could be back any day. James was damned well going to be ready. And David and Jaap were going to help if he had to lock them in a room with the muskets and tools to make it happen.

Jaap elbowed David. "I think he needs a woman to domesticate him a little."

James set down the musket he was cleaning and smacked them each on the back of the head. "Gobshites."

He didn't need anybody, and he most definitely did not need a woman.

As if someone like her would have someone like him.

His mind really needed to stop replaying her calling out his name yesterday. It was a good sign that she might come around soon. Nothing more. Even Sarah had said so when she returned from the kitchens and relieved James of his temporary watch over Faith.

Good grief. When had he started thinking of her as Faith instead of Miss Richmond?

David poked James with his ramrod. "You need to relax, my friend."

"He's lonely and a little rusty, but she could teach him to plow a straight English furrow," said Jaap.

David and Jaap both laughed, and he smacked them again to shut them up. "My cock gets more exercise than yours, so shut up and get back to work."

"Your hand doesn't count," said Jaap.

James shoved him off the step. This pack of fools wasn't ruining his trust with Johnson, even if they were his friends. And dallying with an English lady who had taken refuge under Johnson's roof would definitely do that.

"Not my fault you aren't up to the job," Jaap said, looking up from packed dirt in front of the steps.

For the love of all that was holy. "The likes of you are not her sort," James said, pointing at Jaap. "And her sort might be polite to your face, but if you think she doesn't know her station, and yours, you would be wrong." He tossed the whole pile of oily rags at Jaap. "Now, work."

David and Jaap exchanged looks. Jaap, safely out of arm's reach, opened his mouth. "Aren't we tetchy? I'm not afraid of high-class ladies. I've got the goods to please them — better than stuffy little pricks like that lieutenant." He gestured in the general direction of Albany.

They were halfwits. All three of them were so far below her station, it was laughable. But James had no intention of remaining in his current station, and Jaap wasn't going to blow that plan to hell by seducing a highborn lady whose father would have him shot. "Would you care to give us your estimate on when General Johnson will be arriving?"

David's hands stilled on the musket lying across his thighs. "If Johnson is supposed to be getting hundreds of warriors to accompany him, he will need to call a conference." David looked at them each, and even Jaap's face grew serious as he took in the magnitude of what was coming at them.

James set his ramrod down. David was right. Annoying, but right. A conference was going to make even more work.

"It makes much more sense to do that here than in Albany, where others can interfere," David said.

Which meant delays before they all headed to Albany to join up with the army. But it might also mean more opportunities. He grabbed the next musket from the pile and started cleaning faster.

David nodded. "The sachems will come here to listen to him. Albany would keep many away. It will be here. Johnson is not stupid." David started oiling the gunlock in his hands, leaning into it now. It made sense. The political chiefs of the Iroquois confederacy trusted Johnson, and according to David, they made no political decisions without consultation and agreement. Johnson had to convince them all.

The door opened behind them. Their heads all turned, but their hands kept working.

It was Sarah. Some of her dark hair had escaped its knot. "She is conscious, and a bit put out that her father left without her."

Thank God she was finally awake. James breathed a little more freely.

Sarah sat herself down between James and David on the steps and scratched her chin. "She is feisty."

"James would like to find out just how feisty," said Jaap from the safety of the ground.

Sarah turned her glare on Jaap. "I assume that means it is really you who wants to diddle her senseless?"

Jaap pouted. "You know you are the only woman for me."

Sarah snorted.

Jaap clutched at his heart. He keeled over dramatically and writhed a bit on the ground for effect.

"Is he dead yet?" she asked. "Kick him and see if he flinches."

Jaap popped up. "I am not dead. I do, however, have something that would make you change your mind."

"If you whip that pale little thing out, so help me, I will kick it." Sarah glared at him, her voice level and her face stony.

Jaap waggled his eyebrows at her. Then he reached into a pouch hanging from his belt and made a show of peeking his nose into the pouch.

"Jesus, Mary, and Joseph, you ass." Enough with the theatrics and enough with the interruptions. Jaap had cleaned one musket to his and David's four each.

Jaap finally pulled his hand out of the pouch, and everyone snapped to attention, James included.

"You son of cur-bitch." David launched off the step and tackled Jaap. "You've been holding out on us."

Jaap struggled, but David had him well and truly pinned. Before David could take advantage of that, Sarah jumped down and grabbed the koekje out of Jaap's hand. "This is medicinal. And I might save one bite of it for my patient, because I am the very soul of sacrifice." With that, Sarah climbed the stairs and went back inside.

They all gaped.

"But...." Jaap couldn't even find words to finish his thought. He didn't need to.

"You deserved that, you traitor. You said Oma hadn't baked any." David's tone was flat, and he was apparently too dejected to yell at Jaap.

"I never said she hadn't baked any. I just...let you think it." Even for Jaap, that was pathetic.

James reached over and yanked Jaap to his feet. "I would make you pay by babysitting our fair lady back to Albany, but I don't want to have to send Sarah to piece you back together after Colonel Richmond gets through with you when Faith tells him about whatever groping you do on the trip."

He wasn't letting Jaap touch her.

Jaap's nostrils flared, and he threw his chin up in the air. "You think that soft little man could take me?"

"No, I think he has the full force of the military and judiciary behind him, and yes, they could take you. And we can't spare Sarah, so I can't let them do that. Swine slop." James gathered the muskets that they had finished with.

"She got my last keokje and you care more about *her*?"

"Yes."

David hauled himself back up onto the step. "The roads are going to be less safe now that Braddock has arrived with an army of regulars." He glared at Jaap. "We need to prepare for the conference and then for heading to Crown Point."

Oma Ten Eyck made the best koekjes in all of New York, and she would never send Jaap this way without giving him enough to share. He deserved to have his balls painted with honey and then to be sat on a stinging ant hill.

But James needed him. And David.

David would back whatever the sachems said, but he would join Johnson. No one would stop him. And for that, James was damned grateful.

But what were they supposed to do with Faith Richmond? None of them had time to be traipsing forty miles to Albany and then back. But someone was going to have to do it. Were it just the men, they could push hard and make it there and back in a few days if they had to, but traveling with a lady? It would take at least two or three days just to get there at a speed she could travel, plus a handful of men to protect her with the French swarming through the woods looking for enticing targets.

He needed to not think of her as "enticing."

At least she was conscious now. If her father had just left his aide here until she came to, the lieutenant could have dealt with her. James sighed.

But her father's orders presumably included his staff, such as it was. He rolled his shoulders and rubbed his hands over his face.

"What the hell are you so distracted about?" Jaap asked.

"I am not the one who is distracted."

David grabbed a musket and his cleaning equipment. "We've got a boatload of work to do and not much time to do it in."

At least David understood the larger picture. "Can you make a run to your uncle and see what his men have found in the woods? I don't like that we don't know what the French are doing, and you know darned well Johnson won't like it."

Jaap stood up. "Don't look at me. I'm not going with him. I just got back, if you remember, and I'm tired. I was in Albany—"

"And Schenectady." David glared at him.

"Waiting for news to bring to you two lunkheads," Jaap said, looking offended.

"And chasing Dutch girls," James said.

Jaap's face cracked open in a grin. "Not my fault the assignment came with some inspiring benefits."

No doubt. "Don't let Johnson catch you chasing women here."

Jaap shrugged. "He just doesn't like the competition."

"You are no competition for someone with that much money." Only Jaap was cocky enough to think he was.

"Don't underestimate my prowess."

Jaap was not getting the idea. James grabbed him by the front of his shirt and glared at him until he had Jaap's undivided attention. The rough fabric bit into his skin. He gave Jaap a quick shake. "Even your grandmother's baking won't save you if you dally with Miss Richmond under this roof."

Chapter 12

Faith lay in bed, staring at the heavy brocade bed curtains. She ran her hand over the burgundy coverlet with a gold design woven in.

It was all lovely, and she was sick to death of it.

The room had stopped spinning days ago, and the throbbing in her head had reached a level she could probably function with. At least her vision wasn't blurry anymore.

It was time to try to sit up again.

She started to roll to her left to keep the weight off of her sore leg. If she went just an inch at a time, that seemed to keep her head from going off kilter. At least her stomach behaved.

She made it to her left side, then put both hands down on the mattress to raise her upper body.

Eventually, she was upright—more or less. She leaned onto her good hip to keep her weight off the stitches the woman, Sarah, said were on the back of her leg. She slowly reached her toes toward the floor...but the floor wasn't there.

Carefully, she looked down. The bed was so tall that her feet didn't reach it. She was going to have to slide off the bed for her feet to reach solid ground. That was not appealing. But at some point, she had to make her way to the privy. And she had to get moving before her father borrowed more money from Caleb's family to purchase even more land and get himself too far into debt to ever get out.

She leaned her weight on her left hip and stretched her right toe toward the floor. Just as her left hip started to slide off the edge of the bed, Sarah came running into the room.

"What are you doing?"

Faith grabbed at the bedclothes as her hip slid, but she couldn't stop her feet from hitting the floor.

Sarah grabbed a chair from the corner of the room and set it down right behind Faith. "Sit. Careful of your stitches."

Faith sat, perching only half her bottom on the chair. Even that made the back of her leg and tailbone scream, but she would faint before she let Sarah know that.

"What exactly did you have it in mind to do?"

Faith looked up into Sarah's wide eyes. They were almost as dark as her hair. She didn't look angry exactly, but she clearly didn't think Faith wise just now.

"I have to get up," she said. "I have to get dressed, and I have to get to Albany. I've already caused far too much delay."

Sarah's face softened. "You aren't ready to travel yet. Besides, your father has his lieutenant and the entire army to help him do what he needs to get done. He doesn't need you."

Faith's eyes stung. "Yes, he *does*." She scanned the room for her clothes.

"Is there something else in Albany you're eager to get to? Maybe *someone* else?"

"You don't understand. Caleb can't run his business dealings." Caleb could barely get himself dressed in the morning. "And I have to get my father packed and organized so that he can head out to Fort Niagara with General Shirley."

Sarah shook her head. "With all the thousands of men in the British army, he can't get himself to Fort Niagara? No one else can help him?"

Faith didn't trust herself to answer, and she looked at the ceiling to keep her threatening tears at bay. Yes, they probably could, but they wouldn't stop him from frittering away his salary on things he didn't need instead of paying off his debts. It was bad enough he wanted to marry her off to Caleb, but if they couldn't pay the loans down, Caleb's father would rule them for the rest of their days.

Marrying Caleb was sufficiently uninspiring without the added prospect of their living under his father's thumb.

Sarah knelt down on the floor in front of her and took Faith's hands in her own. "I can see that you want to help him, but he needs to learn to help himself. Or at least his lieutenant needs to learn how to help him. It's his job, after all."

Faith avoided Sarah's gaze. She wasn't going to air her father's dirty linens to a complete stranger, no matter how kind. She had a duty to her family, and in a military family, that was everything.

Sarah shook her head again, then rubbed Faith's back like she was an upset child. "How about we try to get you dressed and see how that goes?"

Faith almost sobbed. "Thank you."

Sarah went to Faith's trunk, opened the lid, and pulled out a blue muslin gown. "This should do for a warm day around the house." Sarah's eyes scanned over the other scant belongings she had brought with her, but she didn't comment as she grabbed her stays.

Faith rocked forward to stand up.

"Keep yourself in that chair while I help."

Faith obeyed. She clutched her stays to her front while Sarah laced them loosely in back, over her shift. The gown wouldn't fit with no stays. Sarah tied Faith's pockets around her waist and slipped a petticoat over her head. Time for the gown itself. She raised her arms so that Sarah could thread them through the sleeves, like she was dressing a little girl.

Sarah grabbed her neckerchief, draped it around her shoulders and tucked the ends into the neckline of the gown. She studied her for a moment. "The embroidery on that is lovely, but the fabric is so fine the men will be staring at your chest right through it."

Faith bunched the fabric up a little more, so it appeared thicker. There wasn't much else she could do about the current fashions and how utterly unsuited they were for the frontier.

Sarah shook her head and let out a gusty breath. "Now we're going to have to see if you can actually stand." Sarah took Faith's arm and braced herself.

Faith planted both feet firmly on the floorboards and leaned heavily on Sarah to get to a standing position. Every part of her body protested in varying degrees.

"You should probably hold on to the bedpost," Sarah said and started arranging the hems of her petticoat and gown so they weren't bunched around her middle, baring her backside. "You're stronger than you look."

Faith wasn't so sure. But she clung to the bedpost because she would be damned if she was going to stay in bed any longer.

"I would very much like to go downstairs," she said.

"If I get you downstairs and you can't get back up, I will have to have one of the men carry you, like James carried you here."

Her head spun, and she worked for balance.

She groaned. It hadn't been a fever dream that he had held her in his arms. The idea of James Carroll's hands on her body shot heat to her midsection and below. She could feel where his hands had touched her, even though it had to be her imagination.

Had he also been by her bedside later? The gentle strength in his voice had made her want to cling to him. *Foolish.* Her weakened state was making her emotional about something that was merely practical on his part.

Her face burned. He must think she was an utterly helpless London miss who couldn't survive outside a drawing room, falling off a ladder like that. The heat in her cheeks spread down her neck. She would crawl up the stairs on her hands and knees before she would let someone carry her.

"You needn't worry," she told Sarah.

Sarah laughed out loud. "You are more pigheaded than half the men in this house."

Faith snorted at that, then stretched up tall. She might not have made a great impression thus far, but she was no fragile layabout. She removed her right arm from the bedpost. The floor was solid beneath her feet.

Sarah stood next to Faith, took her good left arm, and they proceeded to the door.

Chapter 13

"Johnson's back!" Jaap's voice echoed through the blockhouse.

James shot to his feet. He brushed off whatever lint might be on his clothes and then ran his hand over his hair to make sure his queue was still tight and tidy.

Then he dove for the door and led Jaap and David to the main house. They reached the front steps just as William Johnson dismounted his horse.

Johnson was taller than any of them, and dressed in an elegant coat that Sarah had charged him an astonishing sum for. He was a good bit older than them, but still fit and able in a fight.

"We've got business, boys." Johnson handed the reins to a stable lad who had come running from the barn. "I've called a council." He eyed them. "We are going on campaign against the French at Crown Point."

Then Johnson marched up the stairs and in the front door. James, Jaap, and David followed right behind him.

James's eyes adjusted to the indoor light just in time to see Johnson's eyes fall on Faith, sitting in the front room with a book. He had kept himself and the men so busy they only saw her at dinner. It worked to keep the distraction of her existence to a minimum, but he had stupidly forgotten she would be in the front room in the middle of the day.

Johnson straightened, threw back his shoulders, and burst into a smile. "What have we here?"

Shit. The old goat wasn't going to let an impending war distract him from a beautiful woman in his front parlor.

James stepped into the sitting room and stood between Johnson and Faith. "This is Miss Faith Richmond, daughter of Colonel Ebenezer Richmond, who is serving under Governor Shirley in the Niagara campaign."

Faith rose gingerly from her chair. The color had returned to her cheeks over the last few days, and she didn't waver on her feet. She'd proved sturdier than she looked. Even so, she had been knocked senseless, and her leg had to hurt.

He shifted closer to her. She deserved better than to have to fend off his employer's attentions. "Miss Richmond, this is William Johnson."

She curtsied a little stiffly. "General Johnson, I am so pleased to make your acquaintance." She radiated warmth, and Johnson reflected it right back at her. She had remembered his new rank. The woman understood how to flatter an important man, but flattering Johnson came with dangers.

"The pleasure is all mine, I assure you, Miss Richmond." Johnson took her delicate hand in his large one and kissed the back of it. Then he held it and did not seem inclined to let it go.

Wonderful. She was going to be a distraction to Johnson, too.

"She is recovering from a fall," James said. "Her father and his lieutenant had to go on to Albany without her." James looked at Johnson's meaty hand, still enveloping her elegant one. "She was unconscious for three days, and we had to call Sarah Philipse to stitch her up and tend her as she recovers."

Johnson kept his gaze on Faith. "I'm so very sorry to hear that you were injured."

"Sir, we have news about the French." Maybe that would get him to peel his eyes off Faith's neckline.

But Johnson slid his free hand up Faith's arm. "Let us have some refreshment."

James stood for a moment, loath to leave her there with Johnson. But he didn't dare ignore the request. With a last look at Faith, who was laughing and relaxed, he turned and headed out to the hall. Then, as soon as he was out of Johnson's sight, he ran down to the basement kitchens.

Sarah was there, helping Louisa. She wouldn't leave her friend to deal with a houseful of hungry men by herself when she was stuck here anyway, directing Faith's care. "Johnson wants lunch, and if we don't bring him some food quickly, Faith will be on the menu," he told them both.

Sarah stood. "Well, we had better feed him so he doesn't undo my past weeks' work and land her back in a sickbed." She turned and helped Louisa put some food on a tray.

"He steps out of line with Faith, and he'll have a purgative in his dinner," Louisa said.

David stuck his head into the kitchen. "Three more for dinner tonight."

James turned and glared at him.

"Wraxall, Claus, and Farrell just showed up," David said. "Apparently they're hungry, too." He retreated.

This was not good. Faith Richmond was unprotected in a house full of too many men preparing for war. Men who would be itching to release some of the tension of the situation. The fact that most of the newest arrivals were married meant nothing around here.

As soon as the food was done, Sarah shoved the laden tray at James. "You work for him. I don't."

He let Sarah lead the way up the stairs, and he followed right behind. He shoved her with the tray to get her to go faster, and she reached back and swatted at his arm. "I am checking on my patient. Don't make me injure you in the process and feel like a hypocrite."

They entered the hall, and laughter bubbled out of the sitting room. Johnson's dominated, but Faith's laugh was clear and full. They seemed to be getting along marvelously.

Sarah marched into the room. "How are you feeling?" she asked Faith, who smiled back, looking as delighted as a kitten with a piece of yarn. Perhaps she was enjoying Johnson's company as much as he was enjoying hers.

"Very well, thanks to your kind attention."

He should just keep his nose out of it.

Sarah made a show of examining the back of Faith's head, probably as much to remind Johnson that Faith had been knocked insensible as to see how Faith was healing. Sarah knew Johnson and his inability to keep his cock in his breeches.

James set the tray down on the table. David and Jaap had disappeared, and the others must have gone directly to the blockhouse out back.

Finally, Sarah turned and left the room, apparently satisfied that Faith was fine for the moment, and hopefully having underscored for Johnson how seriously Faith had been injured.

James forced himself to turn toward the door.

"Carroll, stay." Johnson grabbed some bread from the tray and gestured at James to sit in an empty chair. "I have a lot of work to do, and I need your help."

His pulse picked up. Yes, war made opportunities.

James sat and schooled his face so as not to look over-eager. The coming campaign and the work that went with it could be his pot of gold.

"I have sent messages to all the sachems," Johnson said. "And I've asked them to convene near the end of June."

That would mean quick preparations. But if anyone could do it, Johnson could. With help. Help that he would be very grateful for.

"I've made Wraxall secretary for Indian Affairs, so he will record the entire proceeding." Johnson took a bite of his bread and cold meat.

The muscle in James's jaw twitched. Because Wraxall could write, he had just gotten a position that would make his career.

James forced his hands to stay still. He could read, more or less, and he was working on writing.

He glanced at Faith, who was listening with rapt attention. His face grew hot. It probably didn't even occur to her that some people didn't get a chance to learn something so critical as writing.

"Claus will be the official interpreter. I can't run the conference and interpret. And Farrell will be my deputy."

Farrell would always be ahead of him, married to Johnson's sister. But Claus was a newcomer from Pennsylvania who had caught Johnson's eye as useful. It served no purpose to be bitter about it. But the purposeless bitterness lingered at the edge of his mind.

Faith leaned in toward Johnson. "This is all fascinating." She looked eager to hear more, and unaware of the dangers. He needed to remove her from Johnson's presence. Johnson liked strong women, and she was distracting Johnson from telling him what role he would get to play.

Johnson smiled at her and adjusted his crotch. "In order to get the support of any of the Iroquois, all of the Iroquois sachems have to agree to support our effort. That is part of how their confederacy works." He took another bite of his lunch and brushed a crumb from his chest.

"Are the Iroquois allied to the Mohawks?" she asked.

Johnson almost purred, obviously pleased with a chance to enlighten her. "The Mohawk are part of the Iroquois, as are the Oneida, Onondaga,

Cayuga, and Seneca." He listed the nations from east to west. Faith was on the edge of her chair and oblivious to the state of Johnson's breeches.

"There are roughly fifty key sachems." Johnson puffed up, always impressed with himself, but his shoulders looked strained. He was confident, and he could get what he needed from the Iroquois, but he knew what a big request he was about to make. He had to.

"I have ordered blankets and guns to hand out. Gifts are critical in diplomacy with the Iroquois. They show care and respect," Johnson said.

Was James just going to be shifting crates of trade goods?

Wraxall could write. Claus could speak Mohawk well. And Farrell had married Johnson's sister, and fine, they were incredibly valuable to Johnson with his trading empire. But there was only so much of other people's good fortune he could stomach at once.

"Carroll," Johnson said. "I'm taking militia from New York, Massachusetts, Rhode Island, Connecticut, and New Jersey. None of them know what they're doing. I need some men I can rely on."

He studied James. James's heart rate kicked up, and he sat up straighter in his chair.

"I'm sure the sachems will send warriors with me, but I don't know how long they'll stay. And they won't be under my direct command. I need some men with their skills who *are* under my command."

He had those skills, and Johnson had seen him use them.

"I need you to gather me up some men who can serve as rangers. They must know how to survive and fight in the woods." Johnson's eyes bore into James. "How long do you think that will take you?"

James kept his face neutral, but his pulse danced. "How many men do you need?"

"I think fifty to start with."

He forced a slow, long breath. Fifty would be a lot, but he would move heaven and earth to do it. "I can think of at least ten right now, and could have a list of likely men for you tomorrow after I've talked with David and Jaap."

Faith had been listening carefully. "Will these men become part of the militia? Or would they be part of the regular army?"

James's and Johnson's heads both swiveled towards her. That was a damn good question. And now James wanted to know the answer, too. He *needed* to know it to recruit the men.

"Well," said Johnson. "I'm not certain yet." He played it off like it was not a major concern. But it was.

"Pardon my question," Faith said. "I grew up an officer's daughter, and sometimes can't help myself." She lowered her lashes demurely. She wasn't calling them out, but James would bet his left nut she not only knew it was an important question, but that he and Johnson had both been about to blunder on without addressing it.

Who would he be asking men to throw in their lot with? Who would *he* be throwing in his lot with? The militia or the regulars? The differences in terms of station were profound.

Johnson turned to Faith and gave her an appraising look from head to toe.

He liked smart women just as much as he liked strong women. And attractive women. His eyes rested on Faith's breasts again, and he shifted his napkin over his crotch.

Now she had done it.

"You may go, Carroll."

James went to the door, then cast a glance back at Faith. Johnson turned and looked at him as if to ask why he was still there.

James gave him a quick nod and headed for the hall.

Chapter 14

A week later, Faith sat alone in the sitting room, reading Bland's *Treatise on Military Discipline*, which she practically knew by heart, much to her father's dismay.

Johnson had been called away, so she had a reprieve from male eyes on her chest. General Johnson was an attractive man, and presumably had no trouble finding female companionship, but she had no illusions about the attentions of the lord of the manor. He seemed to think he was entitled to anything, or anyone, he wanted, and it reminded her too much of Caleb's father. Not that Caleb's father had been interested in her body, but he clearly thought of her as an asset to be bartered rather than as a living, feeling person. And, legally, he was more or less correct.

At least Johnson had kept his hands to himself thus far.

She couldn't concentrate on the book and turned to the window. The river ran past the house, unhurried, ignoring the humans on its banks. A large bird circled lazily in the sky, playing on the air currents, looking for its dinner.

The door to the sitting room opened, and she straightened.

"Sarah had Louisa make this for you."

It was James, dressed in breeches, as he usually was in the house. She preferred the loincloth and woolen leggings he wore out on patrol. Not that it was appropriate for her to have an opinion on the subject.

He carried a teacup on a saucer. His fingers barely touched it, like it might bite him. She couldn't help smiling at his wary expression.

Sarah had taken excellent care of her. Her head was fine now, as long as she didn't move it quickly or touch the spot at the back that hit the floor. Sarah had removed the stitches in her leg yesterday, which wasn't fun, but they had started to itch, which Sarah said was good. Her bruises had gone from dark purple and brown to greenish, and now they were fading to yellow. Not attractive, but healing.

It was time for her to get back to Albany before her father made any more questionable financial decisions.

"Thank you." She took the cup and sniffed the tea. Her nose wrinkled, and she tried not to gag. *Gracious.* That explained James's expression.

"When I was a lad, I fell from the hayloft in Sarah's father's barn. Cut myself open on a pitchfork," James said. He gave her a rare smile, his rich brown eyes radiating warmth. Her belly hummed. "Sarah gave me this after she removed my stitches. I thought she was trying to poison me." He gave an even more rare laugh. "I think the main purpose of it is to be so miserable you forget about your injury."

His angular face was beautiful when he smiled. He probably would prefer to be thought of as rugged, or strong, but he was also flat-out pretty. He was usually so intense she hadn't appreciated the full effect of his smile before.

"I thought you were from Ireland."

His cheeks and the corners of his mouth lowered. "I am. But I came here at the age of ten, and after a year ended up in Sarah's father's household."

She couldn't stop her brows from knitting together. Where was his family?

Before she could say anything foolish, James changed the subject. "I hope General Johnson's attentions haven't been too forward."

Her cheeks burned, and she shook her head. "Isn't there a Mrs. Johnson?"

He chuffed out a laugh. "There is. When the unrest broke out, he sent her to his house in Albany to keep her safe."

So that was why Sarah had been taking care of her. "That explains much."

His expression grew darker. "Not really. The man feels free to help himself, regardless of where his beloved Catty is."

Oh, my. "Does he have children?"

"*They* have three children. *He* has more."

Faith almost choked. Really, she shouldn't have been shocked. "Does he support them?" For a moment, James didn't answer. She shouldn't have asked. He would think her inappropriate.

"A few of them are cousins to varying degrees of David's." He shifted his feet, and she was not imagining the color in cheeks. "Life on the frontier has its own rules. I'm sure they differ somewhat from those in London."

She was about to agree with him, then stopped. How different were those rules, really? His face turned pinker under her gaze. It was hard to know if he was scandalized by Johnson, or just thought she would be. Or at least, should be. "I thank you for distracting him."

He tugged at his collar. She should probably change the subject, but it would be helpful to her father to understand the general better. "How many children does he have?"

"The estimates vary."

She laughed. "That many? Then I thank you doubly for distracting him."

He schooled his face. "Just because he is the wealthiest man in western New York, that doesn't mean he should be able to have his way with whoever he wants, willing or not."

Her chest grew warm and her body thrummed. When was the last time someone questioned the right of a powerful man to behave however they wanted around her, or around anyone, for that matter? James kept surprising her, and, yes, she enjoyed it.

And she liked talking with him. "How long have you known the others?"

He looked at the book in her hands, and she set it down.

James looked back at her. "I've known David and Jaap for years, and I met Farrell and Wraxall when I came to work for Johnson. Johnson just took Claus under his wing in the past year or so. He married Farrell to his sister, and I have seen Claus eying Johnson's daughter. One of his legally recognized daughters."

He was very matter-of-fact.

"Do you think one of the men might be prevailed upon to take me to Albany?" Lovely as James was, she needed to get back.

His face went blank. "Has Sarah said you can travel?"

She chose her words carefully. "I have imposed myself on the hospitality of this household too long, and I am needed in Albany."

"So she says no?"

It probably was funny from his perspective. He didn't understand her position. "I think I am a good judge of my readiness."

"You thought you could travel before you could stand." His tone was softer than his words, but he shifted straighter. "I will ask Wraxall if he can see to your transportation." And with a last glance at the book, he left the room. Had he never seen anyone other than an officer read military strategy?

She huffed out a breath. He probably thought her helpless, when she could very well do for herself.

Outside the window, in the courtyard, a clump of men stood debating something. James joined them, waiting his turn to speak. She shouldn't be staring, especially when she was in plain view through the window. She almost threw her hands up in the air. The piles of "shoulds" she labored under were too much for her to keep track of.

She turned from the window. The sitting room had a chess set on the table, but someone was clearly mid-game, so she didn't touch it.

Footsteps sounded in the hallway, and James returned to the sitting room.

His face was solemn. "I am afraid Sarah says you are not ready to travel. As soon as she says you are, we will get you back to Albany." He paused. "I promise."

She rolled his words around in her mind for a moment. "She out-rules Mr. Wraxall? Does she out-rule General Johnson?"

James laughed loud, the sound of it vibrated right through her. "On the condition of her patients, yes."

Her jaw went slack for a moment before she caught herself. She had never known another woman to command that kind of respect unless she had a title. It was for the best her father was not here to witness this conversation and tell her not to get ideas in her head. He would forbid her from interacting with any frontier women again.

But James couldn't have actually consulted Sarah just now. "I haven't seen Sarah all day. How could she have said no?"

"She had to go home to make sure things were running well there in her absence. She figured you would ask and left strict orders."

How stupid to forget Sarah wasn't part of Johnson's household. And thoughtless of her not to consider Sarah might have other obligations than tending to her injuries. "Does she have a family of her own?"

James laughed yet again. "No one has ever successfully asked for her hand. Not that many haven't tried."

Her cheeks flashed hot. Was James one of that many? Not that any of it should matter to her. She needed to get herself back to care for her own household, not worry about James's interest in another woman.

"James!" Jaap slid in through the doorway. "Johnson wants to talk to you."

"About what?"

Jaap smiled like he had the best gift ever for James. Their temperaments were opposite in every way, and Jaap was clearly delighting in making James wait. "Remember how you said war creates opportunities?"

James nodded.

"Go talk to Johnson. You earned it."

James turned to Faith. "Please excuse me." He gave her a brief tip of his head and strode out the door, his demeanor that of a hound on the scent.

She shouldn't miss his presence. He was a man on the make, and she was leaving. Flights of fancy would get her nowhere. Reality was where she needed to focus her energies.

"I take it Johnson has good news for him?" Faith settled herself carefully back into a chair and busied herself arranging her skirts.

Jaap sat next to her. "The man is a fool to put his career above a beautiful lady."

"I should hardly think so."

"There is nothing I would put ahead of a beautiful lady." Jaap waggled his eyebrows at her.

She laughed at him. He didn't mean any harm. No doubt if she encouraged him, he would be dragging her to the nearest bedchamber, but he didn't seem one to push past a "no." She grew up around soldiers and was confident in her judgment of who to steer clear of.

"I've never seen you put a beautiful woman ahead of your oma's koekjes."

Faith startled at Sarah's voice. The holder of her fate had returned.

Sarah strode into the room. "Did Louisa give you my tea?"

Faith's cheeks burned, and she grabbed the tea, held her breath, and swallowed the now cold concoction. It threatened to come back up, but she swallowed again. Hard.

"Koekjes?" Faith asked. The sooner the tea was forgotten, the better. "I had never heard of them before I arrived here. I must come to Jaap's defense on this, as they are marvelous."

"You only think you have tasted koekjes." Sarah looked at Jaap. "Someday I will cajole the recipe out of her."

Jaap stood and blew Sarah a kiss. "Not even you." And he disappeared out the door.

Sarah turned on her.

Faith held up her hands in surrender. "I drank all the tea, and I'm ready to travel."

Sarah came close, peered into her eyes, and gestured for her to walk across the room.

Faith walked steadily and forced herself not to limp, then she wobbled as she turned.

"You're hiding it well, but no, you're not."

Chapter 15

James swung himself up onto the steps and took two at a time. Johnson was in the attic having a conference with the men. It was the one room big enough to hold everyone.

This might be the chance he had been working for since he arrived in North America.

When he entered the room, Johnson said, "Carroll, there you are." He waved him over to where they were all seated on blankets on the floor.

The back of James's neck tingled as he hurried to join them. "How can I be of service?"

"Have a seat." Johnson pointed to a space next to where Farrell and Claus sat.

Claus bent his head towards Johnson. "You need Red Head. Everyone knows he leans toward the French. But I think he will listen."

Farrell nodded. "We know Hendrick will support you, but so does everyone else. Red Head would make a much bigger impact. No one expects it."

James waited for Johnson to tell him why he was there. Hopefully, Faith hadn't retched after drinking Sarah's vile tea.

"I have sent an invitation to Hendrick." Johnson took a gulp of his beer. "I am confident he will come, and with luck, he will bring Abraham. They will help us strategize. And he had better hurry, or Shirley will have snatched all the available supplies to keep for his own campaign before I can focus on supplying mine and there is nothing left."

James rubbed his hands over his face. He was going to have to talk to David about the politics of all this later, and wouldn't that be fun.

"Hendrick will push for sending warriors, but the Seneca, they will be against it," Farrell said.

"Carroll, this is what I need from you," Johnson said to him.

James squared his shoulders. It had better be good, or Jaap was going to get a fist in his face for getting his hopes up. Because his hopes had reached dizzying heights as he climbed the stairs, and he usually kept them reined in better than that.

"I need those rangers to be militia."

James felt his gut drop. Provincial militia was not as high a step as Regular Army.

"I don't want another general to be able to take my rangers," said Johnson. "So I want you to raise a provincial ranger company."

James nodded. "Of course, sir."

"If you recruit enough men to fill the company, you will be its captain."

James's heart stopped. He wasn't going to be a private, or even an ensign—he was going to be a captain.

Johnson smiled at him. "That's how the militia works, and it does have its advantages over regular army."

James's heart lurched back into motion and slammed against his ribs, which could barely contain it. Johnson had no idea what that meant to him. Or maybe he did.

Holy Mary, Mother of God. He was going to be a ranger captain. For a brief instant, he wished he could tell his parents. "I will talk to David, Jaap, and Okwaho today."

"I don't think you want to sign up any Mohawks without talking to Hendrick," said Claus.

James forced himself not to look at Claus, or at Farrell, or at any of the others gathered. "How many warriors the Iroquois send is going to depend on how the conference goes," James said. "Either way, you know you'll have David and Okwaho. If they are in the militia company, then the sachems can't send them home at an awkward moment."

Johnson looked from him to Claus and back to him. It was hot in the attic, and a trickle of sweat made its way down the channel of James's spine, coming to rest in the small of his back. He didn't shift.

"Farrell, what do you think?" Johnson asked.

Farrell flipped his small knife around in his fingers for a moment. "They both have points."

But James's point was better. "Sir, if David serves with the rangers, he can give you better intelligence on the thinking of the Iroquois as it shifts throughout the campaign."

Farrell let a breath slowly out of his nose. "David does understand the politics extremely well. Perhaps Carroll is right." He glanced at Claus, who shrugged.

James stopped his toe from tapping. "I will ask him for a rundown of the political pluses and minuses." It wouldn't be fun, but David would give it to him, and then join. And he would talk Okwaho into joining, too. With luck, James would survive the political discourse without his brain turning to pottage and dribbling out his ears.

"If Jaap joins, maybe the militia can run on his oma's koekjes," Farrell said.

"Then I'm joining the rangers," Claus joked.

Johnson's laugh reverberated through the entire attic. The mood of the group had lightened.

James took a steadying breath. "We need Leonidas Ten Eyck."

Leo competed with Johnson in the fur trade, and no man was a better tracker. Johnson didn't like competition, so he didn't like Leo. But he also wasn't a fool.

Johnson scowled and said, "He can pay for your uniforms, then."

Leo wouldn't love that, but he would probably do it.

"Someone needs to take Miss Richmond back to Albany," Claus said. "She will only be in the way for the conference."

Right. She needed to go. For her own safety.

Certainly Sarah would declare her fit to travel any day now. And the sooner she was on her way, the better. He should be glad they had finally started to discuss it. But her safety on the road was going to be tricky.

"We can send David and Jaap to take her," James said. David would at least keep Jaap in line, and they would both keep her safe.

Johnson waved his hand vaguely in James's direction. "We'll figure that out when Sarah says it's time."

Never once did Faith play the invalid or complain about anything other than not being able to pull her weight. But now that Johnson was back, that just put her more in harm's way. Her father wasn't here to protect her from Johnson's reputation, let alone the behavior that earned him that reputation. They had to get her back to Albany.

"We need to know what the French have been up to, because I don't want them doing anything that could upset the conference." He looked at James, and then everyone else followed suit. Right—he was supposed to have been figuring that out while Johnson was in Virginia getting his orders.

James looked Johnson in the eye. "We know someone has been scouting. I assume French, but still can't say for certain."

"What have you found?"

"We found more birch bark with markings on it, but we can't decipher them. I also found some parched corn. Could be Abenaki. Could be Canadian."

"I'm sure they already have a map of the house and grounds," Johnson said. "The house is too obvious a target, and it would be too much to hope for that they were so incompetent that they couldn't scout close enough to sketch one with reasonable accuracy."

Yet another reason they needed to get Faith back to Albany.

James nodded, as did the other men. "I think, sir, they are trying to see what you are up to as the preparations for the summer campaigns begin. There is no sign yet of a larger party, but we have to assume they will try to grab anyone careless enough to wander alone to force information from them about the conference and the campaign plans." Before they killed the fool or sent him north as a captive.

"I can't take any chances." Johnson stood and walked to the window, presumably looking at the river as it flowed past. "Carroll, set men to double the scouts. I doubt the French would be stupid enough to attack right now, but that doesn't mean they won't. I am depending on you to find out what they are up to. Go."

James stood. "Absolutely, sir." He turned and headed for the stairs, taking them carefully. Who else could he send on a scout? He was going to have to have David send for Okwaho. He paused on the landing.

Captain.

That had a very nice ring to it. And he would recruit the best woodsmen in the valley to make it happen. He headed down the next flight of stairs and jumped off the last two steps to the second-floor hall.

"Well, don't you have a spring in your step."

He spun, and there stood Faith.

She looked him over from shoes to hat. "Why are you glowing, James Carroll?"

He wasn't glowing, but he was damned excited, and why should he hide it? If he had the slightest idea how to dance a jig, he would be doing it. By

God, he had been so focused for so long, and he deserved to cut loose and celebrate.

"Because I am going to recruit a ranger company for General Johnson, and in doing so, I shall become Captain Carroll."

Her face broke into a smile so broad he would have thought she was the one who was about to become an officer. She clapped her hands together. "That is wonderful!"

It was more than wonderful. It was the opportunity he had worked for years to get. What he had sacrificed so much for. And now that it had arrived, he could barely think his brain was so giddy.

He picked Faith up by the waist and spun her around in the hall. She laughed and clung to his shoulders, holding on tight to him, until he set her down. Then she looked into his eyes, and the temperature in the hall rose. His eyes fell to her lips.

What the hell was he doing?

The scent of roses hit his nose, and the soft fabric of her skirts under his fingers made him want to find the even softer flesh of her hip. The only sounds were their mingled breathing and the mutterings from Johnson's meeting that continued overhead in the attic.

Johnson could take away as quickly as he could give. James would not throw away the opportunity he had just been given.

He removed his hands from her hips. "My apologies."

Then he turned and strode down the stairs to the first floor.

Chapter 16

Faith looked straight ahead as Sarah told her to. Sarah inspected her eyes as though she could see all the way into her mind. She probably could. They had been through this routine every few days for weeks now.

"Hold out your right arm." Sarah took hold of her hand. "Squeeze my hand as hard as you can."

Faith tried to break every bone in Sarah's hand. Not that she would, but if she could make Sarah worry she could, she would have to admit Faith was fine.

Sarah didn't even flinch. "Your arm is much better." She went around behind her and poked her fingers at Faith's back. Faith breathed slowly and refused to flinch at any of her prodding. "And how is your backside? Can you really withstand a journey all the way back to Albany?"

"Of course." It wouldn't be the most enjoyable journey she had ever taken. She must have landed on her tailbone first when she fell, because it was still quite sore. But she had been here for over a month now, and it was time to get back to her father, bruised tailbone or no.

Sarah circled back in front of her, her eyes roving up and down, scanning every inch of her. Then she looked Faith in the eye and gave her a single nod. "I think you'll make it."

Faith's knees went weak. *At last.*

Johnson wouldn't let her leave until Sarah had proclaimed her fit. And now she had. "Thank you." Her throat got tight. "For everything."

Sarah's eyes narrowed. "There must be something incredibly appealing back in Albany beside your father."

"My father needs me to help him prepare...and I need to help Caleb." She took a deep breath. "My father intends for me to marry Caleb."

Sarah raised one eyebrow. "Why?"

Faith shrugged. Marrying Caleb got her father his loan, which her father saw as taking care of their future. Caleb's father only agreed to the loan because if she married Caleb, the money would stay in the family, even if her father defaulted. She would be out on the streets if she defied him. It wasn't as if she had any valuable skills she could support herself with like Sarah and Louisa did, and no man in her circle would marry her without her father's blessing. She would somehow turn their new holdings into something, and it would have to do. With her mother gone, she needed to look after her father.

Yet she couldn't bear to say the words.

Sarah shook her head almost imperceptibly from side to side. "He didn't seem your sort."

Perhaps not, but those were the cards she had been dealt, and without an independent income, she had no others tucked up her sleeve to play at the moment.

Sarah took her arm and led her downstairs and directly into the drawing room and its collection of men. "General Johnson, Miss Richmond is now fit to travel."

Faith stood in the center of the room, many sets of male eyes upon her.

Johnson stood and approached her. "Let me see if I agree with Sarah's diagnosis." He circled around her slowly, never taking his eyes off her body. Her skin twitched, but she stood still. He most definitely was *not* her sort.

"She is ready," Sarah said, interrupting his inspection.

Johnson finally tore his eyes away from Faith and smiled at Sarah. "If you say so."

James was there, eyes narrowed as he stared at Johnson's back. "Sir, shall we let Miss Richmond sit?"

He risked his master's ire by pointing out Johnson's lack of manners. But if he was doing it because he thought she couldn't handle herself, she would have to set him straight. It wasn't as if Johnson was the first man to stare at her breasts. Indeed, she had caught James himself staring at them a time or two, which was far more distracting than when Johnson did it.

James tipped his head and just the merest corner of his mouth tipped up, hinting at a smile, like he could read her thoughts.

Her belly did that flip again. But she was leaving now, and so she was relieved of the temptation to investigate why James set her body to internal acrobatics.

"Yes, Miss Richmond, please do be seated." Johnson gestured to a chair between his and James's. She smiled at each of them and sat with as much grace as her tailbone allowed.

"You have once again worked your magic, Sarah. How would the Mohawk Valley survive without you?" asked Johnson. "When will you relent and become my housekeeper?"

Sarah gave him a stiff smile but shook her head.

That seemed to carry meaning Faith didn't understand. And the least she could do for Sarah was to distract Johnson from pursuing whatever had put her on edge.

"I thank you very much for your hospitality while I've recuperated. I have put you out for far too long, and I fear I must put you out one final time."

Johnson turned and smiled benignly at her. "Whatever is in my power to do for you, Miss Richmond, I am very pleased to do it."

"I have kept my father waiting too long in Albany. And if you would be so kind as to help me return there as soon as possible, I would be much obliged." Johnson said nothing. Had she been a man, she could have just gone. Or at least if she were a man with the skills that James and the others had. But she wasn't. She would need protection and transportation. They could probably all walk it in a couple of days. Life wasn't fair.

Johnson appeared to latch onto something she said, his nostrils flaring like a dog scenting a bone. "Your father is the regular army colonel serving under Governor Shirley, correct?"

He knew that already. Johnson leaned in toward her like she had suddenly become the most interesting person in the room. But this time, he wasn't looking at her chest.

"Yes, he is." She lowered her eyes modestly, since it wouldn't do for her to stare like a man could.

Johnson shifted his chair so it was in front of her, his knees practically brushing against hers, but she didn't pull away. Powerful men's egos bruised easily, and she needed this powerful man's help.

"So your father is serving under Governor Shirley. Has he much battlefield experience?"

"He served in the War of the Austrian Succession, and he studied at Sandringham." He had been an aide-de-camp in the war, not leading men in the field, but Johnson didn't need to know that. And he was very good at training and mentoring new troops.

Johnson studied her for a moment. "Does he have much experience with supplies and logistics?"

She did. "He has some."

"And I hear from my men he has purchased a parcel of land on the Schoharie. Is that correct? Are we to be neighbors?" His eyes had drifted down to her neckline again.

"I don't believe we will take up residence there, no." She leaned slightly back in her chair. "But we do plan for some extensive business operations, so we will certainly pass through."

James leaned in toward Johnson. "We met with them on a patrol. Her father was getting the lay of the land. It was on the first patrol where we found evidence of the French. I am sure that was instructive for him."

Faith glanced sideways at James. He gave her that little quarter-smile. Her heart gave an extra hard thump. From such a driven man, that quarter-smile had more power than a full-on grin from someone like Jaap.

"General Johnson," Sarah said from the doorway. "We still have to address arrangements to get Miss Richmond back to Albany. I am sure her father and his connections are most concerned for her."

David appeared from the front hall. "General, Hendrick sends word he and Abraham will be here well ahead of the conference."

Johnson nodded. "Excellent."

James asked David, "Did he say if they would bring their families? If so, we need to be sure we have enough gifts on hand by then." He turned to Johnson for confirmation.

"The gifts for the conference should arrive from Albany any day now, if Shirley hasn't waylaid the wagons again to supply his own campaign." Johnson surveyed the room, not appearing to really see it. "This is going to be a critical moment for all the campaigns, boys. I will need everyone at their best."

Sarah cleared her throat. "Sir." She tipped her head toward Faith.

He looked back at Faith, and a sly smile crossed his face. "We will have a couple of men take her back as soon as they have unloaded the supplies from Albany. I am so sorry that you will have to tarry here just a little longer."

James made a sound that might have been a groan next to her.

She forced her face not to register her distress.

Chapter 17

A train of wagons traveled along the high road and lumbered, one at a time, into the palisaded courtyard in front of the house. James turned on the front steps to look for Jaap, but Jaap was already heading for the courtyard.

It was going to take them half the day to get the wagons unloaded. But once the gifts for the Iroquois were carefully stored, they could get Faith back to Albany, and then, with luck, he could start recruiting.

There was no way on God's green earth was he going to let this opportunity slip through his fingers. He would exceed all of Johnson's expectations or die trying. And it would be easier with Faith gone. Constantly trying to protect Faith from groping hands, or worse, was doing nothing good for his focus. And now he couldn't even trust himself to not act the fool when he was alone with her, after grabbing and her swinging her around in the house like they were intimate acquaintances.

She kept looking at him like she actually saw him, which was unsettling. Most people looked at him and saw a poor Irishman whose value lay in what skills he could offer. She looked at him like he wasn't an Irishman, but simply a man. And he was a man, for the love of God, which was why having her around was so damned distracting.

Now Johnson was clearly using her to try to slow Shirley down so Shirley couldn't get a head start on Johnson, which was smart, but not very convenient for getting their work done.

Jaap slapped him on the back. "You look like you are girding your loins to take on an entire regiment single-handed."

"As it happens, I was going to let you take on these wagons single-handed while I make a plan for recruiting." He gave Jaap the most beatific smile he could muster.

"Bullshit. You know the lovely Miss Richmond is watching from the drawing room, and you are not about to miss this opportunity to flex your muscles in the sun and impress her."

James shook his head. "Don't accuse me of what you have in mind. You can flex and pose all day long. I have a career to make, and I'll be thanking you not to make that go arseways for me."

Jaap turned toward the house and waved at the sitting-room window.

"She is upstairs with Sarah, you idiot," James said. "You waved at the wrong window."

"So you *did* know which window she is watching from," Jaap laughed.

Jaap was an ass. And yes, he knew exactly where Faith was. And that she was watching.

James walked over to the lead wagon in the convoy, directed the driver to pull up in front of one of the outbuildings, and pointed him toward the stone barn behind the house. "You will find hay and water for your oxen in the barn, and space to let them rest in the shade while we unload."

He turned back to Jaap. "Perhaps you would like to help with the unloading, if you are done wasting time?"

Jaap joined him at the back of the first wagon, and together they untied the ropes and flipped the tarp back to expose the cargo.

"This is going to be a long day." Jaap wasn't afraid of hard work. Boredom, however, would be his undoing.

Sarah appeared beside them. "What is your estimate of how long this will take?"

"I don't suppose you have come to help us unload the wagons?" asked Jaap.

"I wouldn't want to deprive you of your opportunity to show off your boundless strength and endurance," she said. "Are you two actually capable of having all of these wagons unpacked today?"

"How dare you doubt us!" Jaap said.

James rolled his eyes. Jaap was such an easy target.

"Then I shall tell Miss Richmond that she should expect to leave for Albany sometime tomorrow."

James nodded to her, and she stared back at him, tilting her head like she was thinking.

"Hmm," she said.

"What? I agreed with you."

"You are normally smart enough to stay out of Johnson's way when he flirts with women." Sarah's eyes didn't leave his face.

James brushed past her and reached into the wagon for a large cloth-wrapped bundle. He grabbed the ropes holding the bundle together and hoisted the parcel onto his shoulder. Bundles of blankets were always heavier than they looked. He took it to the outbuilding and set it down in the far corner.

As he went out the door, Jaap passed him with a similar parcel on his own shoulder.

"More blankets?"

Jaap nodded.

James pointed to where he had set his down. "Let's stack the blankets in that far corner to keep them together."

James headed back to the wagon. Sarah had cocked her hip and was leaning against the wheel. "You like her." She wasn't going to budge.

"I like you too."

Sarah raised one eyebrow at him. "I think she is more your style, and you're less afraid of her than you are of me." She turned and walked back toward the house.

She was wrong. He was becoming very much afraid of Faith Richmond, which was why he had begun to avoid her whenever he could. He was starting to trust himself even less than Johnson around her.

"Why doesn't she like any of us?" Jaap said from behind him.

He flinched. The bastard had snuck up on him. James swung the bundle of blankets off the back of the wagon and directly into Jaap's gut.

"Oof."

"Add that to the stack. You prefer more compliant women, and you know it."

"And you seem to prefer English women." Jaap heaved the bundle to his shoulder, turned, and headed for the outbuilding.

By the time they were done with the first wagon, they had both stripped off their shirts. Fairer sex be damned—it was getting hot, and he didn't want to have to wash his shirt tonight.

Another carriage rumbled into the crowded courtyard and drew to a stop right in front of them.

James looked up at the driver.

"Muskets and one gunsmith," the man said with a German accent.

James looked into the back of the wagon. "Is the gunsmith in one of the crates?"

The driver leveled his eyes at James. No sign of a smile. "I"—he pointed his thumb at his own chest—"am the gunsmith."

"And you are delivering your wares in person?" James asked.

"I am here to make sure everyone knows how to operate them and care for them properly." He looked at James as though he did not think James knew how to properly care for a musket. "And to repair guns for the Iroquois when they gather."

Johnson had thought of everything.

"And are these gifts for the Iroquois, or are these for the militia?"

"Are you part of the militia?" the man asked.

James straightened. "I am James Carroll, and I am recruiting Johnson's ranger company." He wasn't fool enough to tempt fate, so he didn't refer to himself as captain. He wasn't a captain until he had finished recruiting the company.

"I am Benjamin Dreyfuss, and perhaps I will join this ranger company after the conference."

This man was no woodsman. He was tall and wiry, and his skin was the pale white of someone who spent most of his time indoors. Rangers needed to know how to fight in the woods, not how to sit in a shop and tinker with tools.

Sarah returned from the house and came to stand next to James. Benjamin Dreyfuss asked, "Is she one of your recruits?" He finally smiled.

Sarah ignored him and spoke to James. "General Johnson has decided to keep Miss Richmond entertained, so he sent me to ask you if the muskets have arrived yet. Since this is obviously an excuse to keep me from chaperoning them, I suggest you answer quickly."

"If you will send the wench to fetch a few men, we can unload the muskets," said Dreyfuss.

James winced. He looked from Sarah to Dreyfuss and back to Sarah. Her jaw was flexed tight, and her eyes were cold as flint. "You will do well to remember that I am no one's wench. Paid or otherwise."

James went to the back of the wagon. "Jaap, come here. Right now, please." He dropped the tailgate and slid the first crate of muskets to the edge of the wagon bed.

Jaap appeared next to him. He looked at Sarah, glaring at the gunsmith, and kept his mouth shut. Every once in a long while, Jaap showed signs of intelligence.

James said, "Just grab the other end of this crate so we can get him out of her presence." He slid his end of the crate off the end of the wagon and Jaap grabbed hold of the other end.

"Dreyfuss," James said. "Grab this end and help get this crate stowed away."

The man climbed down from the wagon and grabbed James's end of the crate. Together, Dreyfuss and Jaap carried it to the blockhouse, and Sarah turned on her heel and headed back inside.

David came out of the front door and passed Sarah as she stomped up the stairs.

"Who is that man, and why does Sarah look like she wants to rip his balls off and choke him with them?" David asked.

"Gunsmith who made the muskets. And he called her a wench."

"He better not try that with Louisa, or she will cook him up for dinner. The fool must be an orphan with no female relations."

James rubbed the heels of his hands over his eyes. He really didn't need this today. "He is also here to mend guns during the conference, so we can't let either Sarah or Louisa run him off when we are done unloading the muskets."

He looked up at the house. Faith was watching from her bedchamber. She must have escaped Johnson's company.

David said something, but he missed it. "Sorry, what?"

"You keep complaining that she is distracting us, but you are the one who can't think clearly around her," said David.

He glanced back at the window again. David was more right than he knew.

Chapter 18

The sun shined in the window the next morning when Faith stepped off the final step of the staircase into the hall.

"He did what?" Johnson's voice boomed from the sitting room.

Faith stopped. Jaap came out of the sitting room and spotted her.

"I assume this is not a suitable moment for me to join the gentleman?"

Jaap paused, then gave her an impish grin. "If you are up to it, it might actually be the perfect time."

Faith gave a brief nod. Placating arguing men might not be a relaxing morning's entertainment, but it was certainly within her capabilities.

"Good luck. I have to go check out the gunsmith for James to see if he might be ranger material. Besides, they are talking politics in there. Not my idea of fun." With a jaunty wave, Jaap headed out the door.

She squared her shoulders, then swept across the hall to the drawing room. *Once more unto the breach.* At least Jaap hadn't been avoiding her like James had. One moment James would look at her with those intense eyes that gave her all sorts of impure thoughts, then the next moment he would turn and disappear for hours.

The men all looked up at her. Johnson smiled. "Miss Richmond, pray come sit down."

Then he turned right back to David, as if he hadn't been interrupted. "What on Earth possessed Governor Shirley?"

David shifted under Johnson's gaze. "He claims because he outranks you, he does not need to confer with you to recruit Iroquois warriors to join him on his campaign to Fort Niagara. That isn't sitting well with the sachems."

Johnson sat, stone-like, for a moment. "I sent him word that I have the conference starting in less than two weeks. And now he is bungling it by undermining my authority and recruiting warriors himself." Johnson tapped his hand on the arm of his chair. "In Indian affairs, I outrank him."

James sat silently, eyes narrowed, like he was studying Johnson.

"He has already canceled half of my orders from the Albany merchants and redirected them toward his campaign." Johnson didn't yell, but his voice was stone cold.

Time to intervene.

A tea tray sat on the table in the corner. Steam curled from the spout of the pot. "Perhaps some tea would help solve your dilemmas?" She stood and went to the tea service without waiting for an answer. The distraction would give them a moment to calm down, and at least suggesting tea was something a woman could do without being accused of meddling in men's affairs. Besides, Johnson was apparently between housekeepers.

She bent to hand General Johnson the first cup. He took it and gave her a kind smile. Then his eyes found their way to her cleavage that her neckerchief did little to hide, but at least that distracted him momentarily.

She returned to the tea table and poured a cup of tea for each of the other men in turn. David's shoulders were still bunched with tension.

James's eyes met hers, and he nodded his thanks. Then his eyes dropped a few inches to her lips, and then he seemed to catch himself and look down at his tea. Her body flushed warm, and she straightened a bit too fast, and her head got light.

"Perhaps I can ask Louisa for some food to accompany the tea?" she said, before anyone noticed her loss of equilibrium and declared her unfit for travel.

James and David exchanged glances.

"That would be delightful, Miss Richmond," Johnson said.

"I'll just check with her and be right back."

She trotted down the stairs to the basement kitchen and conferred with Louisa for a moment. The woman's face was bright and rosy, and shiny with a layer of sweat. The cellar was cooler than upstairs, but right in front of the stove, the poor woman must have been roasting. Not that it seemed to bother her.

"I'll send up a tray as soon as I can get it ready," Louisa said, shooing her out of the kitchen. She had long ago figured out that, unlike Sarah, Faith was no help there.

Faith left her to her work and climbed the stairs back to the main floor, her leg protesting only slightly.

Tension in the drawing room had clearly ratcheted up again while she was gone.

She said, "There will be food for everyone in just a few moments."

All the men in the room looked up at her entrance. Some thoughtful, some just grateful.

David turned back to Johnson. "Lydius himself was at the upper castle yesterday."

Faith shot her eyes to David. A man named Lydius had brokered her father's purchase of the land on the Schoharie. Perhaps it was the same man. "John Lydius?"

Heads swiveled once again in her direction.

"Are you acquainted with him?" Johnson asked.

"My father had some dealings with him."

Johnson's brows knit together, but then he turned back to the men. "Shirley appears to be trying to undermine my campaign to Crown Point and my efforts to recruit the Iroquois to our cause."

James looked from David to Johnson. "It wouldn't serve his purpose. He needs both campaigns to be successful, especially since he fancies himself in charge of both. Doesn't he?"

"He is not in charge of my campaign," Johnson said.

David tilted his head. "I hear Braddock was rather vague on that point."

Johnson grunted and glared at David.

She felt James's eyes on her, and her skin grew warm under his gaze. The man's behavior had grown unpredictable lately, but his effect on her body had not. Whether he was being kind and attentive or avoiding her like she had the pox, her body grew feverish every time his eyes landed on her.

But she needed to pay attention. A rift between Johnson and Shirley wouldn't do. "I trust General Shirley is competent enough to understand how foolish it would be to hamper either campaign." Faith looked at Johnson and smiled. "You are clearly the gentleman who has the respect of the Iroquois nations. Is Shirley not from Massachusetts? Surely when he is in Boston he does not interact with the Iroquois, who live in New York?" She made her eyes as wide and innocent as she could make them.

"No, he most certainly does not." Johnson beamed at her.

Flattered men were always easier to handle.

James's eyes met hers for a moment, which did nothing to bank the fire his presence already fanned, and then he turned to Johnson. "All the gifts are in the outbuildings. And the gunsmith brought enough guns for an entire militia regiment, not just the rangers." He clearly understood the need to redirect Johnson's attention to what he *had* accomplished.

"Good, good." Johnson's mood brightened as his ego was soothed.

James shifted in his chair, which seemed closer now. Heat centered in her midsection, and threatened to dip lower, but she forced herself to ignore it because she needed her wits about her right now.

A maid entered the room carrying a giant tray laden with bread and jam. From the aroma, the bread was just now fresh from the oven. She took a deeper breath. The scent of freshly baked bread was its own divine life force.

It looked like there was enough food on the tray for ten people, but men on the frontier seemed to have rather more appetite than those in the city. For everything.

Faith rose to help the maid serve the food. Her father would have had fits to see her helping the staff. But he was not here, and someone needed to hostess.

She handed James a small plate, and her hand brushed against his. Heat raced up her arm, and she wasn't sure whether to yank her arm away or savor the sensation. He stared at his hand. He had to have felt it, too.

Good gads. The man was the most distracting person she had ever met, and he would be her undoing if she didn't set her mind to rights.

She served the other men quickly. Then she returned to her seat and tried not to look toward James.

"We will be sorry to see her go," James said, "but we do need to get Miss Richmond back to Albany now."

Her heart squeezed. She shouldn't feel hurt. She needed them to get her back to Albany, and once she was away from here, she could sort out her addled mind before her father frittered more money away on some new flight of his fancy.

Johnson took a bite of his bread. He chewed slowly, then swallowed. "Governor Shirley is making me rethink my planning."

Her breath caught. How could Shirley's doings have affected his willingness to have her taken back to Albany?

"Where are the best gifts?" Johnson asked.

"The gifts for the sachems are in the attic," James said. "We figured you would present them while you met up there."

Johnson nodded. "That is well."

"Hendrick is not happy that Shirley has sent Lydius into the area," said David. That idea made all the men scowl.

"If Mr. Lydius is not the right man, I would be happy to relay that message to General Shirley when I reach Albany," Faith said.

Footsteps sounded in the hall, and then Jaap re-entered the room.

"Excuse me, sir," he said, "but the gunsmith was showing me one of the new muskets, and while we stalked a rabbit, we found this." Jaap held up his hand.

James walked over and looked at what lay on his palm. His whole body went rigid. "More parched corn."

"Did you see signs of more than one man?" Johnson asked.

Jaap shook his head. "Only one set of tracks."

"No doubt they have seen all our preparations," Johnson said. He rounded on James. "I can't have the French skulking in the woods while I focus on the sachems. You are supposed to be catching one for information and then driving the rest off."

Faith looked at James, who braced himself and looked fully at Johnson.

Johnson stood. "Carroll, you need to find them and put the fear of God into them. I will not have the conference compromised."

"Yes, sir."

James was already turning for the door when he glanced her way and stopped. "Before I head out, sir, who shall I send with Miss Richmond?"

He had just been dressed down, but he took the time to ask. Was he being kind, or did he want her gone?

Fine—she needed to get back to her father, anyway.

Johnson swung his head around and looked at her like she was an intriguing puzzle piece. Then he slowly shook his head. "No one. I'm sorry, Miss Richmond. I can spare no one to take you to Albany until after the conference."

She snapped her mouth shut. Surely, he wasn't intentionally toying with her. The conference was important, and they were busy preparing for war. She forced her face to remain neutral and refused to let any tears escape.

James stalked out the door, not looking any more pleased with that answer than she felt.

Chapter 19

For at least two miles now, James had been following the prints Jaap had found, with Jaap and David covering him from behind.

If the man they were tracking joined up with others, he was going to be in a mountain of trouble, having stormed out of the house with just Jaap and David. But he'd been so rattled by Johnson's rebuke that he had just grabbed his musket and hatchet and charged out the door with the two men who were already there. He hadn't dared risk Johnson's further ire by losing the trail because he was too slow.

Now Sarah was the only one left to protect Faith from Johnson or any of the other men in the household. He had wanted to punch Johnson, commission be damned. They were all wound too tight to be trusted around her.

Of course, he was, too, at this point. Everyone was right. He wanted her.

He forced his mind to focus. The tracks led west, but that meant nothing. Any experienced raider would have circled around to make it hard to figure out which way he was heading.

He stopped to listen for anything out of place so they didn't run straight into an ambush, and the others halted behind him. The usual chaos of birds flitted through the trees, and the rustle of ground animals scuttling through leaves sounded from every direction.

No sign of disturbance. He pushed on. Eventually, a lone man would have to join up with a group if he was traveling from Canada. They had to catch him before he did.

His moccasined feet made no sound as he began to run. Leo would be proud.

No, Leo would think he was a jackass for getting all tangled up in his head about Faith while he was in the woods. She was not here, and someone else was. Most likely someone who wouldn't hesitate to shoot him. And to shoot David and Jaap.

He scanned the undergrowth as he ran. Breathing silently while running took a hell of a lot of control, and his lungs burned from the effort. It helped get his head back in the moment.

They followed a bend in the deer track, and it sloped uphill.

The woods opened up on a granite expanse, and he slowed to a walk. There was less cover here, and they were more visible, but they would lose the trail if they hurried, tracking over rock. An eagle screamed overhead, and they all flinched. They were too exposed.

Some of the lichen growing on the rock was compressed. Someone had stepped on it when there was no way to avoid it. But there were large stretches of bare rock between each print, and they all had to cast around to find each one.

It was taking too long. He had to catch the man before he rejoined his party. And they had to take him by surprise, or they wouldn't be able to capture him and gain any intelligence. They couldn't just kill a man running through the woods, even if they wanted to.

Where was Okwaho when he needed him? James could outrun David and Jaap, but David's cousin was, if anything, faster. Together, the two of them could run pretty much any single man to ground. But he wasn't here. And they hadn't got a good enough trail now to follow at a run, anyway.

Either the man was lucky, or he'd intentionally aimed for this rocky hillside to lose anyone tracking him. And if he knew the area that well, he was either an experienced raider, or he was local, which was worse. If any of the Iroquois were spying on Johnson, that would mean Johnson's status among the Iroquois was not what everyone thought it was. And that would be very bad for them all.

Sun glinted off the rock, and he squinted. Where was the next damn print?

David gave a low call, like a crow. He was pointing at some moss off to the right.

A print heading toward two boulders. And then the next, a few feet away. That must have been how he intended to circle back, because his trail was aiming northeast now. Which meant they really had to move fast.

He hustled to the small pass between the large rocks and then stopped so suddenly, he almost over-balanced. In the space right between the boulders was a single copperhead, sunning itself on the warm rock.

Shit.

Jaap came up behind him. "What...oh."

At least he had pitched his voice low, so no one beyond James could have heard him.

David joined them.

Jaap pulled out his hatchet and flung it at the snake. The handle landed an inch from its long body, but the business end of the hatchet clanked to the rock behind it.

Jaap swore quietly in Dutch, then turned to James. "Give me yours," he whispered. "I'll get closer and just hack its head off."

"You most certainly will not." James whispered back. "I am not explaining to Leo why I wasn't able to stop his cousin from dying of stupidity."

David nodded. "And I'm not carrying your dying self back."

A bear would have been better than a snake. And now it was an agitated snake, since Jaap had used it for axe-throwing practice.

Shit, shit, shit.

Leo always said snakes would rather leave in peace if you gave them the opportunity and incentive. Its eyes reflected the sunlight, but still seemed dead. If James's gut kept churning like it was doing, he was going to shit himself.

The snake's tail rattled. He jumped back. The others stepped back more deliberately. He took several deep breaths, and sweat trickled down his temples, past his ears, and onto his neck.

But they couldn't stand there all day, and they couldn't let the trail go cold. They had already made too much noise. And they had wasted too much time. Leo would have been around and past the snake long since.

James swung his musket off his shoulder, grabbed the butt as close to its end as he could, and edged the muzzle toward the snake.

The snake stared back with its eyes that practically blended into its coppery scales, and it rattled its tail again. Leo was full of it, because the damned thing was very much not scared.

Fine. He took a step forward and got the muzzle within a foot of the snake.

It reared up and whipped forward, striking at the barrel of the musket with its fangs bared.

James jumped back so violently he dropped the musket with a loud clatter. "Jesus, Mary, and holy Saint Joseph!"

The snake slithered off along a crack in the rock. It only went about ten paces before it stopped.

"Well, they know we're after them now," muttered David.

James looked around them on the ground. Not only had they made a racket that could've been heard all the way to Schenectady, but they had also obliterated any sign of the trail. Damn it.

David carefully retrieved both Jaap's hatchet and James's musket. There was no point in going any further. Either the man was long gone, or he had joined his fellows and was staging an ambush if they kept following.

A scream of utter frustration welled up in James's chest, but he clamped his teeth together and didn't let it out. He yanked his musket from David's hands.

He circled east to take a different path back, just in case they picked up another trail. It never served to return the way you came if someone might be hunting you. The others followed wordlessly. He trudged through the undergrowth for at least a mile, careful to leave as few signs of their passing as possible.

A giant tree lay across their path. James went to step over it and stopped.

The ground was disturbed. Whoever had been there covered their presence well, but the leaves were damp, like they had been moved from wherever they had been decaying on the forest floor.

He knelt down and sniffed.

Burnt wood.

He carefully removed the leaves and some soil. There was the char. And a small, ragged piece of birch bark.

The others looked over his shoulders as he carefully withdrew it from the leaf litter. With great care, he blew some of the clinging soil off it.

Letters.

He grabbed the end of his queue and used his hair as a fine brush to remove more dirt without damaging the bark. His breath came faster.

The bark was burned and filthy, but there was definitely writing on it. He concentrated hard on it and finally worked out "nson." Johnson? There were other letters, but he couldn't make sense of them.

"That's Dutch," said Jaap.

James whipped his head around. "What does it say?"

Jaap shrugged. "There's only a couple of words. Looks like 'late June.'"

The conference was in late June. Dutch? Were they following Leo? That made no sense. Leo had no love for Johnson, but he would have just showed up at the blockhouse after dark if he was in the area. He always had when he wanted to visit Jaap or the rest of them.

Who else?

He looked at David, who shook his head, like he couldn't make sense of it either.

They needed to get this back to Johnson. This was not the French. This was a Dutchman.

Chapter 20

Faith slipped out the rear door of the house and quietly shut it behind her. Sarah was stitching up a fancy coat for one of the sachems. She was a magnificent seamstress. Yet another womanly task at which Faith had no skill.

Johnson was in the front hall talking with Mr. Wraxall, but that would only last so long, and he had adjusted his crotch almost every time he looked at her. She had managed to avoid being left alone in a room with him all morning, but Johnson was sending Mr. Wraxall on an errand, so remaining in the sitting room was no longer a wise option. Standing in the busy space between the manor house and the outdoor baking kitchen wasn't exactly going to make her difficult to find, either.

Sarah had said some mild exercise wouldn't hurt her and might do her good, so it was time to take a walk. She wasn't keen on leaving the immediate grounds, but she needed to be a little braver. There was a creek off to the east, a river to the south, and deep woods to the north. The woods to the west had some lovely flowers growing on the verge, and some well-worn paths, so that was where she headed.

Bluish-purple flowers, perhaps irises, grew low along the woods' edge. But maybe irises were taller. She wasn't sure. This was the first time she wished she could identify flowers. They looked so pretty when they grew wild.

She headed to the broad trail next to the flowers. It would be easy to keep her way and not get lost.

The more she studied the underbrush as she walked, the more she was struck by the variety of the plants. Sarah knew how to use plants to heal, like so many women at home. Perhaps Sarah would teach her if Faith was going to be stuck here until after the conference.

She needed something useful to do or she would go mad. She could never abide sitting around doing nothing, and her father would no doubt point out that her lack of patience got her into worlds of trouble. He had never had to spend an afternoon in a room full of vacuous neighbors gossiping over needlepoint or he might have understood.

A flash of red and yellow caught her eye.

More flowers. They dangled elegantly from their stems and had four bits that poked toward the sky like an upended table.

She held one to her nose and drew a deep breath, smelling its faint, sweet perfume. Divine.

She glanced back toward the house. It was out of sight beyond the trees, but she could still hear the activity around the outdoor bake house and ovens.

The woods were thicker than any she had encountered at home. Trees towered over her, and shrubbery crowded the base of the trunks. How did James patrol out here when there were so few trails? Maybe the heavy leggings he wore protected him from the brambles.

Her face grew hot as she pictured his thighs, visible between the leggings and the breechcloth he had been wearing when she first met him.

London would be scandalized. Oh, what a sight London was missing. She was in favor of the fashion that left so little to the imagination. Even the memory of that view turned her core molten. And at that, her father would be scandalized. Heaven forbid women feel passionate urges like men.

She picked a lacy looking flower and twirled it in her fingers.

Yes, she was definitely feeling passionate urges toward James. What would it be like to indulge them? Would she actually like to find out, or was she just lonely?

The sounds from the house didn't reach her anymore, but the general din of the forest sounded the same.

She sniffed. Wet leaves, flowers. She smelled lavender. That must grow here, though she hadn't seen any.

Then there was movement in the corner of her eye. She turned her head to the left.

Behind a large tree that she couldn't identify, someone's shoulder was just visible. Her heart took off like a jackrabbit in her chest.

It was likely someone from the household. This was obviously a path that people used every day. But she wasn't an army officer's daughter for nothing, so she looked around for something to use as a weapon. There were broken branches all around from spring storms. She quickly scanned the nearest branches for one that was both stout and jagged.

There. Only a pace or two to her right. She silently moved her feet and wrapped her hand around the branch and pulled it free from the undergrowth. She shouldn't have come this far. Fantasizing about James had been an unwise distraction.

A crinkling sound, almost like paper being folded.

She faced the man who was presumably attached to the shoulder that she could just barely see. "Show yourself."

She tested the weight of the branch in her hands, waggling it in front of her. It had enough heft that it could do damage, but was still light enough that she could give it a good hard swing.

The tree chuckled.

Growing up around army encampments meant she wasn't fool enough to trust a man chuckling like that in the presence of a lone woman. She glanced back up the trail. Too far from the house to run for it, and she wasn't going to turn her back on him.

The chuckle echoed in her mind and sent a chill racing up and down her spine, lifting the hair on the back of her neck as it went.

Her hands trembled. Not telling anyone where she was going was less wise than it had seemed when she thought she was escaping the men in the house. Stupid.

With one hand, she felt on the ground for a rock. Her fingers found a sharp-edged one, and she picked it up and hurled it behind the tree. It made a thud, but she couldn't see what it had struck. From the sound, it might have struck a person, or it might just have struck the ground. She grasped the branch with both hands again.

Her heart pounded, and she broke out in a sweat. Something sounded off to her right. Footsteps? She swung around toward the footsteps, but the brush was so dense she couldn't see anyone.

She spun back toward the tree, and the shoulder was gone. Then someone grabbed her around the middle from behind and pinned her arms to her sides.

She screamed. Birds launched from their perches in the trees at the sounds of her voice. She wrenched her arms, trying to loosen the grip on them, but she couldn't free them.

Tears streamed down her face. What a stupid way to die. She kicked back and caught a leg, but no matter how hard she struggled, she couldn't loosen the grip on her arms.

"Faith, it's all right."

Her brain sputtered for a moment. The full length of a man pressed against her, his arms holding her tight against himself.

"What were you about to take a swing at? Were you trying to get yourself killed?"

Then Jaap and David appeared in front of her, muskets at the ready.

Her mind reeled for a moment.

James.

His hard body was glued to her back and hips. His arms still held her, and his breath was quick and hard, like he had been running. Her body melted, pressing back against his. His breath tickled her neck.

She looked from Jaap and David to the tree.

She could barely draw breath. "Someone was behind that tree," she said, her voice raspy.

Jaap and David both slunk around the tree and disappeared into the woods, muskets at the ready.

Her muscles trembled, and she leaned her full weight back against James. Then she turned and buried her forehead in his chest.

"You're all right," he said. Then his lips brushed her forehead.

She held him tighter. Her face pressed against his rough hunting shirt, and his heart beat against her cheek like a steady beacon.

One hand slid up and down her back, then up to the nape of her neck. His other hand cradled the back of her head, and her legs trembled with relief. She was safe.

Then he pulled her tighter against him, like he needed her touch as much as she needed his.

"He ran west," David's voice sounded behind her. She flinched and felt heat race up her neck to her cheeks.

"You can peel yourself off her now." That was Jaap.

James looked down at her again, still holding her. "You shouldn't stray this far from the house." His face was strained.

"Thank you. I had already come to that conclusion."

He spared her a tight smile, then turned to the others. "Who was it?"

Jaap answered. "Could be who we were tracking earlier, but could be someone else. Hard to say, but he joined up with at least four more men."

"Might have circled back when he met up with the others, so we didn't dare push too far with only two of us," said David.

Even Jaap was frowning, and their concern was contagious.

Her hands began to tremble again. "Do you know who you were tracking? Was it a French soldier spying on General Johnson?"

The men all looked at each other, lips tight.

James answered. "We've been tracking someone, but it seems that someone is Dutch."

"What do the Dutch have to do with the French invading British colonies?" she asked.

"The only Dutch in the area are New Yorkers," said James.

Chapter 21

James stayed a few steps behind as Johnson swept down the front steps of the house to greet his guests. Everyone else who had been in the sitting room followed. Johnson had not been happy about their findings, but at least the arrival of important guests had distracted him from the worst of his anger.

Faith stood at the back of the group, and he could only imagine what she thought as Hendrick, Abraham, and their entourage entered the courtyard. David's cousin Okwaho had arrived with them.

Hendrick and Abraham dismounted from their horses, clad in breeches and jackets with silver buttons and medals presented by various governors over the years.

Johnson approached and greeted them. Hendrick clasped Johnson in his arms and spoke to him like a son. "You have done well for yourself, Warraghiyagey."

Faith was suddenly at James's shoulder. "What did he call him?" she asked in a low voice.

"His Mohawk name. 'One who does great things.' At least that's how Johnson likes to translate it." He couldn't help the smile on his face. According to David, that was a slightly grandiose translation. But somehow that suited Johnson.

Hendrick's gaze swept over the group that had emerged from the house. He knew all the men, but then his eyes lit on Faith.

He approached her, with his brother Abraham right behind him. Hendrick had aged since James had last seen him. Not too surprising, since the man had to be around sixty-five years old. He still looked every inch the impressive warrior, despite his increasingly stout girth.

The Bear Clan chief ran his eyes up and down Faith, and James's back stiffened. The poor woman had been leered at by enough men in the past few weeks. She didn't need yet another one who was old enough to be her grandfather staring at her lovely breasts, and frankly, James didn't need it either.

He was in no position to have a say in who coveted her body, but he definitely coveted it. He pulled his own eyes away from her. He was worse than Johnson.

"And who is this lovely addition to your household?" Hendrick asked.

Johnson beamed at him. "This is Miss Faith Richmond. She has been staying with us recovering from an injury, and her father is a British colonel who will serve under Governor Shirley in his campaign to Fort Niagara."

James inched closer to Faith. Two powerful men vied for her attention, and they both held more power in their little fingers than James could ever hope to hold in a lifetime. He really needed to back off and let it go.

Faith dropped into a formal curtsy in front of Hendrick and Abraham. "I am pleased to make your acquaintance, your majesty." She remained in her curtsy, head bowed low, waiting for Hendrick's reply. James almost choked.

"I am most delighted to meet you, as well, Miss Richmond." Hendrick said.

She rose back to her full height with an elegant, sweeping motion. If she was uncomfortable meeting the great Mohawk leader, she showed no sign of it. The woman knew how to handle people, from her father, to Johnson, and now Hendrick.

Johnson turned to James. "We must show Hendrick and Abraham the fabulous new muskets that our king has sent us to fight against the French."

James kept a snort from escaping. The king had done no such thing. Johnson had paid for the muskets. But at least it would get James away from Faith before he did something stupid like plaster his body up against her again. "Yes, sir, absolutely."

James turned to David. "Would you help me choose a mark?"

David gave him a nod, and they left the group and headed for the outbuilding where they had stashed the muskets.

Inside the building, next to the crates, Jaap was helping the gunsmith, Dreyfuss, unload and inspect the last of Dreyfuss's handiwork.

"Now we get to see how well your guns work," James said. "They had better be impressive, because our recruitment of Mohawk warriors might hinge, at least in part, on how impressed Hendrick is in the next few minutes."

"My muskets are the best," Dreyfuss answered simply.

Jaap handed James a pouch full of cartridges. James took it from him and then reached for a musket.

He stopped. If Johnson wanted an impressive demonstration, he had better have them all shoot together. "David, Jaap, grab a musket."

Dreyfuss handed one to each of them and then took one himself. "If you need to make a display, four is better than three."

They eyed the gunsmith. "I know you can make guns, but can you shoot them?" James asked.

Dreyfuss loaded the musket in his hands without even having to glance down at what he was doing. He could certainly handle a musket with ease, but that didn't mean he could aim worth a damn.

James, Jaap, and David loaded their muskets and set their flints.

"Everyone ready?" James asked.

The other three men nodded. The fact that neither David or Jaap was talking just underscored how important they knew Hendrick's opinion was for the fate of Johnson's campaign.

James led them from the outbuilding into the courtyard and lined them up in front of Hendrick, Abraham, Okwaho, and Johnson. And Faith.

James pointed to a large maple tree near the bank of the river about a hundred paces away. "That's our target, men." He added in a lower voice that their audience couldn't hear, "Aim for the lowest limb on the left, where it branches out from the trunk." As long as they hit the tree, their audience should be pleased, but if they could break the branch, that would be a better show.

"Take aim." The other three men all aimed at the tree, and so did James. "Fire."

All four guns blasted in unison. The leaves on the maple shook from the impact. Then the branch gave a final shudder, and the end tipped toward the ground.

Dreyfuss reloaded. "One or two of you missed."

Before James could speak, Dreyfuss raised the musket to his shoulder again and fired.

The remaining fibers of the branch exploded, and the entire thing dropped to the ground. Damn.

"Good shot, Dreyfuss." James said.

"You can call me Ben, since we're going to be comrades-in-arms." The man looked at James, daring him to disagree.

James gave him a nod. "You can call me James." Then he gestured to the others with his chin. "The blond one is Jaap, and the one who won't shut up about politics is David."

David and Jaap both laughed. Ben gave them a rare smile. He seemed a fairly stern sort of man, though that might just be because he didn't know them yet.

James turned back to Johnson and Hendrick. They were talking and gesturing, their attention still on the tree that had been their target. Faith stood behind them as they spoke, and slightly apart. She was staring straight at James and the men, and gave them a small nod and a smile.

"Faith seems to think they were impressed," said David.

Jaap elbowed David. "But is she impressed with James?"

"I thought we were preparing for war," said Ben. "Not the marriage market."

"We are," said James, "and one of the key requisites for joining the ranger company is that you ignore these two idiots."

Ben looked at Jaap and David, then looked back at James. "Shouldn't be hard."

James laughed. He was beginning to appreciate Ben Dreyfuss.

"Shoulder your muskets, men," James said. "Let's look disciplined and military as we head back to Johnson." And he led them back to the group in front of the house.

Johnson thumped James on the back. "Lovely show. Well done."

Hendrick reached out a hand for David's musket. David handed it over to him with a slight bow of his head.

Hendrick examined the musket closely, running his fingers over the trigger and other workings, then he turned to Johnson. "Our English father has done well sending you these."

Ben took in a breath, no doubt about to correct him, and James kicked him in the ankle. Ben closed his mouth.

Faith smiled at James and held his gaze for a moment. His pulse picked up its pace, and he forced his focus back to his employer. Thank God Johnson didn't see her smiling at him. The man was already irritated with him for not finding whoever was spying on them, and she could cost him his position. Johnson was fickle that way.

He looked away and tried to ignore her. He lowered his musket and held it in front of his crotch in case it got ideas he couldn't control. This had to stop.

If he didn't steer clear of her, either Johnson would kill him, or he would die of frustration.

Chapter 22

They had shot the branch of the tree clean off. Faith had never seen anything like it. Not that the British army did much in the way of marksmanship practice.

James's command of the situation had been...inspiring. She fanned herself with her hand in the June heat. The men might all be friends, but they clearly looked to James for leadership. Did he even realize how they instinctively took their cues from him?

But he confused her. One moment he acted like he wanted to wrap his entire body around her, which was an idea worth exploring, no matter how inappropriate, and the next he avoided her like she hadn't bathed in a year.

He was maddening.

The entire household buzzed like a beehive since Hendrick and his brother's arrival, and the preparations for the conference seemed to take on a new intensity. And since Johnson couldn't spare anyone to take her back to Albany, or just *wouldn't*, she ought to join the worker bees and make herself useful.

Faith headed down the earthen ramp to the basement kitchens and went inside, looking for Louisa or Sarah, but neither was anywhere in sight. She went back outside again and around the house to the baking ovens. There was Sarah, working at a large table.

"If you have idle hands right now," Sarah called to her, "I can put them to work. Louisa had to go borrow her aunt's giant kettle to have an extra during the conference, and I am trying to keep her work from piling up while she is gone."

Faith went to her and held her hands up as an offering. "What can I do?"

"What do you know how to do?"

Faith's shoulders sagged slightly. "I am a very fast learner."

"That is what I guessed." Sarah shook her head. Then she grabbed a large bowl that was filled with flour, as best Faith could tell. "You are going to learn to knead bread."

At least she had seen that done a thousand times. It was simple enough.

Sarah added water to the bowl full of flour. "Stir that around once or twice."

Faith reached her hand in and carefully swirled it through the flour. "It isn't as soft as I expected."

"This is for the men, not for the main house. The men will be just fine with the coarser bread." Sarah added a little more water to the bowl. "Stir."

Faith did. And this time the water made the coarse flour stick to her hand in a glob. More water. Now the mixture stuck to her fingers, coating them like thick woolen mittens. She tried to scrape it off.

"Don't bother yet. Here's more water."

Faith had to work her arms harder now. And she almost tipped over the bowl. Sarah grabbed it and steadied it.

"I'm so sorry."

"You're a quick study, remember?" Sarah raised an eyebrow at her. "Everyone should know how to make food to feed themselves."

Heat burned Faith's cheeks. She was useless compared to Sarah and Louisa and the others. But she could learn, and she spread her feet for a more solid stance and leaned in hard.

She kneaded what was becoming a leaden paste. Surely half of the contents of the bowl now coated her hands and wrists in a layer more than an inch thick.

A shadow crossed the table, and she looked up. There was James, not two paces in front of her. If her cheeks were hot before, they must be glowing coals now. By instinct, she lifted her hand to give him a little wave. Her hand was so heavily coated in dough that she struggled to lift it, and she almost toppled the bowl again. She must look a joke.

If he didn't set unmentionable parts of her glowing hot, she would be better able to laugh it off. This was a very inconvenient time to find herself in lust. The man should have had the decency to be less good-looking.

"Hello, Faith," James said. "Sarah, we are sorting through the blankets and linens for gifts."

"Do you need Faith?" Sarah asked. "You can have her if she would be helpful."

Clearly Faith was not being as useful learning to knead bread as she had hoped. Maybe she could sort blankets and linens and figure which would be good gifts for which sorts of people. Then she might be less of a burden.

"No, you can keep her," he said quickly. "But I need you to send some bread to us as soon as you can. The men are getting hungry and irritable." With that, he turned and left.

Faith jammed her hands back into the dough. "Well, *someone* is certainly irritable."

Sarah threw her head back and laughed.

Faith asked, "Is he always like that when he is hungry?"

"I've known him since he was eleven years old, and truth be told, yes. The man can be a cranky old badger when he's hungry."

"And I am a hindrance rather than a help in the kitchen." Faith sighed.

"You are. But you're growing on me."

Faith leaned into the dough and tried harder. Then another shadow crossed over her work. She looked up. It was the gunsmith who had brought the muskets and made the last shot that sliced the branch.

"Oh good, it is dark bread," he said to Faith. "I would like a loaf, please."

"You will have it with the rest of the men," Sarah said, smacking his hand away as he tried to take some bread from a cooling rack.

Oh my. Even Sarah was on edge today.

Sarah turned to Faith. "Lift your hands." Sarah dusted her own hands in flour and then scraped the dough off of Faith's wrists, hands, and fingers, and back into the bowl. After five or six passes, Faith's actual hands became visible. "There's a pail over there," Sarah pointed to a bucket near the closest oven. "Go wash."

Faith turned and doused her hands in the bucket. She scrubbed vigorously until at least most of the residual dough was gone. She lifted her hands and gave them a few quick shakes, then she dried them on a rag that was tied to the pail's handle.

When she turned, the gunsmith was inspecting rows of bread cooling on the table. He went to reach for one again, then made a show of clasping his hands behind his back and leaned over and sniffed the bread instead. He was lucky Sarah wasn't close enough to the collection of wooden spoons at the far table, because judging by the scowl on her face, she might have cracked his knuckles with one.

Sarah went to a table on the far side of the ovens. She grabbed a tray and filled it with small loaves of bread. She slammed each one down with such force that everything else on the table jumped each time.

Then Sarah grabbed the tray and thrust it into Faith's hands. "Take these to James and the men. And take that with you."

Presumably "that" was the gunsmith. "Let us go feed the men, and then you, too, can have the bread you came for," she said to him.

Before he could answer, she turned and walked briskly toward the front of the house. She could at least do that for Sarah, who had clearly had her fill of annoying men for the moment. The gunsmith followed her.

James and the other men were in front of one of the outbuildings that flanked the courtyard. Sorting gifts sounded like pleasant enough work, but the men were hauling huge bundles out of the building and a few of them, James included, had removed their shirts in the heat.

She paused to enjoy the view. It was not one she often saw in London, more was the pity. Yes, he did stir something in her, and since she was staying through the conference, she might finally have to figure that out.

Then James looked up and caught her gawking.

Chapter 23

James dropped the bundle of blankets he'd been carrying so it fell next to the rest of the blankets. Sweat channeled in between the muscles of his chest and across his stomach to his waist. He needed water. And he needed food. He looked toward the house, and he almost choked.

There was Faith, a huge tray of bread in her hands and her lips parted in a delicious little O. Her tongue darted across her bottom lip.

The feel of her body plastered to his in the woods sprang to his mind for the hundredth time. She looked like she wanted to lick the sweat off his chest, and his body was more than interested in any licking she would like to do. She was the answer to his basest fantasies.

Except she wasn't. She was an English lady and wasn't about to lick anything off of anyone.

Giving her father a reason to want him dead would not be a good career move, now that he had the hope of a military career beckoning him. He wouldn't let anything but the head on his shoulders determine his actions. He hadn't come this far to be run through by an angry father.

Ben walked behind Faith, which explained where he had disappeared to. Perhaps he had expedited their dinner.

Faith approached them, and James went back into the outbuilding to grab another bundle of blankets and get his head on straight. He hoisted the blankets up to his shoulder, then leaned against the wall and softly hit his forehead against it. Maybe she would leave the tray and go back to help Sarah.

Bread. Water. Then back to work.

When he returned to the late-day sunlight, Jaap, David, Okwaho, and Ben were each sitting on a bale of blankets with a small loaf of bread in their hands. Faith stood, eyes already on him, showing no sign of heading back.

The stirring in his breeches determined his actions. He set the blankets down. "I have to go back to the blockhouse and do something," he said to the men. "Finish your bread and get some water before you get back to work. I'll be back to help before you're done eating."

He turned and headed for the back of the house. He passed the ovens where Sarah pounded the life out of a bowl of dough. She didn't look up. He continued toward the blockhouse, then footsteps sounded behind him.

He stopped and turned.

It was Faith. She was an officer's daughter, for the love of God. She should know better than to bait a man. Especially a man alone on a secluded path.

"Have I done something to upset you, James?" she asked. "It seems in the last couple of days that you have worked very hard to avoid my presence."

"You should go back to the house."

"Why are you avoiding me?"

She was becoming as direct as Sarah and the other women out here in the valley. But she wasn't a tough frontier woman. She was a well-bred English lady, and he would do well to remember that, even if she didn't seem to.

He ran his hand over his head as if that would make him think more clearly. "I'm not avoiding you, Faith, but we have a lot of work to do to get ready for the conference, in case you haven't noticed." If that sounded rougher than he intended, it was probably just as well. If she was insulted, maybe *she* would start avoiding *him*.

She tilted her head like she was studying him.

His skin grew hot. He had forgotten to grab his shirt when he left, and he was standing there half-naked in front of her.

"I think you *have* been avoiding me."

She had definitely been spending too much time with Sarah and Louisa. That was no longer a question. "It's for the best."

"That is nonsense. I enjoy your company, and I did think you enjoyed mine."

His heart stopped for a moment, then banged against his ribs as it restarted. He enjoyed her company more than was good for either of them. Could she read his mind? No, she had no idea what he was thinking, or she would not have said what she just said.

"You really should go back to the house."

"I don't want to."

Picking her up and carrying her kicking and hollering back to the house was a temptation. But if he did that, they would end up on the nearest patch of soft grass with her on her back. He was only human.

"Why shouldn't we enjoy each other's company?" Her eyes were wide, and she was breathing heavily. Her lips were slightly parted, and the swell of her breasts heaved up and down above the neckline of her gown.

Fine. If she was going to continue to insist on playing with fire, it wasn't his fault if she got singed. He reached out for her arm and drew her up against his body.

She looked into his eyes, almost daring him. She didn't even pretend to resist, God help him.

So he pressed his lips against hers, and when she gasped, his tongue seized the moment and began exploring between her parted lips.

She tasted like fresh bread and honey.

He cupped his hands around her ass and tugged her against his cockstand. His tongue thrust into her mouth in the same rhythm, mimicking what he would really like his cock to be doing to her.

The heat of her body almost seared the hair off his chest.

She was probably terrified. And he was acting like a buck in rut.

He peeled his lips off of hers while he still had the presence of mind to do it, then looked her in the eye, their noses still almost touching. "This is why I've been avoiding you."

She blinked.

So help him, he ground his hips against her again. "This"—he rubbed his length closer to the juncture of her legs—"is not a good idea. For either of us."

Her eyelids were half closed, and the breath entering and leaving her delicate mouth tickled his bare neck.

He pushed her away from him, breaking their connection, and stepped back. He should never have done that to her.

Her mouth closed. Her brows lowered. Her lips formed a thin, tight line.

Good.

"I see you understand now," he said. She had to know this could go nowhere.

She looked at him, her face tilted up toward his. "I do not."

His chest tightened, and he wanted to pull her back into his arms. "Now you really need to go back to the house." Before he did something even more asinine.

Her arms dropped to her sides, and her hands clenched into fists. If she went to hit him, he would let her. He deserved it.

She took a step toward him, and he stood his ground, every nerve in his body springing to life.

She stopped, her delicate brows slashing angrily down over her eyes. "How dare you?"

Then she turned on her heel and ran back down the path toward the house.

He dragged his hands through his hair and then over his face. This was why he stuck to brief encounters behind the barn with women who weren't interested in anything more from him than blissful release for a respite, and never someone he was likely to cross paths with again.

Or whose father outranked him and could legally have him shot.

And now she was furious with him. Maybe even frightened of him. Furious was more likely.

When she had stepped toward him, part of him thought she planned to kiss him. His brain knew she should hit him, but another organ had hoped otherwise. And that scared him to the deepest part of his being.

Now she likely thought he was a coward and a lout.

He tipped his head back and stared up at the sky. People had thought worse things of him.

And he shouldn't care what she thought. She was leaving. Behaving like a fool with her could put him on the wrong end of military justice to say nothing of what consequences it could have for her.

And now he was paying the price for having plastered his body to hers again and showing her what he really wanted. His cock strained so hard against his breeches that he had to bend slightly at the waist to relieve the pressure of the fabric constraining it.

He deserved the torture, but if he didn't take care of that, his stones would turn blue and he wouldn't be able to return to the men and finish their work.

That obviously would not do. He needed to get over himself and he needed to do it now.

The creek ran off to his right. He turned off the path and tromped through the underbrush into the woods. He swatted the branches away from his face as he plowed on. Crows laughed at him from the branches overhead. "Feck off." He flung his arm up and gestured in their general direction.

Clearly she was affecting his brain if he was swearing at birds.

He smashed through another pine bough, and there was the creek. He stopped and stared at it for a moment.

"This is absurd."

The crows called in agreement. He bent over and yanked his shoes off his feet. Then he removed his rough stockings and stuck them in his shoes.

He listened for a moment. Only the overbearing crows were there to witness his stupidity.

He unbuttoned his breeches, shoved them down, and tossed them aside. Then he waded into the creek and sat down in the water, waiting for the current to ease his agony. But the creek was shallow, and the weather had been unseasonably hot.

The crows laughed at him again. He groaned.

This day was not going to plan. And the water was not cold enough to do its job.

He reached down between his legs and grabbed his cock. He gave it a hard pull and immediately the image of Faith's face appeared in his mind.

He groaned again and began yanking with purpose.

Chapter 24

Sarah handed Faith another divided tray of beads as they sat on the ground in front of one of the outbuildings, sorting gifts for the conference.

"These are so much prettier than I expected," Faith said. "My father always referred to them as cheap trinkets and trade beads. I had no idea they could be so lovely."

Sarah looked at the beads like she hadn't seen them before. She picked a red one up and held it to the sunlight, so it glowed like a gemstone. "I never really thought about them that way." She handed the bead back to Faith and reached into another crate. This time, she pulled out a handful of tortoiseshell combs.

"Here," Faith said. "I have a pile of those started already."

Sarah handed them to her, and Faith set them down in the right pile, next to the stack of small looking-glasses.

There were more goods here than she had seen in even the largest shop in London. How many people were coming to this conference? "Will the sachems and warriors take these home for their wives?"

Sarah laughed. "Would you let your husband pick out beads and combs for you?"

She wouldn't let anyone do that for her. But it wasn't like they had a choice, did they?

Sarah handed Faith more combs. "The wives will be here too."

Her eyes widened. "They are coming to a war conference?" She at least kept her voice from squeaking in her surprise.

"And the children."

"How very civilized." Her father would have quaked at the thought.

"Yes," Sarah said. "But it makes for one hell of a guest list. There will be hundreds of people here next week."

Faith's jaw went slack. "Hundreds?"

Sarah nodded and grabbed another handful of combs out of the crate.

"Where will Johnson house so many guests? I realize I will have to give up my bedchamber." Who knew where she would sleep, but the house only had four bedchambers, and obviously the Iroquois chiefs were more important than she was.

Sarah's face grew ashen. "They won't stay in the house. There isn't room."

Faith laughed. "Obviously, they won't *all* stay in the house, though perhaps the house could hold all the chiefs and their families if everyone slept on the floor next to each other. Johnson sounds like he might approve of that if any of the chiefs have pretty daughters."

Sarah shook her head. "You are wasted on London."

Faith laughed again. At least here she didn't have to pretend to be oblivious to carnal activities.

Her body chose that inopportune moment to remember how James's obvious carnal desires had felt as he had ground himself against her, and how her own had threatened to flare out of control in response, despite his then pushing her away like she wasn't worth the trouble. She ducked her head and grabbed another handful of combs.

Sarah said, "They will camp around the grounds. You will be surrounded by people and unable to take three steps without running into one."

No privacy. Which was fine. She shouldn't be doing anything that required privacy, anyway. This conference could apparently affect the success of the upcoming campaigns—her father's, and Johnson's. It was critically important. She looked up at the stone house and then around at the outbuildings and grounds. This isolated house was about to become a small city.

Sarah pulled the last stack of looking-glasses out of the crate. She handed them over to Faith. And Faith put them in the correct stack.

"Ladies, you have done wonderful work. I thank you," Johnson said, approaching them.

She and Sarah both stood. She gave Johnson the slightest bow, but Sarah did not.

He poked through the beads and then pulled out random blankets, running his hands over them to feel their texture and the heft of their weave. His face was a portrait of serious study.

James and Sarah both told her how central these were to the success of the conference, but she had still framed them in her mind as small tokens.

But the blankets and cookware the men had laid out earlier, and everything she and Sarah had sorted, were not trinkets. They could keep a large village not only fed and warm through the winter, but elegant and festive.

Johnson said to Faith, "It's a shame we have to send you off to Albany after the conference."

He was a tall man. His shoulders were broad and his face open and charming. His behavior, however, was that of an entitled lord, and she got enough of that in London. Even among officers, it was the lords who treated women the most like playthings, all the while referring to their enlisted men as animals.

"My father needs me."

"He will be off to Fort Niagara with General Shirley."

Sarah stepped between them. "You have guests waiting for you in the house."

Johnson laughed. For all his lordly behavior, he handled Sarah's rebukes shockingly well. Frontier hierarchies were less stratified, apparently. Sarah certainly could not say whatever she wanted, but she obviously felt much freer than Faith did. Everyone here seemed to speak their minds more freely, even in front of Johnson.

They turned back to the piles and surveyed their work. Johnson stepped behind Faith, then a hand patted her backside.

She schooled her face and turned to look. He smiled and then turned to head back to the house. It wasn't nearly as intimate as what James had done earlier, but it was far more irritating.

"He grabbed my bum," she said as soon as he was out of hearing.

Sarah shook her head. "If he did that to me, I would grab his stones and twist them right off."

A laugh exploded out of Faith's mouth. It was followed by another, and another, until she doubled over with tears running down her cheeks. It was time for her to learn to be more like Sarah and the other frontier women. The idea of just grabbing a man's giblets the way they grabbed her bum sounded very satisfying, indeed.

She wheezed and gasped until she could regain her breath, then thought of grabbing James's giblets, and her face heated. She looked up.

Sarah was grinning. "One thing the old goat is right about is that it will be a shame when you return to Albany."

He wasn't exactly old, but the goat part rang true. "Does he do that to every woman who comes to his house?"

"He has some standards, though they do not relate to a woman's marital status."

In London, he would probably get away with that for years, but one day, someone would call him out. Pistols at dawn, and that would be the end of that.

Sarah linked her arm through Faith's. "When I first saw you lying in that bed in your lacey chemise, I thought you were going to be a prissy hot-house flower. Thank you for proving me wrong."

In fairness, it was what Faith expected from most young English ladies, as well.

And most of them were—by training, if not by natural inclination. But eventually, she was going to have to find a way to fit in with them. Once her father married her off to Caleb, she would have to deal with the ladies, despite not having mastered any of the feminine skills they had acquired. They would no doubt find her a burden, too. And there was an unhappy thought.

"Why did the light just go out of your eyes? You can't possibly be offended."

She breathed deeply, then smiled at Sarah. "I was just thinking that once I marry Caleb, I'm going to have to deal with all of those women who do act like you thought I would."

Sarah snorted. "Sounds boring as all get-out." She started leading Faith back toward the house. "If you follow through with that plan, you will lose your mind in less than a year."

Probably.

Faith bumped her shoulder against Sarah's in a sisterly way. When they got to the house, Faith headed upstairs to her bedchamber to rinse the sweat off her face.

When she reached the room and closed the door, she hoisted herself up to sit on the edge of the bed. She thought about James kissing her in the woods. Her lips tingled at the memory, and muscles fluttered, rippling through her midsection.

He had looked so righteous when he pushed her away. Like he had taught her a lesson.

Did he think she was a prudish London Miss as well?

Arrogant man.

She groaned and flopped back on the bed. An arrogant man who had taught her in a few brief moments that kissing really could live up to her fantasies...and then he rejected her. Yes, his hard manhood pressing up against her frightened at first, but her body had been gleeful, and her body had been in the right. She had grown up around soldiers, for heaven's sake. It wasn't as if he was the first aroused man she had ever encountered. She just hadn't known what to do about it.

Perhaps she was more of the London Miss than Sarah thought she was. Her only personal experiences of kisses were Caleb's clumsy efforts and a few young army recruits over the years who managed to evade her father's eagle eye.

Caleb had certainly never ground himself up against her. Indeed, he had not seemed to find their kisses any more inspiring than she had, and had long since given up trying to catch her alone. And she had certainly seen no evidence of inspiration attempting to escape his breeches.

James, on the other hand...yes, inspiring.

But so very irritating. Why did men always make it out that they were doing you a favor when they yanked something away after dangling it in front of you? She would not be thinking of him the next time she touched herself. She would not.

She was getting heartily tired of spending her life pretending to cheerfully bend her will to men.

She slid back off the bed, went to the washstand and washed her face. Then she marched to the door and out into the hall.

Chapter 25

James set the last bundle of blankets down in the outbuilding. They had been carefully sorting the gifts for days.

Hopefully, all of that bounty would do its job. It would have kept his entire village from freezing for years, back in Ireland. It should do the same for all the various Iroquois nations. It had better, because they needed their support.

He returned to the doorway of the outbuilding and looked out at the courtyard. It was already vibrating with last-minute preparations. By tomorrow, it would be packed with people.

Then it would be hard to get five minutes to himself, at least during daylight.

He had gone over the security plans with David, Jaap, Ben, and Okwaho. Jaap and Okwaho had agreed to start teaching Ben the basics of tracking and finding his way. If he showed any aptitude for it, James was signing him up. They were going to need marksmen, and someone who could mend their muskets would be mighty handy as well. In close fighting, sometimes you had to use a musket as a club, and that wasn't exactly healthy for its mechanical works. Last summer, on their scout around Lake Champlain, James has bent the hammer of his musket on the head of a French ally. The weapon had then been useless until they got to a gunsmith back in Albany.

A light breeze blew, and for a few moments, he closed his eyes and savored the air currents moving over his skin, cooling it.

He opened his eyes again, and Faith and Sarah had come out and sat on the front steps.

Heat rose up his neck to his face, undoing the work of the cool breeze. Some of it was the memory of Faith's body up against his, her lips soft and yielding.

But it was mostly shame.

He had been a jackass, and he needed to apologize. He wouldn't be able to focus on his work if he flinched every time he saw her.

He marched across the courtyard to the stairs. "May I borrow Faith for a moment?" he asked Sarah.

"Ask her yourself." Sarah laughed.

They must not be in the middle of any critical preparations if Sarah was laughing at him instead of giving orders. Johnson had offered her a more than decent wage to stay on and help direct preparations.

He turned to Faith. "Do you have a moment?"

Faith stood. "Of course." She smiled and behaved as if all was normal and he hadn't had his hands all over her the last time they were alone. The woman could've bluffed her way out of the Tower of London.

He raised his hand up to her so she could balance as she descended the stairs. "This way." He led her around to the barn, and she followed without resistance. She should have resisted, given their recent history.

James stuck his head into the barn door and looked around. "Hello?" Only the sound of horses and oxen munching their fodder answered. He led Faith inside. The sweet smell of dried hay filled his nostrils.

"I owe you an apology."

She waited silently.

He shifted from one foot to the other.

"Oh, was that the apology?" She was smiling, which took the edge off the barb.

"I behaved like an ass yesterday, and you deserve better. I am very sorry to have forced myself on you and kissed you."

She narrowed her eyes at him and tilted her head sideways. Apparently that wasn't enough of an apology, and really, how could it be?

He went on. "No one has a right to grab you like I did yesterday, and I am ashamed of my actions."

Her eyes grew a little harder. "You have no idea what it's like to be on the receiving end of that, do you?"

No, he didn't. Nor should she, but he couldn't very well undo that.

She took a step toward him. Her body was close enough now that its heat reached his. Their toes almost touched. So did everything else.

Then she flung her arms around his neck, hauled him down to her, and kissed him. He tried to pull back, but she slid her arms down his back and grabbed his arse.

This was not his fault. His cock did not think there was any fault to be found.

As she kissed him, her hips pushed against his, and she groaned. Her groan triggered one of his own, and his cock was now painfully hard. She had no idea what she was doing, or she most certainly wouldn't be doing it.

He concentrated all of his willpower and pulled his head back to look at her. It took everything he had.

"This wasn't quite the apology I had in mind."

She gazed up at him. "I've been busy, but I have thought about this from time to time."

"And when in particular were you thinking of it?" He really needed to shut up.

She traced her finger from the base of his throat down his chest and then circled it around his belly. His brain sputtered.

"I did think of it last night after I closed the bed curtains."

Good God, she was not saying what it sounded like she was saying. Surely proper English women didn't do that.

Her finger kept circling his belly, and the various muscles under his skin jumped in anticipation as her finger came near them in turn. If she was working up the nerve to do something more, he was in trouble.

He growled low in the back of his throat. "Faith...."

Her finger skated over the button at his waist, and he shivered. Then, with her whole hand, she cupped his cock through his breeches.

She smirked like she was very pleased with herself. His thoughts jumbled together, and instead of protesting, he asked, "Does that meet your expectations?"

She squeezed tentatively, and his vision got momentarily blotchy.

"Hmm. I suppose so."

She would be the death of him, and probably in the next few moments. But at least it was better than being killed by a Frenchman.

"Dare I hope this means my apology is accepted?" He should not be egging her on.

"You have apologized for kissing me, which you do not need to do."

James opened his mouth, "I did—"

"You definitely needed to apologize, but for how you behaved afterward." Her hand slid further south and cupped his ballocks.

He had underestimated her. Obviously.

He had nothing to offer a woman, and until he met Faith, he hadn't realized how much that bothered him.

She asked, "Why did you act like an ass afterward?"

Was she seriously asking that? "Because I am one."

Her eyes bore into his, and she still held his stones in her dainty hand, which was absurdly arousing. Her eyes grew hooded, and his cock twitched.

"Damn it, James, where the hell are you?" David's voice bounced around the interior of the barn and James jumped back away from Faith.

His balls ached and were no doubt turning a nasty shade of blue.

Faith turned to David, calm as could be. "He is over here."

The barn was silent except for the fidgeting animals. James held his hands together in front of himself in a feeble attempt to block David's view of his cockstand. How in hell could she act so unruffled?

"Uhhh...."

"Stop gaping and use your words, David," James said. "Is there a reason you came looking for me? Or were you just lonely?"

James moved toward the doorway of the barn, and Faith's footsteps followed behind him. Not that he needed to hear them to know exactly where she was. "We were just trying to have a conversation where we wouldn't be interrupted."

"Well, I'm sure this will be an anticlimax, but I came to tell you that Leo has arrived."

Leo. The lingering sensation of Faith's hand blocked his brain from summoning what he needed Leo for.

Uniforms. "Has anyone told him he has to buy our uniforms?"

Faith looked utterly unaffected by the interruption. Maybe she wasn't affected by their interaction at all. Maybe she had planned to get him irreversibly aroused and then leave him there, unsatisfied, as punishment.

She asked, "Who is Leo, and why in heaven's name does he have to purchase your uniforms?"

She was all business, and apparently no more aroused than a priest at mass. Did he really think she had been after a quick knee trembler in the barn? What a gullible fool he was to let his body talk him into believing that. He gave up wishful thinking years ago.

David answered her. "Leonidas Ten Eyck is Jaap's cousin. He is a fur trader, and he has to pay for our uniforms because Johnson doesn't like him."

"And General Johnson doesn't like him because...?"

James took Faith by the arm and led her past David. "Because Leo makes a lot of money trapping furs he won't trade with Johnson."

"Well, that sounds like standard London intrigue. At least I'm in familiar territory now."

David laughed from behind them. He jogged to catch up. "Frontier intrigue is more fun. You'll see."

"We really don't need any intrigue at all right now, in case I need to remind you," James said to David. "We need a successful conference so the sachems will send warriors to Crown Point with us."

"And with Shirley and my father to Fort Niagara, yes?" Faith asked.

David opened his mouth to say something, but James cut him off. "Of course."

Chapter 26

James surveyed the colorful sea of humanity. More than a thousand people had convened at Johnson's estate for the conference.

All the Iroquois nations were represented, as were some of their client nations. People filled the fields around the house and buildings, and the sachems were gathering in the courtyard. At least that had kept him too busy to think about Faith.

Much.

"Carroll." Wraxall came up behind him. "I need you to fix this and get me an extra pen." He held up a quill with a broken point, then shoved it into his hand. "Hurry."

James took the pen and turned to the house.

How the hell was he supposed to know where to find a pen? And he certainly didn't know how to fix the broken one clutched in his hand. He ran up the steps and into the sitting room. The desk was open, and he rummaged around its boxes and cubbies. No luck.

"What's the matter?" asked Faith.

He jumped out of his skin. Only panic would have kept his body from feeling her presence behind him.

He held up the pen.

"I can fix that." He had never met anyone who looked so happy about being useful. She crossed the room and took it from him, her hand brushing his. The color in her cheeks was all in his imagination, just like the heat where her finger had touched him. Everywhere those fingers had ever touched him.

"I need my pen knife to fix this, and it is upstairs." She turned and left the room.

He hurried up the stairs after her and then stopped outside the door of the bedchamber she had been staying in. Which was stupid. He needed pens, and he needed them now, so he followed her in.

She sat down at a writing desk and began working the pen with a small knife. Then she handed it to him with a flourish. It looked brand new, to him at least.

"I need another."

"Do you not have any?" she asked.

He shook his head. His face and neck flushed hot. He was only just teaching himself how to write, and it wasn't as though he could afford pens. He used charred sticks on birch bark.

She rummaged in a small box on the table, then straightened, holding two pens. "Which would serve your purpose better?"

One was larger than the other, so he pointed at that one. She handed it to him with a smile.

"Thank you," he said. "Wraxall has to write down everything they say, and his pen broke. I had better take these to him."

She looked up at him with bashful eyes. "Do you think it would be terribly inappropriate for me to come outside and listen? From a distance and out of the way, of course."

He could at least help with that. "Come down to the door while I get these to Wraxall. Then I will come get you."

She jumped up from her chair and clasped her hands together in what looked like an attempt to not clap them like an excited child. His heart gave a little extra beat. He led the way down the stairs, and she followed right on his heels, her steps light and quick.

He motioned for her to sit on the front steps while he delivered the pens. Wraxall took them without looking at him, checked them over, and finally looked up. "Don't go far. I may need you to mend them again. Someone's dog must have run off with my other pen."

With that, Wraxall turned back to the table he had set up as a desk for recording the proceedings. Entire villages were now in attendance, and many had, indeed, brought their dogs. And horses, and children, and the list went on. The grounds about the house would take a long to time to recover. Johnson was already grousing about it, not that anyone could blame him.

Johnson descended the stairs from the house, barely seeming to notice Faith sitting there. As soon as he had passed her, James hurried over. "Do you have that little knife you used to mend the pen?"

She pulled it out of her pocket. Either pens broke often, and she knew that, or she had decided to go about armed. A pen knife could do some damage if anyone grabbed her. Which he would do well to remember.

"Come," he said, and took her by the arm. There was still some open space near a tree right behind Wraxall. "It is better than being in the full sun."

She gave him a quick smile, then turned to the proceedings. It could have been the latest London play, she was so engrossed.

Johnson raised his hand for attention. A hush fell over the crowd. Then he launched into the presentation he and the others had been working on since Hendrick arrived over a week ago.

"Brethren of the confederate nations here present," he said. He held up a string of wampum. "With this string of wampum, I wipe away all tears from your eyes."

Faith looked at James with her brows furrowed. He leaned over and spoke quietly in her ear. "It is part of an Iroquois mourning ritual."

She nodded and turned her rapt attention back to Johnson and his audience. Every so often, Johnson would offer a string of wampum, or after a particularly important passage, a belt of wampum.

One of the sachems went through a demonstration of how sticks together were unbreakable. As he banged a bundle of sticks against his knee, they held strong. But sticks on their own would break, just like people. He pulled a few sticks from the bundle and smashed them to splinters over his knee.

Faith watched and listened, eyes wide. She wasn't the only one hanging on their every word and gesture. The stick trick wasn't exactly original, but it was very dramatic, and the entire audience leaned in like he was turning water into wine.

Wraxall wrote so fast James was sure he could hear the pen scratching the paper from where they sat under the tree. He was going to stab the pen right through the paper if he wasn't careful.

The point of his pen finally snapped. Wraxall dropped it, grabbed the stout pen Faith had donated, dipped it in ink, and began writing again without missing a word. When Johnson paused for breath, Wraxall tossed the broken pen at James.

He caught it. What was he supposed to do with it?

He knew what to do with a musket or hatchet. He could survive in the wilderness, hunt, and fight. But he didn't know what to do with a pen. Johnson needed Wraxall to have working pens to keep the record of the conference.

Faith nudged his arm. She smiled at him, took the pen from his hand, and silently began mending it. He could only watch. People probably had to mend pens all the time if they wrote. She had probably realized back in the house that he didn't know how to use a pen. That he was just a poor, uneducated, former indentured servant.

She handed the pen back to him and gave him a gentle shove toward Wraxall. "He may need it."

His face must have gone redder than an apple. He stepped over to Wraxall and put the pen down. He was Irish. Maybe people would just think his skin was burned by the sun.

He returned to her side, and she squeezed his arm. "I could teach you if you want."

His breathing got tight, and he waited for her pity about his not being able to write.

It didn't come. She just continued following the speeches. Did she really not find his lack of schooling significant?

Then she leaned her head against his shoulder.

His heart stuttered, and the earth shifted a little. He looked down at her hand, still on his arm, then put his own hand over hers and held it.

Johnson continued to speak, with pauses for Claus to translate his speech into Mohawk. Johnson could have translated it himself, but it would not have had the same ceremonial impact.

He talked about the king sending a great warrior, General Braddock, and then said he was done.

Hendrick stood. "Brother. We return you our most grateful acknowledgment to the speech you have made to us, and also for the promise of the further speeches you mention, and for the present, we take our leave of you." With that, the sachems began to leave the courtyard.

Faith asked, "They will answer him and he will give more speeches? Will they answer those, too?"

James smiled. "This will take a least a week, probably longer."

"I'd no idea," she said. She still held his arm, looking on at the dispersing leaders in wonder.

James squeezed her hand. "Don't worry, you needn't sit through the whole thing."

She popped her head up to look him in the face again. "But I would like to." They were making war plans, and she wanted to listen to it all. He had never met a woman like her.

David appeared at James's elbow and nodded to Faith, who kept hold of James's hand. David had developed very bad timing.

"So far the conference is going well, but Jaap is eyeing my cousin Caroline's—" David cut himself off and glanced at Faith.

Faith laughed. "I've met Jaap. You mean he is staring at her breasts."

David grinned. "Yes, you have met Jaap, haven't you?" Then he turned back to James. "But Johnson is eyeing them too. We need to get Jaap out of the way so he doesn't get himself sacked."

Faith's brows knit together in concern. "Shouldn't we be worrying about your cousin?"

David shook his head at her. "My cousin is no fool, and if she gets half a chance at Johnson, she will take it. Jaap is the idiot I am worried about just now."

Faith was silent for just a moment, then offered her own solution. "Well, I can go distract him if it will be in his best interest."

"You most certainly will not." James said, a bit too loudly.

Chapter 27

She should not be happy that James sounded jealous, but it sent a little thrill to areas that she had only ever explored on her own.

James found Jaap in the crowd, which wasn't easy in the fading light, and sure enough, the man was chatting up a tall Mohawk woman with a buxom chest.

"Jaap!" he called.

Jaap ignored him. Faith pressed her lips together so she didn't laugh. James wasn't used to Jaap ignoring him, but Jaap would probably ignore Johnson himself right now.

"Jaap!" This time James bellowed.

Jaap turned a glare on their little group, and James gestured for him to join them. He said something to the woman and came their way.

"Leo needs you." James said when Jaap was close enough to hear. Faith still hadn't met the mysterious Leo, who apparently kept a low profile around Johnson.

"Now?"

"He's in the blockhouse," said David.

Jaap turned and stomped off.

"How do you know Leo is in the blockhouse?" she asked. "You two have been out here all this time."

David shrugged. "I have no idea where he is."

The sun had set, and the brightest stars shone in the gloaming.

"I see one of my uncles, and I think I will pick his brain and see how he thinks the sachems are feeling about day one." David gave them a big wink. "I will leave you to it." And then he slipped off in the darkening shadows to join an older Mohawk man by a campfire near the edge of the woods.

David was clearly aware of what he had interrupted the day before, and he probably thought she was a shameless harlot.

James said, "I should get you back to the house before anyone gets designs on you. The stress of these conferences seems to bring out...a need in some to relieve stress."

She couldn't see his face, but she could feel the heat radiating off it. The man was blushing again, or she was Archbishop of Canterbury.

Men often felt awkward around her, because she took an unwomanly interest in things only men were supposed to be interested in. Caleb always looked at her like she had just let a frog loose in a punch bowl when she asked about military matters. But no man had even been awkward around her because they found her tempting. She usually didn't care, because she was usually trying to have an intelligent conversation. This evening, she cared very much.

And she found James tempting. Caleb was never going to give her the same shivers of anticipation that he did. Not being able to satisfy her curiosity was not something she took well generally, and with this, well, no one was here to stop her. She should be allowed to learn what she would be missing the rest of her life.

Fires were being lit in various spots around the grounds, and the occasional giggle, both male and female, sounded in the night. But no one could see them.

She leaned in and kissed James.

For an instant, he went still under her touch. Then he pulled away. "If Johnson sees you, he will yank you out of my arms and drag you to his bedchamber."

Her brain spun for a moment. "No, he wouldn't." Yes, he probably would, but she still had her pen knife and would use it if she needed to.

James sighed in the dark, and Faith's hopes waned.

"You are a great temptation," he said in a voice so low she almost didn't hear him. "But I am in no station to have you." His fingers brushed her cheek.

She leaned her face into his touch. "I am not proposing marriage to you," she said. She tried to keep her tone light.

The sound of his breathing got louder, and his fingers burned hotter against her cheek. Her own breath got short and quick.

"What are you proposing?" he asked.

A very good question. She reached out and touched his chest, letting her finger trace a circle there. "I believe you mentioned something about relieving stress?"

"You know I wasn't talking about a moonlit stroll or prayers, yes?"

"I've never found either of those things to relieve stress very well. Have you?"

He grabbed the wrist of the hand that had been touching his chest. The heat of his fingers scalded her. She tipped her head back to look up at him, and the reflected flames of campfires danced in his eyes.

"You have no idea what you are doing," he said.

She pulled her hand from his grasp. "You seem to be the slow one just now."

He grabbed her hand again and pulled her along, past the house, into the darkness of the trail toward the blockhouse.

He stopped once, turned to her, and asked, "Are you sure?"

"Are you questioning my decision-making abilities?"

He half-groaned and half-growled, and then he started leading her down the path again. They reached the blockhouse. "Wait here." And then he disappeared inside.

The door stood open and voices spilled out of it.

"Okwaho and Leo are on watch right now, circling behind the camps." That sounded like David. "Go get some sleep, you grumpy old mule." Definitely David, laughing as he insulted James.

She swatted at an insect in the dark, then fanned herself. She had thought London was hot in summer, but New York Colony in late June was much hotter.

James emerged with a small lantern and a rolled blanket. He took her arm again without speaking.

The touch of his skin on hers sent hundreds of butterflies fluttering through her chest and down through her belly. Her whole body seemed to flutter as she followed him down a narrow path to a little clearing in the woods.

The air smelled of pine. He let go of her hand and set the lamp down on a small rock, and he spread out the blanket on the soft ground. Then he lowered himself to the blanket and patted the space next to him.

She sat.

"I am in the provinces to make a career, and I am about to go to war." He looked into her face like he wanted to be certain she understood the implications of that statement.

"And I have to get back to Albany to run my father's affairs before he bankrupts us." This might be her only chance to know true pleasure with a man she actually wanted.

He stroked her cheek. It was a simple gesture, but it set her body fluttering again. She turned into his hand and kissed its palm.

He sucked in a breath. But he didn't grab her face or kiss her. He lay down slowly and pulled her with him until she lay across his chest. Their hearts pounded against each other, and his hand caressed her hair.

"You are a beautiful woman, and you drive me to distraction."

"You are a fascinating man, and you drive me to do this." She cupped his face in her hands and kissed him. Her lips explored his, and she pulled at the string that contained his hair in a queue and set it loose. It was thick and wavy and luxurious.

Her body moved over his, and his cock stiffened against her.

Then he rolled her gently over until he was atop her, kissing her, exploring her mouth with his tongue and stealing her breath. His hand ran up her ribcage and began massaging her breast through her clothing, and she arched into the pressure that shot heat straight to her core. Every inch of her tingled, and she couldn't push herself close enough to him.

His hand reached between them and dipped beneath her stays, freeing one breast. Her nerves grew more sensitive than she would've thought possible. His rough-skinned fingers sent ripples of a sensation through every inch of her body in a way touching herself could never have prepared her for.

Then he lowered his mouth and began to suckle her, flicking his tongue over her nipple and teasing her skin with his teeth. Her mind lost its ability to function. Her body bucked against him, out of her control.

He lifted his head and whispered in her ear. "Please tell me if I need to stop."

She could barely form words. "Don't you dare."

He smiled against her cheek, then his mouth returned to her breast more forcefully.

She clutched his back to pull him closer, and his hand skimmed down her side. Then it was on her leg, under her skirt. Her whole body quivered, and it was delicious. She had never brought herself to this intense a state of arousal, and certainly no one else had.

His hand shoved her petticoat to her waist. She gasped. He went still, and she grabbed him and pulled him closer. He began teasing the hair at the juncture of her thighs, and she gasped again. His thumb found that very sensitive spot that only she had ever touched.

His finger slipped inside her. "You are magnificent, Faith Richmond."

And she cried out and came apart in his hand.

Chapter 28

He pressed his mouth over hers to swallow the cries she made. Those cries were his, and he didn't want to share them with anyone else who might be out in the woods this evening.

She arched against his body and shuddered. Her arms almost squeezed the breath out of him. He kept his left arm wrapped around her, holding her together, and continued to bring her to pieces with his right hand.

He hadn't expected her to come apart so quickly. She didn't hold herself back, or pretend she wasn't affected, or try to shield herself in any way. She just gave herself over to him completely.

His heart reached out to hers, and he couldn't let her go.

Slowly, her body subsided under him, and he nuzzled her neck under her ear. She kissed his cheek, still breathing hard. Her breath against his skin sent his heart rocketing.

She relaxed in his arms, sated and content. His body was anything but.

But he wasn't about to risk getting her with child. It would upend her life and probably simply end his. But he was going to have to figure something out soon.

She reached down and caressed his rock-hard cock through his breeches. His whole body jolted in response. He pressed into her hand. The heat of her caress almost burned the fabric.

Her fingers then went to the buttons at the waist of his breeches and began unfastening them. She had them undone faster than he could have.

She touched the soft skin of her finger to the head of his cock, and it jumped in response. Then she thrust her hand into his breeches and grasped his throbbing flesh in her hand, pulling him gently toward her.

His brain went blank for a moment as his hips thrust into her grip. God, he wanted to bury himself deep inside her and never emerge.

"We can't." He grabbed her wrist. "It is too great a risk for you."

She groaned and pulled again at his cock.

He almost came undone right there in her hand. He was so far past any stopping point.

"And my father might shoot you."

There was also that.

She kissed him and still didn't relinquish her grip. And really, she could lead him around like that for the rest of his life and he would be a happy man.

"But this isn't fair to you," she said, circling her thumb around his head, exploring it by touch. She was going to kill him faster than her father's bullet.

She sat up, hand still in his breeches. "What do you do to relieve yourself when you are alone?"

He almost choked. Women weren't supposed to know men did that.

"Don't get all proper on me, James. I have spent most of my life around army camps. Men talk. And surely you know women do that too?"

His jaw went slack. Images of her own hands where his had just been made his cock dance with joy. Or maybe that was because she was still caressing it.

She pushed him down on his back and grabbed his hand with her free one. She brought it down over the hand she still held on his cock as he lay there on the ground.

The light of the small lantern reflected hot in her eyes. "Show me."

Jesus, Mary, and Joseph.

His hand began to guide hers as they pulled at his cock, then slid back to its base. Pulled and slid back.

Holy Jesus.

She leaned in like she wanted a better view.

He grabbed her free hand with his and brought it to his aching stones. He caressed her hand as it caressed his stones, and together they brought him to the brink of madness.

His ballocks tightened, and his hand made hers pull him faster and harder.

He stopped breathing and thrust into her hand like he was going to punch a hole in the sky. Then he exploded. His seed shot up onto his belly and almost reached his chest.

They both kept pulling his cock and squeezing his ballocks, and his hips bucked out of his control.

The pulsing began to subside, and his vision returned to normal. He had never experienced anything so erotic in his wildest fantasies.

Her mouth hung open, her lips full, and her face flushed. Good God, she was astonishing.

He kept his own hand wrapped around hers on his cock, and took her other hand and shifted it up under her skirts as she knelt above him.

Her eyes shot to his. The flames there looked like they might consume both of them.

He guided her hand to her throbbing flesh between her thighs. She was so wet with excitement, his cock began hardening again. He dipped one finger inside her and then spread her juices across the bundle of nerves at the front of her opening.

Then he pressed her thumb over it, and she immediately began to circle it and rub. So he slid a finger back inside her, then a second, and watched her eyes grow wide.

Her hips bucked against his fingers and her own as they both began to speed their motions. The hand she worked his cock with mirrored the rhythm of his fingers, and he grasped his own stones with the hand that had been covering hers.

They both gasped and muttered nonsense as they brought each other to the brink.

She was the first over it, letting out a strangled moan as her body stiffened and pulsed around his fingers, which he kept working to keep her going as long as he could. Then his own cannon went off, shooting his seed up his belly again, throbbing into her hand.

She collapsed down on the blanket next to him, her hand still caressing his cock.

She lay there, breathing hard. "I never..." Her voice trailed off like she couldn't form any more words yet.

He pulled her toward him. "Me neither." He kissed her forehead and tucked her head against his neck, under his chin.

He smoothed her hair. It was silk under his hand. Softer than anything he had ever held.

She snuggled up closer and wrapped her arms around him like he was her anchor in the roiling seas their bodies had created.

He pulled her in even tighter. If he could have wrapped his body around her entirely, he would have. He wouldn't let anything hurt her. He would just keep her here.

He kissed her hair. His lips got to feel its silky smoothness. He kissed her again.

She was amazing. If she had danced naked in front of the sachems, she couldn't have shocked him more than she just had. English women were not as he had imagined. At least this one wasn't.

Indeed, this one began to snore in his arms. His heart melted. At least he had worn her out as much as she had worn him out.

He couldn't figure out how to think of her except as a treasure.

He lay there, listening to her.

After a while, it occurred to him that his ass was hanging out, bare to the world, and his breeches were somewhere around his knees. But he couldn't bring himself to move. He reached for her skirt and pulled it over him like a blanket. It would do.

He drifted off to sleep.

Chapter 29

The moon had risen when he woke, and Faith was watching him.

"Was I snoring?" he asked.

She smiled. "No, was I?"

He kissed her. "Just a little."

She burrowed into his arms, and he kissed her again.

"All my life I wished I had been born a boy so I could join the army and go off on adventures." She looked up at him. "But then I never would have ended up here in these woods with you."

He chuckled. "This feels like quite an adventure to one Irish lad."

She smiled against his neck. "A rather magnificent adventure."

He stroked her hair. His hands couldn't get enough of its feel under his fingers. "When I first came to the provinces, I had no idea what was in store for me. I just knew it couldn't be worse than what Ireland had to offer me."

She propped herself up on her elbows. "What made you leave?"

He shouldn't have said anything. She didn't really need to hear his sob story. It wasn't unique to him, but she had loosened his tongue and he couldn't stop it.

"When I was ten, we were starving. My parents couldn't feed my sister and me, and my other siblings had already died. Someone offered a few shillings for my sister, and my parents considered it. I told them not to, that they didn't have to feed me anymore, and I ran off to Dublin to sell myself to a ship's captain to come here. I traded eleven years of labor just for passage across the ocean in the stinking hold of a merchant ship." He buried his face in her hair. "I hope they never had to sell her."

She held him tight. "You are an amazing man, James Carroll."

No, he wasn't. He was just one of thousands like himself. But in that moment, he wanted to believe her.

She stroked his face again and kissed his neck. She was the amazing one, and a very lucky Englishman was going to get to spend his life with her.

That sobered him up.

"Your future husband is going to be delighted on your wedding night." He tried to keep his voice light, but his gut felt like he had just swallowed glass.

"Hardly. I don't think Caleb particularly likes me."

His chest crushed in on itself. She was going to marry the damned lieutenant. How stupid could he be? Now two officers would form a line to run him through.

But what kind of fool didn't like her?

He took her face in his hands. "Then why are you marrying him?"

The lamplight shone in her eyes, and he could see them filling with tears. "I have a duty to my father."

She ducked her head and spoke into his chest. "I was supposed to be a boy. He named me Faith because he had faith his next child would be a son. But there was no next child. Then my mother died, and he couldn't bring himself to remarry."

His mind flashed back to the woods when they first met. She had reacted oddly when David said something about how she got her name. But that didn't mean her father could take his disappointment out on her for her entire life.

He really didn't like that man. "But why did you agree to a marriage that obviously makes you unhappy?"

She stiffened in his arms, then raised herself back up on her elbows. "You may have only been a boy, but you still had a say in your fate. Do you think for one moment that anyone asked your sister? Do you think anyone asked me?"

"But—"

She slapped her hand over his mouth and almost growled at him. "I am legally my father's to do with as he pleases until I am married, then I am legally my husband's responsibility. Do you not understand that? Even if I defy him, I have nothing to live on. Nothing in this world is legally mine."

He stared at her. That couldn't be right.

Finally, she shook her head, like she couldn't believe what a fool he was. Then she shoved herself off his body and curled up on her side with her back to him.

Chapter 30

Faith stepped up to the house, and the lingering smoke of hundreds of campfires from the previous night settled heavily in her lungs. Her muscles were stiff, and she had not gotten much sleep, but at least James had gotten her back to the house as the sun came up, which was absurdly early in June.

They hadn't spoken since he had asked her about why she agreed to marry. After what he had told her about his sister, she thought he would have understood how few choices she had. She hadn't even had the opportunity to decide to marry to bail her father out of his debts. Her father had claimed that decision for her.

But no. It didn't even occur to James that she didn't have the same legal say in her life he had in his. He probably thought her mercenary, choosing to marry for money. Yes, she could have found some willing man somewhere to elope with, but she hadn't found one worth abandoning her father for. She wasn't fool enough to marry someone she didn't like out of spite, just avoid her duty to her family. Her mother would weep in her grave.

Expecting James to understand was a flight of fancy. She had fewer choices than he did, but she was going to use the choices she did have as wisely as she was able. She wasn't helpless.

She stood for a moment next to the front steps. It was the quietest it had been since people began gathering for the conference.

The faint hum of the river reached her ears. It flowed fairly slowly here, but the water was deep and wide, and its quiet strength moved her. Tenonanatche, David had called it. She didn't know what the word translated to in English, but the sound of it suited.

Voices from the campsites intruded and grew closer, so she hurried toward the kitchen. At least there she could see if Louisa had some menial task she could do, and everyone would be too busy to pry.

She went down the earthen ramp and in the cellar door. The kitchens teamed like a London dockyard as a ship came up the Thames to be unloaded.

"Is that you, Sarah?" Louisa asked.

"No, it's Faith. What can I do to help?"

"Where is Sarah? Johnson needs her to mend his suit."

"I can try," Faith said.

Louisa looked at her like she had sprouted a second and third head on her shoulders. "I am sure you can mend well enough, but this conference is too important to trust his appearance to anyone but Sarah's needle skills."

Faith had terrible needle skills. It bored her, so she never applied herself. Another womanly failing. "I can go search for her if you would like."

"What does the old goat need now?" Sarah's voice boomed so close behind Faith it made her jump.

Louisa explained Johnson's sartorial emergency, then mumbled something in Sarah's ear, glancing Faith's way.

Sarah laughed. "Faith, I need your help."

Tears prickled at the back of Faith's eyes, which was ridiculous. "Have you been charged with keeping me out of the way?"

"I do need company." Sarah squeezed her shoulder like she was a little girl with hurt feelings.

James had thrown her completely off kilter. It was disconcerting to have her nerves so exposed.

"Hello, Miss Dreamer, are you coming?" Sarah was already out the door.

"Of course." She hurried after her.

They went into the house and threaded their way through the crowded hall. Wraxall and Claus were there, as well as Farrell and a minister, and they were all deep in conversation.

Faith followed Sarah up the stairs, and they almost collided with Johnson as they made the turn at the top of the stairs.

"Thank God," Johnson said. "My brown suit has a large tear, and so does my shirt. I caught them on the gate post last night in the crush and need them this afternoon, and they can't look patched. Not now."

His mind was clearly focused on the conference. His gaze didn't wander to either set of breasts before him.

"I will take care of it."

Johnson gave Sarah a nod, clearly trusting her to make sure he looked the part of the great Indian Commissioner and general by the time his audience reconvened.

There were blankets neatly folded on the floor. "Yes," Sarah said, "folks were sleeping here last night, which you would know if you had come home."

Faith's face burned like she had stuck her head into the bake oven.

"I don't blame you. He's a far better match for you than that dim lieutenant." Sarah led the way into Johnson's bedchamber and closed the door.

It was quiet in here, and it seemed odd to have so much space with only two people in it after the crowds everywhere else inside the house.

But she had gone to help in the kitchens so she could do some mindless work and think about last night. Not to be grilled about it.

"How can I help?"

"I don't need anyone's help to sew. I just need some entertainment, because this is some picky work."

"I could read to you as you stitch. I have one of Shakespeare's comedies in my trunk."

"I don't need comedy right now." Sarah grabbed the suit from off the foot of Johnson's bed. "James is a fine man, if a little Irish around the edges."

Faith could leave the room, but Sarah would just corner her again.

"When my father bought his indenture, James was so eager to prove himself, he insisted on doing the work of two men. He never rested. My father felt so lucky, he joked about having a team of laborers but only having to feed one."

Sarah's family had *owned* James? She hadn't even considered that people who were now his friends might have owned his indenture. She almost groaned out loud. She had tried to learn everything possible about the area and yet had fundamentally misunderstood the basic social order.

"You all must have been so horrified to be saddled with a clueless chit from London when I landed in your laps." How awkward she must seem to them all.

"Hardly. You read people faster than anyone I know." Sarah's needle flew in and out of the front of Johnson's suit. "Which is why I can't imagine you married to that lieutenant."

Faith fiddled with her skirt, then forced herself to let the fabric go. "My father's estate started to founder after my mother died, and he needed to borrow money to see to my future. I was just another expense, being female, and couldn't earn anything to help out."

"Nonsense. You run his holdings. Any fool can see that. Does Caleb come with money?"

"Marrying me to Caleb was the only way Caleb's father would agree to the loan. If my father defaulted, he would still control the property. My father expects me to do my duty in return and keep up the family name."

Sarah's needle stopped. "You are the security on a loan?"

Faith tried to smile. "I propose we change the subject."

Sarah studied her own needlework on the coat, then set it aside. "If he wouldn't be so careless, his clothing would last longer."

Then Sarah threaded her needle with white thread to match the shirt and began to work on it. "So you headed into the woods and diddled James to give yourself a little excitement before a life of lying back and surrendering to boredom?"

Faith gawked at Sarah.

"You both looked spent as you crept back to the house this morning."

"I was..." Gads, there was no appropriate way to end that sentence.

Sarah's needle paused. "Your life could get a little complicated if you are with child."

She sighed. James had been too thoughtful.

"I am impressed. He left you speechless. I doubt many people do that under any circumstances." Sarah snipped off the thread and held up her handiwork to the light of the window. "Come look. Tell me if you can see where the mend is."

Her brain wasn't reliably functioning, but she looked at the shirt. And looked again. There was no mend. She took the shirt from Sarah's hands to look closer.

"Good." Sarah nodded. Faith's searching must have answered her question.

Faith handed the shirt back. "How did you do that?"

Sarah smiled and waggled her fingers. "Magic." They both laughed.

Then Sarah gathered her mending materials into their basket. "Don't let your father hitch you to someone who bores you to oblivion, to anyone if you don't want. You don't need anyone. Stay with us. We are going to need more women willing to roll up their sleeves and get their hands dirty when the troops head out."

"I can't cook. I can't sew. I don't think the army would pay to feed me just to read Shakespeare to the officers." Even if she had Sarah's skills, she had a duty to her father. His finances weren't just her future, after all, they were his, too. He had barely been able to function when her mother died, and he had never really recovered. She couldn't leave him to ruin. So she would marry Caleb and find a way to make this latest investment turn a profit. For everyone's sake.

"I am glad you at least got your world turned upside down once before you commit yourself to an eternity of tedium." Sarah left the room and closed the door behind her, leaving Faith alone in Johnson's bedchamber.

Somehow Caleb didn't seem like the sort to bring her to oblivion with his hands while she pulled his manhood, watching it throb and explode in her hands. Then again, she wouldn't have imagined herself engaging such things until last night, so maybe he would surprise her.

No, he would find her unladylike for even suggesting such activities.

Voices sounded on the stairs. She jumped for the door and let herself out in case it was Johnson.

He, no doubt, engaged in all sorts of behavior when his wife was not at home. Perhaps even when she was. Perhaps his wife did too.

Gads, her brain was truly addled this morning.

She dove across the wide hall to her own bedchamber. Maybe they hadn't seen her.

Chapter 31

At last, the conference seemed to be winding down. James was ready for all the talking to be done so they could go take Crown Point. How David could be so enthralled by the verbal sparring was a mystery of Biblical proportions. James preferred action to talk.

Unless the sachems had done a significant about-face overnight, they were ready to send most of their young men. They were negotiating time for them to return home and put their affairs in order before they headed to face the French. So they were down to debating when, not if.

He had no affairs to put in order before they headed out.

He couldn't afford any land. He couldn't afford anything. He certainly couldn't afford a wife.

His chest felt like an ox was sitting on it. Perhaps by the time the war ended, he would have gained enough rank and saved enough money to purchase a small farm and think about a family.

Faith would long since be married off. And didn't that thought just turn his stomach.

But he had never needed anyone before, and he wasn't going to start now. He rubbed his hands over his face until he rubbed the image of a family life right out of his head.

Now the conference was almost over, it was time to recruit in earnest for the ranger company. That was the opportunity his ten-year-old self had exchanged his childhood for, and it was time to get on with it.

He looked over as Johnson opened the day's proceedings, and then at the table where Wraxall sat recording the day's speeches on paper.

It was just as well that he couldn't write worth a darn. As much as he coveted the titles and prestige of Wraxall and Claus's positions, he would have had to stab himself in the eye with a pen to keep himself awake during all the ceremonial to-ing and fro-ing.

At least he now knew how to mend a pen if he broke the tip smashing it in frustration. Thanks to Faith.

David appeared next to him. "Okwaho decided not to wait for the rest of the negotiations. He went back to Canajoharie to pack his things. He will fight under Johnson instead of Hendrick."

James turned to David. "With Hendrick's blessing?"

"Yes." David smiled. "Unless you ask Hendrick in public."

The wily old bastard. "I don't understand half of this, but I'm grateful Okwaho is with us."

And, of course, David could not let him remain blissfully ignorant of any possible political lesson. "Leaving out the details that will make you complain of bleeding ears, Hendrick wants some men helping Johnson, even when the rest of the Mohawk are not there, and Okwaho would rather spend his time with us than with our sixty-five-year-old uncle."

"He just wants to be where the food is better."

"Yes," said David. "That too."

The man's stomach had no bottom. His name meant "wolf," and despite what Okwaho said about some childhood incident that gave him the name, James was convinced he got it because of the way he tore into food. David refused to confirm or deny either version.

Red Head, the Onondaga sachem, stood to give the Iroquois response to Johnson's latest speeches. This should be the grand climax of the conference. Then they could be done with endless deliberations and get ready to march to Crown Point, and he could finally start to prove himself.

David's face grew more serious. "The Kahnawakes are going to be difficult."

They were Mohawks who had moved close to Montreal and become Catholics, and Johnson had been reluctant to say he would leave them be unless they agreed to come south, away from the French. With the sides in the coming war dividing down religious lines, James couldn't blame him.

"Will they come south?" James asked.

David shrugged. "At least they will have fair warning. Red Head just agreed to Johnson sending a messenger to them."

Red Head had been leaning toward the French himself, and it was a stroke of genius that Johnson had gotten him to agree to take a lead in getting the Iroquois to support the British.

Johnson had a way with people, much like Faith did. He could speak to the Iroquois like the brother they saw him as, and turn around and speak to Governor Shirley like a born aristocrat.

James's eyes went to Faith as she sat off to his right, near Farrell. She found the negotiations fascinating, and he hadn't had a moment alone with her over the past few days.

Farrell said something to her, and she smiled. James stiffened.

"Easy, there. She has no interest in him. Have a little faith." David poked his elbow into James's ribs. "Or have you already had our pretty little Faith?"

James said nothing.

"Perhaps I should ask her." David was having too much fun, but before James could tell him where to put his asinine ideas, David's face went serious again. "Oh shit, here we go."

Red Head stood. "Brother. You promised us that you would keep this fireplace clean from all filth and that no snake should come into this council room. That man sitting there" —James couldn't see who he was pointing at—"is a Devil and has stole our lands."

James's view was blocked by a head in front of him. David swung up into the branches of a tree some children were sitting in, where they respectfully made room for him. From there, he could see over everyone's heads.

He scrambled back down. "Lydius."

"What? When did he get here?"

David shrugged.

The man had been adopted into the Turtle Clan many years ago, but had recently gotten a number of people drunk, then sold their lands for them. To more than one group of investors, for good measure.

Faith had stopped talking to Farrell and stared hard at Lydius as Red Head went on at length about the man's failings.

James looked at David, who looked back at him.

Her father had recently purchased lands along the Schoharie. Lands that David had said no one had sold. If he purchased them from Lydius, that would be a financial mess, to say nothing of the political fallout.

"She didn't," David said, like he was trying to convince himself.

"No," James said. "If anyone did, it was her father."

David made a low grumbling growl.

"She did nothing." He grabbed David's shirt and pulled him close to make his point.

David started a moment, then laughed. "I wasn't going to call her out for pistols at dawn, you ass. Besides, she would probably shoot a hole through me before I could even fire. I can't work those stupid little guns."

He let David's shirt go.

"You should marry her before her father marries her off to that convenient subaltern."

He didn't even look at David. "I can't afford to marry." But his gut gave a slow, threatening lurch. The lieutenant was possibly the only person he had ever met who was dim enough not to like her. James was going to pound him into dust if he ever saw him again.

"I'd marry her in a heartbeat. She understands important things," David said.

James smacked him in the chest. "No, you wouldn't."

"No, but it was fun to see your reaction."

"Screw you."

"How about you screw her instead and leave me out of it?" David danced away from James's elbow as it jabbed at his ribs.

After the other night in the woods, he wanted nothing more. But he wouldn't.

And he would not let her yank him off again, even if she was willing, no matter how badly he wanted to make it worth her while. And he wasn't at all sure she would be willing after he had so spectacularly ruined the moment by proving his ignorance.

He still couldn't wrap his head around the idea that someone of her station might have less autonomy than him. Was that possible?

David heaved a big sigh. "Don't tell Okwaho that she might have bought land from Lydius."

"Her father might have bought land from Lydius."

David shook his head. "Okwaho won't be interested in the difference."

He was right. Neither would most of the people in attendance, including the Germans, English, and even the Dutch, even though Lydius was one of them. The shitehawk had managed to make enemies wherever he went. He was lucky there was such a large audience, or Johnson would have thrown him out bodily the moment Red Head pointed him out in the crowd.

Johnson and Lydius had gotten along well enough early on, but Lydius was a competing trader, in addition to being a snake in the grass, so Johnson had long since crossed him off his guest list. The bastard must have snuck in overnight when everyone was exhausted.

Johnson was talking again.

James smacked David's arm to get his attention. "Did he just call Lydius 'colonel'?"

David rubbed his arm. "He did. Must have been promoted since King George's war."

"Is he here recruiting for Shirley again?"

David's eyes went wide. "You are better at this politics stuff than you let on. If he is, Shirley could undo all of Johnson's work over the last two weeks of this conference. What an ignorant jackass. Everything they just agreed to will fall apart if it looks like the British can't possibly stand up to the French."

"Why would it mean we can't stand up to the French?"

David jabbed him in the ribs. "'We' now, is it? Your swearing really is the only Irish Catholic part of you left."

James ignored the barb. He wasn't going to be deterred by David's ribbing. "Why, David?"

"Would you fight for men who can't even agree on which of them is in charge?"

James would not.

"Exactly. Even Hendrick might choose to sit that out. He might not side with the French, but why risk his life for the British when he can simply continue to play the power balance between the two? He's been doing that in this region since before Johnson and Shirley ever set foot in North America."

James rubbed his hand over his face. "We don't know if that is why Lydius is here."

"True," David said. He looked dubious, but he was too smart to assume their fears were facts. "But we did find the paper with notes about the conference in Dutch the day we found Faith alone in the woods."

He hadn't even considered that Lydius could be the man spying on the conference. They were both trying to get ready to fight the same enemy, for heaven's sake. "We need to find out."

David nodded.

"Lydius is a wily bastard." James added. "We need someone he doesn't know to talk with him. Does he know Okwaho?"

David looked heavenward. "Okwaho might have knocked out two of Lydius's teeth last winter."

"All right, not Okwaho."

People rounded the corner. The speeches must have finished for the day.

James grabbed David's arm and pulled him back to the front of the house. "We need to see where he gets to." He scanned the crowd, looking for Lydius.

"Uh, James?"

"What?"

David pointed to Faith, who walked right up to the little weasel.

James launched himself in their direction.

Chapter 32

"Colonel Lydius, how lovely to see you. I didn't realize you had been promoted. My congratulations."

The man looked to see who had called to him. He looked older than Johnson, and far less prosperous. His hair was gray and greasy, and he was looking around like he was in a hurry to leave. But she couldn't let him because she wanted to better understand what Red Head had meant.

Surely her father had made sure the deeds were legitimate before borrowing on her future to buy land from him. But he hadn't let her attend that part of the deal-making, and why would he be more careful about that than he was about anything else with his investments?

A glint of recognition shone in Colonel Lydius' eye. "Ah, Miss Richmond. How lovely to see you. Whatever are you doing here? I saw your father not a week ago in Albany."

He smiled at her. He was missing two teeth, right in front. "Yes, well, I met with a bit of an accident, but as you can see, I am well now and I will be returning to Albany as soon as the conference wraps up."

Lydius looked her up and down, a smirk on his face that made her want to knee him in the crotch.

"I heard Red Head's claim," she said. As if anyone had missed it. "I am certain a misunderstanding lies behind it all."

Lydius snorted, just as her father would have.

She persisted. "I have come to know a number of the Mohawk while I have sojourned here. Perhaps I could put in a good word if you could explain to me the nature of the misunderstanding?"

Lydius moved closer and spoke in a low voice. "I am recruiting scouts here for Governor Shirley and his campaign to Fort Niagara."

Well, that couldn't be right. After two weeks of the conference, she understood how this was supposed to work. "But isn't Johnson to handle all interaction with the Iroquois?"

He patted her on the arm like she was a child. "General Shirley outranks Johnson. And he is your father's commander. We need to get some warriors to make certain your father makes it safely to Niagara."

"But Johnson has already handled that. They will be traveling through Iroquois territory. Who would bother them?"

Lydius glanced around them, apparently making sure who was and was not in his audience. "You are sweet, Miss Richmond, but people don't always do as they promise, do they? Your father needs protection against any Seneca who might have sided with the French, does he not?"

David had said the Seneca were not as well represented here, as they were the farthest western nation of the Iroquois, and tended to lean toward the French. But he also said if the council decided to give Shirley safe passage, they would stand by that.

"Are you saying they are not good to their word?"

"You heard them here pretending they had not sold what they received good payment for."

She didn't like what she had heard, but not because she didn't believe it. Nothing anyone had said led her to believe the Mohawks were deceitful in their dealings. It was Lydius she distrusted.

"Yes," she said. "They say the land you sold us wasn't yours to sell."

He didn't even bother to look offended. "Of course they do. But that doesn't mean your deed is not good. Courts would never side for them."

"I didn't ask how courts would side."

Lydius waved his free hand as if he was shooing a fly. "Don't you worry, Miss Richmond." He put his second hand on her other arm as he moved in just a shade too close. His breath stank of rotten teeth. "You say you have gotten to know many of the people here."

She stood her ground. "Of course. One could hardly stay here for weeks and not get to know people."

"And have you gotten to know any of the Onondaga or Oneida? Or just Mohawks?" He seemed oddly eager, and it set the hairs on the back of her neck on end.

"Mostly Mohawks. Why do you want to know?"

"I told you, I need to recruit for Shirley, so he has scouts. Don't you want to see your father get safely to Fort Niagara?"

"Of course I do. Let's go find General Johnson. I am sure he can help you."

"No, no, Johnson is too busy right now." And then the man melted into the crowd.

James and David came up to her side, somewhat breathless. "Where did he go?" asked James.

She scanned the crowd. He had completely vanished. "I have no idea."

James took her hand and gently pulled her under a tree, so they wouldn't have so many people around them, and David followed. "What did you ask him?"

Had they been watching her? "I asked if the deed he sold us was good, and he said it would hold up in court."

David and James exchanged glances, then James turned to her. "But you don't think he is correct?"

"I am confident that Red Head would not have made a public accusation founded on nothing." And she was not so naïve as to deny people were defrauded intentionally. The possible implications for her father's finances made her gut plummet.

David spoke up. "As much as I wish to hang Lydius by his privates for his fraudulent dealings, we have a more pressing issue."

If he had defrauded her father, she would gladly participate in the hanging.

James took both of her hands in his and gazed into her eyes. "What else did he say?"

"He is recruiting for General Shirley. But I thought General Johnson was supposed to do that, and I offered to take him to Johnson to sort that out, but he mumbled something about Johnson being too busy and then vanished. That was right before you two arrived. Did you scare him off?" She tried to make the last bit light, but as she said it, it struck her that they might have.

James still held her hands in his, but he spoke to David. "You tell Hendrick, and I will get the word to Johnson."

David turned and went off toward where Hendrick was camped.

James turned back to her. "Thank you. This is bad news, but it is very important for us to know."

"I understand that he seems to have skipped the chain of command, but I assume Johnson is going to send some of the Iroquois with Shirley, isn't he?"

James pulled her closer to him. "Probably not yet. He doesn't need them. Once he gets to Oswego, the Cayuga and Seneca will help him get to Fort Niagara. He doesn't need protection going through Iroquois country."

She pushed back. "But Lydius said not all the Seneca would agree to that."

James shook his head.

"My father will be with Shirley, James."

He pulled her into his arms. "He will be safe," he whispered in her ear.

She tipped her back to look at him. "How do you know?"

"If the council says they have safe passage, they have safe passage. That is law."

And any group of people might break the law if they felt their interests sufficiently threatened.

Chapter 33

James watched as people from the various Iroquois nations and client nations began to disperse from the grounds. It would take all day, and they had to make sure everything went smoothly. People were people, and that meant none were immune to petty jealousies that could flare up into something bigger with bad timing, so he had to be ready to break up any fights before they became full-blown diplomatic incidents that would undo the careful accord Johnson had just achieved.

David pointed up the road to a choke point that was slowing the flow of people west. A simple but sturdy German cart was partially blocking the way.

"Let's clear the logjam before it gets worse." James motioned David to join him and waded through the stream of humanity on the road. "I thought more came by canoe."

A young Oneida man bulled his way through on horseback. David pointed. "Can't bring your horse in a canoe, and what's the point of the biggest conference in human memory if you can't show off your new horse and see if it is faster than everyone else's?"

Some things were universal. It would have been the same in Dublin or London.

They reached the back of the cart and peeked over the tailgate. No driver. What the hell?

James circled to the front. The break was set and the two mismatched horses stood patiently for the moment as the people and other horses streamed past them. Horses, as a rule, panicked at the idea of being left behind.

He looked out toward the river, but there were only Iroquois trying to go around the traffic. No German faces. Or English, or any other Europeans.

He gestured to the woods on the right side of the road, and David gave a little shrug and followed.

They hadn't gone ten paces when voices reached them. They both stopped and listened.

"Sign up for the campaign to Fort Niagara. It will be much faster and easier than trying to take Crown Point. And Shirley knows how to run a campaign. Good money, too."

James looked at David, whose set jaw and flexed fists confirmed what James thought. It was Lydius' voice.

James held out his hand to signal David to stay still. Better to get a sense of who Lydius was recruiting before they blundered in.

"Ya, that's what you said, but Johnson led Iroquois in the last war and did pretty fine."

David relaxed, but only a fraction.

Lydius wasn't recruiting a Mohawk. He was recruiting a German from up the valley. Probably the owner of the cart blocking the road.

But that gave them less ground to run Lydius off. Johnson was in charge of all English interactions with the Iroquois, not with the Germans.

He motioned David to lean in. "Let's circle around and see if it is just the German before we interrupt." He kept his voice pitched low so that it wouldn't carry.

David replied just as quietly. "We can't just bash him for recruiting Germans. We could cause political fallout for Johnson."

True. But they couldn't just let Lydius sashay into the valley like he ran things. "We can't bash him, but I am recruiting a ranger company, and this German might prefer our company to Lydius'."

A devilish grin spread across David's face. "There is hope for your political education yet."

"Let's just circle round until we can make sure it is only the two of them, so we don't have any surprises."

James stepped off the path, feet making no sound, and David did the same in the opposite direction. He went about twenty yards, until he could see Lydius and another man. No one else.

A crow cawed. Well, it was David, but crows were the only birds he could imitate. With no crows in sight, it was presumably a sign that David saw the same thing he did, which was just the two men they expected to see.

James made the call of a cardinal and retraced his steps to meet back up with David on the path.

"We have got to get Okwaho and Leo to teach you more calls before we head to Crown Point. Even the French will figure out that the crows aren't invading. All that time learning Latin left a huge gap in your useful education."

James turned and headed up the path to where Lydius and the German stood.

"Hello there," he said. "I thought that fine pair of horses had to have an owner nearby."

The German and Lydius both looked up, their faces in complete contrast to one another. The German, a giant of a man, smiled like he appreciated the compliment to his somewhat scruffy team, and Lydius snarled, like he had been interrupted doing the Devil's work.

"What do you want?" Lydius said.

James summoned all he had observed of Faith's charm and subtle flattery when she handled Johnson. "Well, we saw that sturdy team, and figured the owner was someone we would want to talk with as we are recruiting a company of rangers to lead the way to Crown Point under General Johnson."

The German topped James by half a head. He was also tidy and well-dressed for someone from the Palatine towns to the west.

He smiled at James. "I've seen you. You trapped with Leo Ten Eyck for some summers. You are good in the woods."

Lydius scrunched up his face like he had eaten a worm.

James held his hand out to the German. "James Carroll, of Johnson's Rangers. Pleasure to make your acquaintance."

"I am Dieter Klein. I have a farm at German Flats, but I also trap and hunt with Leo."

That explained how he could afford horses instead of just oxen.

Lydius shifted uneasily, and David stepped next to James, which meant he could keep a better eye on the snake.

Lydius wasn't going to give up so easily. "You don't want to run around in the woods and sleep in the elements. You want to join Shirley's forces and be treated to proper food and shelter on the march."

Klein gave a belly laugh. "I served in King George's war. I've seen English proper food and shelter. I lost so much weight I had to tie my breeches up with a rope."

"Wouldn't you rather put your tracking skills to work? Leo will be joining us."

His eyes lit up at that.

"You are not yet a married man," said Lydius, "and Governor Shirley's officers have very pretty daughters." He made a rude gesture toward his privates. "One of them has been staying with Johnson, but she will likely be accompanying her father on campaign."

James's breathing got short and fast, and his hands clenched into fists.

David elbowed him and spoke for the first time. "I am sure Johnson's forces will have plenty of pretty women about. You know Johnson. He would not be a happy man without ladies around, but even he doesn't have the stamina to service them all."

James calmed his breathing. Lydius was a pig to use Faith as recruitment bait, and he couldn't let the pig have his way.

"Have you met David White?" he asked. "He is one of Hendrick's nephews. He will be fighting with us, too."

David reached out to shake the big man's hand.

"Shirley will have Mohawk scouts, too," said Lydius, "Don't worry about that."

No, he wouldn't. "David is not a scout. He is a member of the ranger company."

Lydius waved his hand like there was no difference.

The big German brushed a small leaf from where it had fallen on the lapel of his jacket. "You say Leo will serve with your rangers?"

Technically, Leo hadn't said yes yet, because he didn't like Johnson. "Of course. He's the best tracker in New York."

Dieter Klein's eyes went distant for a moment. "One time I met him trapping, and he shared with me the most wonderful small Dutch cake." He sighed, like it had been a spiritual experience.

James was not above using Leo and Jaap's grandmother for recruiting if it would deprive Lydius of a recruit at the same time. "We will pass through Schenectady on our way to muster in Albany. That is where his grandmother lives, and she is the one who bakes the koekjes. She would never let Leo pass by without baking for him. And for everyone with him."

Lydius's eyes were narrow slits, and his hand rested on the knife in his belt. "You will regret interfering with my work." Then he turned and disappeared down the trail.

Chapter 34

The day after the Iroquois had left to return home, Faith watched James engage a tall, wiry Black man in heated conversation. Now that the conference had ended, Fort Johnson had a much more focused energy.

With the support of the Iroquois secured, all the contained tension of the diplomatic negotiations exploded into action.

And so many people had arrived in conjunction with the conference that she was only now realizing how many of them were actually not part of the conference itself, but of the larger preparations for war with the French.

Or at least battles with the French. The two nations were not technically at war, despite the Virginia militia attacking and killing the French diplomat.

She had served as her father's unofficial secretary long enough to understand that both sides would use their armies to push and shove each other in the provinces, but war and peace would be determined on European issues.

Britain had sent a massive number of troops to North America, and the French would do the same, and that meant there would be fighting. Her father's cronies insisted that if they thumped their chests hard enough, the French would suddenly see they had encroached on King George's territory, apologize, and leave.

Men could be very stupid.

She had watched armies in action most of her life. That many armed men in close proximity to each other would start fighting, even if it was just over food or a woman.

"What are you all pucker-browed over?" Sarah came up beside her.

"Men." She paused. "War." She pointed to where James still spoke with the tall Black man. "Who is that James is talking to?"

"You've not met Leo yet?"

She shook her head. Then stopped. Leo was Jaap's cousin, but he clearly had at least one Black parent, while Jaap was as pale and blond as could be.

Sarah laughed. "It's legal in New York."

"What's legal?" Faith had missed a step somewhere.

"Leo's father and Jaap's father are brothers. Jaap's father married a Dutch woman. Leo's married a Black woman. It's not so uncommon among the Dutch."

Faith looked back at the man James was talking to. Leo. His entire demeanor was different than Jaap's, but now she knew to look for it, there was a clear resemblance in their faces and builds. "Didn't someone say he and Johnson don't get along?"

Sarah shrugged. "Leo is a very successful trapper and fur trader. That makes him competition. But they are both smart enough to stay out of each other's way so they can stay cordial." She turned to go, then stopped and groaned.

Benjamin Dreyfuss, the gunsmith, was right behind them. "Good morning, ladies." He gave them a little bow, which seemed sincere enough. His nails were dark with the oils he used in cleaning and mending guns. He had worked non-stop during the conference doing repairs and maintenance on hundreds of Iroquois guns at Johnson's expense. It was a miracle his fingers hadn't simply fallen off from all the work. "Would one of you minxes mind fetching me bread?"

Sarah's whole body stiffened.

Faith jumped up. "We would be happy to, Mr. Dreyfuss." She grabbed Sarah by the arm and dragged her toward the house.

"Minxes? Insufferable ass," Sarah muttered.

He was from Manhattan. They might be more forward there. "Come on, let's get them all something to eat."

Sarah grumbled something unintelligible. They reached the kitchens and Louisa gave them some coarse bread for the men.

Sarah emerged from her funk once they were away from the gunsmith. "Pile it all up on a platter and take it to them. I have to finish adding trim to Johnson's uniform."

Faith was realizing just how sought after Sarah's skills were. People from as far away as Schenectady came to her for their most intricate sewing needs. But now she was in full preparation for the campaign, just like the men.

Faith heaved the tray up and held it still while Sarah added a few more loaves. Then she went back out into the hot sun and looked for where James and the rest had gotten to.

Ben Dreyfuss was showing them something on one of their muskets. She headed their way.

"Faith," James welcomed her.

Dreyfuss handed the musket to Leo. "They made you carry that out here all by yourself?" He came and took the tray from her. "You are all barbarian frontiersmen. No manners."

That was not what she had expected after he ordered the bread like she and Sarah were the help at a tavern. Perhaps he was making up for his rudeness.

"You underestimate her, Ben." James came to her defense. Or perhaps his own, since he hadn't offered to help. "She is a strong one."

Heat flooded her body. How long could she really be angry with him for not knowing what it was like to not be a man? How could he know? It wasn't like he had his mother and sister around to tell him.

"Leo, this is Faith Richmond. Her father will be serving under Shirley."

Leo gave her a friendly smile and a nod. "Well, that is not her fault." He took her hand and gave a little bow over it.

What wasn't her fault? That her father was serving under Shirley?

She studied him more closely. He wore the long shirt and leggings she had come to think of as typical among the men who did their work in the woods. The only thing that indicated he wasn't a poor woodsman was a gold signet ring on his left hand. He had strung pouches around his waist, presumably with cartridges and flints. And he had tucked a hatchet in his belt.

All the men seemed to carry weapons now. Especially Jaap, who had a knife tucked in his belt that looked too long to be safe there without a scabbard. He would un-man himself if bent over too quickly.

They all grabbed bread and sat, so she sat with them.

"Shirley is siphoning off supplies for his campaign," said David. "Doesn't matter how much Johnson offers, there is only so much to go around. But it gets much worse. Shirley was at the lower castle himself trying to get people to join his own campaign, and he was telling them he could make or break Johnson."

"Shit," said Leo. Then he seemed to remember she was there. "My apologies, Faith."

She raised her hand to stop him. "I have spent my entire life around the army. If I fainted every time someone swore, I'd have long since been exiled to some distant relation's country cottage to die of boredom."

David and Leo laughed.

James looked at her, head tilted like he was trying to sort her out. Then the corner of his mouth tipped upward, and she almost laughed. At least he didn't seem to mind that she would rather hear men swearing than languish with a spinster cousin and her own appallingly bad needlework.

David sobered. "Shirley is undermining Johnson. Mark my words, there will be fewer Mohawks marching to Crown Point now."

"Shirley is a fool," said James.

This was her father's commanding officer, and second in command under Braddock of all the British forces in North America. She asked, "Can't Johnson explain the situation to him? They are on the same side, after all." But they were men of power, and maybe that was why they were butting heads. The higher the rank, the more inflated the sense of self-importance. Men like them could turn anything into a pissing contest.

James looked at David and Jaap, who looked back at him.

"What?" she asked.

"Speaking of Johnson. He leaves for Albany tomorrow," James said. His face was strained. "And he says he will take you in his carriage. We are to follow with the crates of muskets and recruit our way to Albany after we wrap things up here."

Tomorrow? After waiting so long, it felt sudden. "He did?"

"Yes." They all were quiet for a moment. She was going to be stuck in a carriage with Johnson and no chaperone, and they all knew Johnson well enough to know what his agenda for the trip would be. But no one could do anything about it.

Perhaps she could somehow make Johnson think she had the pox.

It was Jaap who finally spoke. "Now we have to start training Ben here how to fight with his hands and a hatchet, since he only knows how to shoot things." Apparently he didn't like awkward silences.

Faith looked to the gunsmith, who looked resolute, if a little leery. "I don't want to learn to speak French," he said. Presumably he meant in a prison if he were captured. These men were not high-ranking officers who would be protected by opposing officers from their men. She swallowed hard. Even if they were captured in battle, and not injured, their odds of survival were not very good.

"And we need him to keep our muskets in good repair, because we can't replace them," David said quietly. "There are troops mustering in Albany with no weapons at all."

"What?" How could they fight with no weapons? "Why haven't they been supplied yet?"

"Do you have any idea how long it takes to make a single musket?" Ben asked.

Were they were raising troops so fast they couldn't arm them? How on earth could they fight back if they were attacked before they had muskets? She looked from one of the men to another, her throat closing around a knot that tried to choke her.

James shoved David aside. "Don't worry. We have the best gunsmith in New York, or so he claims, and we aren't letting him go." Thank God for that.

But Ben Dreyfuss was with the rangers, not the regulars. "My father doesn't." Her father could train new recruits, but he couldn't magically provide them weapons to fight with.

James looked at her. "True," he said. "But your father is serving under Shirley. He has all of New England's resources behind him. They will be fine." He stood. "Now, we need to get to work." He seemed to linger just a moment, then he gathered the men and led them away.

James was right.

And she was leaving them tomorrow. She looked after them and took a big, slow breath. She had known the day would come, but not how much it would wrench her guts when it did.

She watched them head to the palisaded courtyard. James stripped his shirt off and stood half naked, as did the others. He signaled for David to go at Ben and yelled instructions to Ben as he figured out how to defend himself with just his hands. Then James stepped in to demonstrate some hold. Sun glistened off the muscles of his back.

He wasn't hers to keep.

She headed to the house and climbed the stairs to her bedchamber to pack.

Chapter 35

The door to the room opened behind her.

"What does your lieutenant have to offer that that man doesn't?" asked Sarah.

She should have known Sarah would just barge in and ask. Again. And she wasn't really certain how to answer.

Sarah came and stood next to her at the window. "Look at him."

As if she could pry her eyes away from his muscles, flexing as his fair skin turned pink in the sun. He and David were wrestling now, stopping every once in a while for James to point something out to Ben.

They all deferred to him, even though some of them had taught him the skills he was now passing on.

Sarah asked, "Is your lieutenant smarter than him?"

She snorted. "Caleb probably needs to hold on with both hands to avoid pissing on his own foot."

Sarah doubled over, laughing. Faith couldn't help chuckling, too.

Sarah finally said, "That is not a ringing endorsement, but at least we have livened up your vocabulary while you have been here."

"Considering my upbringing, I suppose it was only a matter of time before I started sounding like one of the enlisted men." Her manners really had declined a bit since her arrival in the wilderness, but she would do her duty and pull herself together when she returned to Albany.

James huddled the men together to talk through something.

"Does Caleb make your toes curl when he kisses you?"

"No."

"Does James?"

James did far more than make her toes curl. James made the earth tilt. Her eyes closed, and she imagined his lips on her breast. His tongue circling her nipple. Tugging at it.

"I can see that is a yes."

Heat rushed up her neck and caught fire in her cheeks.

Sarah looked her up and down, then dragged her away from the window. "Did he get you with child, after all?"

Faith's jaw dropped. "He did not."

Sarah's eyes narrowed. "How can you be sure?"

"He was too much of a gentleman to risk such a thing." Her nostrils were flaring, but she couldn't stop them. "I'm not such a fool, and neither is he."

Faith pulled her arm out of Sarah's hand and walked back to the window. James had the big man pinned to the ground and straddled him. What she would give to trade places with the big man right now.

"James is no gentleman, and I want to make sure I understand why you are so sure you are not with child."

Sarah pulled Faith away from the window again, and this time she forced her to sit down on the edge of the bed.

"You do know that even if he spills his seed outside you, he might have spilled just enough inside without either of you realizing it?"

"He did not have the opportunity to spill anything inside me." And this was an absurd conversation. "I need to pack."

Faith went to the cupboard in the corner of the room and yanked a gown off the peg.

"You are leaving tomorrow, so what are you going to do about him?"

Faith began folding the gown so it would fit in her small trunk. "There is nothing to be done. I will leave tomorrow with General Johnson and return to Albany, and someday soon be married off to Caleb."

"You care nothing for James beyond his skilled hands?"

Faith's own hands stopped folding. "I didn't say that."

"And what do you feel for Caleb?"

She thought for a moment, then sighed. "Boredom."

But sorting their finances was a challenge. It would keep her occupied the rest of her living days. And she owed that duty to her father. Or at least her mother.

She dropped the gown into her trunk.

Who cared about clothes?

She turned to the table next to the bed and grabbed the copy of Thucydides that she had been reading. She lay the book carefully in the small satchel that lay next to her trunk. Already inside was her copy of *As You Like It*. Her books might be the only thing between her and madness once she was married.

"I have a suggestion for you," Sarah said.

"No. James is a man on the move. Battle lines are being drawn between Johnson and Shirley, and through no fault of our own, we are on opposite sides of it. It is time for me to get back to my family duties."

"Don't be so dramatic. This isn't *Romeo and Juliet*."

Faith looked at her in surprise.

"What? We have Shakespeare out here on the frontier. This house does have books. Even my house has books."

"I'm—"

"Enough. Just listen to me. You don't leave until tomorrow. Tell James you want him to kiss every private inch of you until you see stars tonight."

"What?"

"Just be prepared to do the same for him. Then we'll see how you feel about going to back to that lieutenant."

Sarah turned and headed for the door.

"Sarah?"

Sarah stopped. "I just hate to see you bore yourself to death. You obviously love adventure and a good challenge. Decide for yourself which man offers more of both. You aren't property for your father to gift someone. And if you are married, your father has no power over you."

She turned again to go.

"Wait."

"Do yourself a favor and listen to me. Then good luck getting your toes uncurled."

And she left.

This was stupid. She had to finish packing and get back to her life. Her real life.

Her father was going to war, and she had to help him prepare. No one here needed her. Even if she was stuck in Albany while her father was gone, she had business plans to make.

James and the others still wrestled in the courtyard.

Ugh. She shouldn't have looked.

She went to the cupboard and grabbed her other gown. She folded it and stuffed it in the trunk on top of the first and slammed the lid. Which was silly and over-dramatic, because she still had her brush and comb and other things that needed to go in it.

When she married Caleb, she would have lovely dresses. And not be able to do anything that mussed them.

Maybe Caleb would surprise her. He might reach into the neckline of her gown and pull her breast out to suckle it as he ran his hands up between her legs.

She closed her eyes and imagined the feel of lips on her flesh, and hands pulsing into her body. And James's face, inches from hers.

"Gah!" Not James. Caleb.

She opened her eyes, and James was looking up at the window. She started to raise her hand to wave, then dropped it. The others all looked up to see what he was looking at. Then Jaap blew her a dramatic kiss. James punched him, but probably not as hard as Jaap's reaction implied.

James got the men back to their training, and he glanced once more up at the window before he joined them. She did give him a little wave then.

His lips had felt divine on her breast, and now she imagined them between her legs.

She was leaving tomorrow.

But she was here tonight.

Chapter 36

James stood in the sitting room, looking out at the courtyard as the sun began to lower in the sky.

Johnson was leaving tomorrow, and he was taking Faith.

It was a good thing.

The conference was over. He had to recruit the rest of the company, and then they were going to Crown Point.

Britain and France might not be at war technically, but Johnson's army was most certainly going to meet French forces somewhere in the woods north of Albany, just as Braddock's had no doubt already clashed with the French near the Monongahela by now. This was the chance he had bargained his life for all these years ago. It was not time to be mooning over Faith, no matter how deeply she had burrowed into his consciousness.

Johnson had called them all to the sitting room. Between that and preparing to leave for Albany, he should be busy until evening.

Johnson entered the room. "I've sent Farrell to meet Okwaho and dance a war dance with the men joining us from Canajoharie," Johnson announced.

David entered the room, followed by Faith and Sarah.

"Everyone, come sit. I need to get you all sorted before I leave."

A maid entered with a tea tray laden with food as well as tea. Faith was on her feet before the maid could set the tray on the side table.

"Thank you, Miss Richmond." Even Johnson had grown used to Faith providing the hospitality to smooth the social gears of all the people coming and going under the stress of preparing for the coming campaign.

Faith handed Johnson some tea, then David and Leo. Then she took a cup to Jaap, who took it in both hands, like he was afraid he would break it if he breathed on it—which, since he was Jaap, he probably would.

"It is already July and we need to take Crown Point before winter." Johnson had dark smudges under his eyes, even though James knew he had rested since the conference. The war was an opportunity for Johnson, too, but it must also be a heavy weight to carry. Especially with Shirley, his commanding officer, now trying to undermine him at every turn.

"James." Johnson turned to him. "I need my rangers to scout ahead from Albany. I need you to be up to strength and ready to move within two weeks."

"We will be ready." He didn't know how, but they would.

Faith handed him a cup of tea. Her hand brushed his as he took it, and he briefly caught her little finger with his, then let it go before anyone noticed.

She held his gaze just a heartbeat longer, then turned back to the tea service.

Johnson turned his attention to Sarah. "I don't have faith in the New Englanders to bring enough women. And they seem to think God will protect them, because they haven't sent enough surgeons."

Sarah held up her hand and stopped him. "I have already spoken with Louisa, and she sent to Stone Arabia and German Flats for more cooks."

Faith looked to her. "Are you traveling with the army?" Then she turned to Johnson. "I'm so sorry, I shouldn't have interrupted." If James wasn't mistaken, under her surprise was something more like curiosity.

"The Mohawk Valley doesn't go to war without someone to stitch up our wounded." Johnson beamed at Sarah like he was her father.

Several emotions flickered across Faith's face, but James couldn't interpret them. Surely the daughter of an officer knew no army traveled without a large contingent of women to keep them fed and otherwise occupied. But then, a woman of her status was probably sheltered from that.

She looked at Sarah for a long time, narrowing her eyes and pursing her lips, and if he didn't know any better, now he would say Faith was flat out jealous.

The idea of Faith around an army of lonely, randy young men made his grip tighten on the handle of his teacup. Surely her father wouldn't let her join him on the march? He set his cup down before he broke it.

She glanced at him, and her gaze grew more intense. If only she could join them on the march to Crown Point, having her underneath him when he got back from a scout would make the scout go significantly faster.

"You said you sent Farrell to Canajoharie today?" David asked.

Johnson nodded.

"Lydius headed that way when we chased him off from recruiting after the conference. He hasn't returned this way."

Johnson slammed his fist on the arm of his chair. Then he stood and paced to the front window. "That son of a bitch. There has to be a way to put an end to this."

David was thinking, which was always obvious because he moved his jaw like he was talking, even though his lips stayed shut. "If he is still trying to recruit, that is going to shrink the number of men willing to fight even more."

"I will strangle the whoreson. He needs to be stopped before he undermines the entire Crown Point campaign."

Johnson might have meant Lydius, or he might have meant Shirley. It didn't really matter.

Then Johnson's brows lifted, and his face brightened like he had just had an epiphany. He turned to Faith. "My dear Miss Richmond, I am so sorry, but I believe I don't have room in my carriage to take you to Albany tomorrow."

Faith stood, teapot in hand, jaw slack. Then she snapped her jaw shut, too diplomatic to let her face continue to show her dismay.

Before she could speak, Johnson went to her and put his hand on her arm. "Fear not. I shall send to Lydius right away and let him know he is ordered to take you back to Albany post haste."

"Lydius?" James couldn't stop the word before it was out of his mouth. The man was offering Faith up as recruitment bait, so why in hell would anyone trust him to protect her?

"Yes, he serves with her father, and I am sure will be most anxious to be of use. He needn't do any more recruiting here in the valley, and like us, Shirley needs to get his campaign under way."

It would have been genius if Faith were not the pawn in play. She would be alone with Lydius and at his mercy.

Jaap leaned in. "Lydius wouldn't dare," he said in a low voice. "Her father would have him shot and would have the full weight of the law behind him. And we will make sure he understands we will rip his ballocks off and choke him with them if he so much as touches her."

Jaap was right. Besides, it could be days before they found Lydius to give him Johnson's orders.

Faith wore a neutral expression that had to be a mask. She had been used as pawn, again, and was too smart not to know it. And as she had said, no one had asked her, and she had no recourse short of begging and crying, which she was too much the officer's daughter to ever resort to.

But she would be here a little longer.

He was a selfish bastard to be happy about that, and his cock was about to start dancing a jig. Maybe her molten look from earlier meant that he would at least be able to say a very improper goodbye.

"Keep it in your breeches, boss." Jaap whispered.

"Carroll," Johnson said.

James flinched. "Yes, sir?"

"You and David go now to Canajoharie. Find Lydius and give him his orders, then help Farrell finish up there so you can all get to Albany."

James blinked. "Right now, sir?"

"What other now is there?"

James set his teacup down and stood. "Of course. David, gather our gear." He turned back to Johnson. "I'll just ask Louisa to pack some food for us and we'll be off." It was a twenty-mile walk, and they wouldn't get there until the middle of the night. They would find Lydius and send him here, and then help Farrell. Faith would be gone before they got back.

Faith's eyes shone glassy, like she was on the verge of tears, but her chin was firm.

"In case you have left for Albany by the time we return, Miss Richmond, I wish you safe travels." He gave her a little nod, which she returned.

His chest was caving in. He looked back at her once more.

Then he turned and left the room before he embarrassed himself in front of everyone.

Chapter 37

The moon loomed over them, glaring down.

James kept pushing toward Canajoharie. He had to find Lydius and give him his orders...and not think about the fact that the bastard would be alone with her.

"That's it," said David. "Stop. I need to take a piss and I don't feel like running to catch up with your miserable self." He stepped off the side of the road and began watering the grass.

James swung his tumpline pack around in front of himself and jammed his hand between the folds of his blanket until his finger reached some dried venison. He pulled it out and tore off a strip with his teeth.

David rejoined him. "You are so distracted by Faith you are going to piss yourself or get shot."

James didn't answer, since he was likely right. They kept walking in the moonlight. Only about another mile to go.

"You need to make a choice, my friend."

James grunted at him. The only choices he had were made back in Ireland. Now he just had to follow through.

"Either tell Johnson to go to hell, or let her go."

James turned on David. Goddam him. "I have nothing to offer her. Not even a bed to sleep in, let alone a roof. Nothing. I would ruin her life even if she was fool enough to accept me." He turned away.

"If she was married to you, her father would have no more legal power over her."

It wasn't that simple. "Just let it be."

"Excellent. Make the choice for her. She seems to love that."

"Shut up. I have to plan what to do about Lydius." David seemed to have forgotten they had orders.

David sighed. "Since you are choosing Johnson, at least save the disemboweling for the French. Lydius is a snake, but we are technically on the same side."

He had no choice. James kept putting one foot in front of the other. "Damaging Lydius is not good for my prospects, so I will not damage him. The war is going to create opportunities for men like me to pull ourselves up a rung or two. I am aiming for three at least."

"So you keep saying."

And if the war gave Lydius a chance to get shot, so much the better. Maybe the blasted lieutenant, too.

They reached a path to the river and pulled one of Hendrick's canoes from the underbrush. They both got in and paddled their way across to Canajoharie.

The palisade around the upper castle rose in front of them. David led the way in, and they found the longhouse Okwaho's mother owned and slipped in. They would be welcome, and they could sleep more soundly because a hundred people would be walking around them as soon as the sun rose. They didn't need to worry about oversleeping. Or keeping guard, for that matter.

They stretched out silently on the floor by the embers of the fire and bedded down.

J ames groaned and stared at the smoke hole in the bark roof when the sky grew light and people around them stirred.

A toe dug into his ribs.

"Up, you hibernating bear." It was Okwaho.

James stretched.

Okwaho asked, "What are you two doing here lying around on the floor when everyone is supposed to be heading toward Albany? Did you get turned around?"

James climbed to his feet. "I'll be back."

He waved to some of the little children in the longhouse as he walked out the door at the end and headed for a tree. He leaned his head against the trunk, letting the bark dig into the skin of his forehead as he pissed on the roots.

David came up behind him and found another tree to relieve himself behind.

"Has Okwaho seen Lydius?" James asked.

"Yup. Over with the Turtle Clan," Okwaho said, joining them.

James almost pissed on his own foot. "He's still here?" Damn. That was easier than they expected. He gave his cock a shake and then did up his breeches. Of course, if Lydius was still there, he was likely recruiting, and that meant more trouble for Johnson. "Hurry up."

"You can wait a minute." David stuffed himself back into his own breeches and did up the buttons.

An unintelligible bellow rang out from near the center of the village.

James and David looked at each other for an instant.

"You don't belong here," said an Irish accent.

"Sounds like Farrell found him," said James, and they took off at a run to find Farrell.

They rounded the end of a longhouse, where Farrell and Lydius glared at each other next to the remains of the previous night's fire. The ground all around was trampled from the dancing.

Farrell's eyes were bleary, and his movements labored. The dancing had no doubt lasted for hours. The man had to be exhausted.

Lydius looked well-rested.

Farrell pointed at Lydius's chest. "You go. Now. Only Johnson negotiates with the Mohawks for the British."

"I'm just visiting my clan while I am in the valley." Lydius smiled and slithered around, out of Farrell's range.

"I heard you trying to get the Turtle Clan men to join Shirley instead of Johnson. Shirley doesn't need Mohawk warriors to get through Iroquois territory to Oswego, and then he can get support there from the Cayuga and Seneca. Johnson has arranged it. You were there. You heard him."

Lydius circled around behind Farrell. Farrell turned and kept an eye on him.

"Just because you lick Johnson's boots doesn't mean everyone else does."

Shit.

Farrell launched himself at Lydius, and James took a step forward. David and Okwaho pulled him back.

"Turtle chief," David said quietly.

In the doorway at the end of the longhouse stood the broad-shouldered leader of the clan Lydius had been adopted into years ago, before he started his fraudulent land dealings. They didn't dare interfere in front of him. If they did, they would make Johnson's man look weak, and therefore Johnson, too.

Farrell took a swing at Lydius, but Lydius dodged and Farrell only landed a glancing blow.

Farrell staggered when his fist skimmed past Lydius's body. Farrell looked drugged, he was so tired. He must have danced all night with the men preparing to follow Johnson.

"Don't," said Okwaho to James. "Anything we do could only make things worse."

Lydius stepped behind Farrell and, before Farrell could turn, Lydius swept the man's legs out from under him, and he went down with a thump.

"Where's Hendrick?" James asked. He wouldn't let Johnson's envoy be treated like this.

"The lower castle, making sure the men stay true," Okwaho said.

Farrell grabbed Lydius's ankle and pulled him down. The two threw punches at each other from the ground until they both managed to scramble back to their feet. Lydius was not a young man, but he was scrappy.

The Turtle chief came out of the longhouse, and Farrell glanced his way. Lydius took that moment to sweep his legs from under him again.

Before Farrell could go after Lydius or get back to his feet, the Turtle chief stepped to his side. Farrell tried to stand to acknowledge the important man properly, but the chief had two men grab Farrell's arms and pin him.

Farrell protested. "I am here on behalf of Warraghiagey." He used Johnson's Mohawk name.

The Turtle chief stared at him, then, when he had Farrell squirming under his gaze, the chief slowly dumped ashes from the fire on Farrell's head.

No one breathed for a moment.

"Sweet Mary, Mother of God." James knew enough from David to understand that was not only an insult, but one aimed at Johnson. What the hell had Lydius gone and done? Was he trying to get the Mohawk to completely abandon Johnson's campaign? Lydius and Shirley had managed to sow discord in the unity Johnson had worked so hard to build at the conference.

"Fucking bastard," David said so that only James and Okwaho could hear. Lydius just walked away and disappeared around the side of a long-house.

He was not getting away so easily. James circled around and then cut him off, stepping out from around the end of the longhouse just as Lydius passed.

Lydius flinched, but said nothing. He squared himself as if for another fight, but James was bigger than Farrell, and Lydius glanced around like he was looking for backup.

James's fists itched to lay the older man out. "Your clan brothers are still insulting Farrell. But I have orders for you to return to Albany immediately. Shirley needs you. And I am told he is getting impatient."

Lydius curled his lip at James. "You are a bag full of shit."

The bastard could spit whatever insults he pleased. "Johnson is already in Albany, getting ready to march on Crown Point. We head out to join him tomorrow. We agreed to deliver your orders against my better judgment. But if you want to be the one who delays Shirley's march, be my guest."

He turned on his heel and left Lydius to think about it.

David and Okwaho were right around the corner. "Nicely played. He doesn't dare risk upsetting Shirley," said Okwaho.

David looked less excited. "You didn't say anything about Faith."

James poked him in the chest. "That man goes nowhere near her. We will take her and we need to leave now."

He walked right past them, stopping only long enough to grab his pack and musket before he headed out of the palisade to the canoe. David and Okwaho caught up to him, and they paddled across and dragged the canoe back into the bushes. James headed for the road.

"Would someone like to explain what that last bit was about?" Okwaho asked.

"No," said James.

David ignored him and explained. "Johnson wanted Lydius to take Faith to Albany to get Lydius out of the valley while still slowing his return to Albany. Not sure this is going to go well."

But he would at least get to say goodbye.

Johnson would be plenty angry at him for improvising, but apparently he was willing to risk it to have two nights more before he had to let Faith go.

"Walk faster, you two."

Chapter 38

Faith tapped her finger against the edge of her book. Leonidas was a brilliant general, and the way he held off the Persians at Thermopolis was nothing short of genius. If the Persians hadn't spotted goats on the hidden path around the pass, the Spartans might have won, despite being so massively outnumbered. But even the great general himself couldn't keep her occupied today.

Sitting and waiting for her fate to happen to her made her want to throw something. She had to get to Albany, but she didn't want to leave, and she certainly didn't want to leave with Colonel Lydius. But anything she might try to do about it could only make matters worse for people she cared about. This was misery.

Leo and Jaap entered the room. "Oh, I'm so sorry, Faith," said Leo. "We didn't realize you were in here."

"Morning, Faith," said Jaap.

"Good morning, and I welcome the interruption. I was just reading, and I have read this book many times before." She smiled at them.

Leo approached and looked at the book. "Ah, Thucydides."

"Have you read much on the Peloponnesian wars?" She had given up guessing who might and might not have had a chance to go to school or have tutors.

"Had to learn about the man I am named for," said Leo with a smile. "And learn his lessons. They apply to life, not just battle."

How true. "Beware innocent goatherds going about their business."

He laughed. "Indeed."

Jaap looked from one to the other and threw up his hands. "What are you two babbling about?"

Faith said, "I take it you have not studied the classics?"

Jaap's face contorted in horror.

"I suppose they aren't to everyone's taste." She couldn't very well hold it against him. "I am told you two are cousins?"

"I'm the smart one," said Leo with a grin.

"I'm the dashing one." Jaap jabbed Leo with his elbow. "And Oma loves me best."

They all laughed at that.

Despite their different colored skin and hair, they looked alike, and had a similar sense of humor, even though Leo was clearly a grown man, and Jaap, well, was Jaap. The family resemblance was obvious to anyone looking for it.

Something outside the window must have caught Jaap's eye. His face went serious. "They're back already, and they look like shit. And no Lydius."

Leo turned to her. "Excuse us."

Then they both rushed out the door to greet James, David, and Okwaho.

She followed them to the door, then stopped. James and the others looked like they had been fighting with Leonidas and his outnumbered Spartans at Thermopolis all night. Her eyes pricked with tears. He was here. She got to see him one more time before she left.

She called down to Louisa for food and drink, then hurried after the Ten Eyck cousins into the courtyard.

James had dark smudges under his eyes, and his hair stuck out of his queue in a few places. Had they been attacked overnight? At least he was apparently unharmed, and here, and Lydius was not.

David's shoulders sagged as much as James's, and his head hung in a way that made her think his neck was not quite able to hold it up. Okwaho looked like he had at least had time to wake up and put himself in order before they took to the road.

"How are you already back?" asked Jaap.

"No reason to linger," said James.

They all waited, but James didn't elaborate. He might have simply been too tired to form any more words. He needed to sit, and he needed to eat. She wasn't going to let the men keep him out here on his feet.

"Come inside. Louisa is putting together a meal for you." She shepherded them toward the door. "You look like Philippides after he ran from Marathon to Athens to deliver news of the battle."

"And only right before he keeled over and died," said Leo.

"I liked her before I knew she read that old Roman stuff," Jaap said.

"Greek," said Leo, cuffing Jaap on the back of the head.

She herded them all in front of her to the house and into the sitting room. James and David both flopped into chairs with enough force to skid them an inch or two back on the floor. Okwaho managed to sit with a little more decorum. They were all filthy and stank of sweat from traveling all night and all day in July, but they were here.

James lifted his head. "We sent Lydius directly back to Albany."

Her chest tightened. Lydius was supposed to take her with him.

"We will take you," he added.

The others looked at James with raised brows. That wasn't what Johnson had told him to do. He was defying orders to take her.

"But aren't you supposed to recruit on your way?" she asked.

"Yes, I'm afraid we won't be the quickest escort. But Lydius, well, I don't trust Lydius." For all that James's face was exhausted, his jaw was set, and his brows cranked down in an angry V over his eyes.

Okwaho said, "He started a fistfight with Farrell, and the Turtle Clan chief dumped ashes on Farrell's head." He scanned the group to see if they understood the import of what he had just said. The men all nodded.

"I'm sorry, I don't quite follow," Faith said, keeping her voice even.

David took pity and explained. "Dumping ashes on someone's head is an act of extreme disrespect. Lydius riled the Turtle Clan chief to turn on Johnson's man in favor of Shirley's."

James rubbed his dusty hands over his face. "Shirley is making the British look divided. The Mohawks are not fools. Fewer men are coming to fight with us now."

"But why would the Turtle Clan leader do that when everyone was just here saying they would do as Johnson asked?"

Okwaho said, "Lydius was adopted into the Turtle Clan many years ago, before he started dealing in lands. The Turtle chief had to look out for his own, which Lydius knew."

"Bastard," said Jaap.

That seemed to apply to everyone in this scenario.

Leo said, "With apologies to Miss Richmond, now that clear lines are being drawn between Johnson and Shirley, wouldn't delaying Faith's return slow Shirley? Then Johnson could get his troops on the move and out of Albany before Shirley could leave?"

Faith's heart pounded. She wanted to scream at him, but she couldn't. Not just because she would make a fool of herself, but because, from their perspective, it made sense.

Except they were wrong.

"My father left Fort Johnson without me, and he would certainly leave for Fort Niagara without waiting to see me." She let her head drop into her hands. It was too much.

"She is not a pawn in this fight." It was James's voice.

"Johnson won't be happy," said Jaap. "He would want us to leave her here. Sorry, Faith."

Her head was still too heavy to lift, but she gave a nod to the floor, so hopefully they knew she understood. It wasn't their fault.

"No," said James. "We take her back. We are not leaving her here unprotected when Lydius comes back this way. Johnson will survive us doing this one thing for her."

She lifted her head. He shouldn't be risking Johnson's wrath for her. He couldn't afford it on so many levels.

David rolled his eyes.

James gave her a nod, not a smile. "We will all be leaving for Crown Point as soon as the troops are mustered, so even Johnson won't have time to sit around and think on it. She'll be back with her father"—he looked away—"and his lieutenant."

Who were leaving for Fort Niagara. They were going to deposit her in Albany and all march off, leaving her behind. Albany had been her focus for so long she had not given enough thought to what happened after she got there. And even though James had risked Johnson's wrath for her, he was still leaving her. And, in his mind, leaving her with Caleb.

Officers would not be taking their families on this sort of campaign. Her father might very well be gone before she even got there. They might none of them come back. And she would be in Albany. Doing nothing. She couldn't even work on her father's new holdings. She didn't trust Lydius enough now to believe their deed was legitimate, even if it did hold up in court, because the courts favored Europeans over the Iroquois.

A hand touched her shoulder. She looked up, and her heart jumped. James. His finger traced her chin, and he smiled. She wanted to fling her arms around him and curl herself into his chest.

"We will get you safe to Albany. It will take a few days, but we will be with you."

It would also take a few nights.

He brushed his fingers over her lips.

Chapter 39

Faith watched from the front steps as the men got ready. Dieter, the large German man, brought his pair of mismatched horses around to the courtyard and hitched them to a wagon that already stood loaded with her small trunk and satchel, and with the crates of muskets Ben Dreyfuss had brought, and whatever was in the men's packs, which were piled on top.

The air was hot and sticky, and the sun shone mercilessly on them.

"I am so sorry," said Sarah next to her. "They are going to stink before they go a mile down the road in this weather." She fanned her face as if waving away the stench of sweaty men. "I'd give you a lavender sachet to drown out their smell if I could get it to grow around here."

"I thought it did," Faith said.

"I wish. It is good for burns as well as for covering the stench of these sweaty rangers." Then she stopped and tilted her head, like she was looking from an intentionally new angle. "But they are a fine-looking lot, even if I am biased toward their sorry selves."

The seven men all swarmed around, tying down crates and packs so they didn't fall off as the cart hit ruts. Two Mohawks, two Dutchmen, two Germans, and one Irishman. Off to fight for the British Empire, or at least for their place in it.

She glanced at Sarah, whose dark skin glistened with sweat from her own preparations. In another day or so, she would follow the men as they made their way to face the French. Helping to keep them alive. Another Dutch person joining the cause.

Faith was the only English person present, and the only one who would be staying safe and sound in Albany. The one with no real role to play. She couldn't even travel with the women because, as an officer's daughter, she would make them a target.

Dieter waved her over. She went to him and had to tip her head back so far to look him in the eye that her neck muscles protested the unaccustomed strain.

"You have driven horses before?" he asked.

"A pony. When I was a girl. But I ride, back home."

He gave her a kind smile. "That will do. You know how to talk with them. It doesn't matter so much in what tack." They would walk, and she would drive the horses alongside, since the wagon was so laden, they didn't want more than one person adding to its weight, and she was the smallest and lightest of them all, and had therefore been designated the driver.

He took hold of her arm and led her around the front of the wagon to the horses's heads. His hand completely encircled her arm.

"This is Goldie," he scratched under the chin of the chestnut horse, "and this is Marzipan." He scratched the shorter roan's chin.

She stroked each horse's cheek and rubbed under their manes. They had to be itchy under there on such a warm day. Each horse leaned into her scratches and she had to brace her feet as they began to lift and lower their necks and lean in, helping with the scratching.

"You understand them. You will be friends." Dieter patted her on the head like she was a lap dog. It annoyed her when her father did it, but she couldn't be offended when Dieter did. The man clearly liked animals at least as much as people.

"That's the last, James," said Leo.

Ben came past her and circled to the rear of the wagon. "Are the crates secured?"

It made sense that Ben didn't want months of his painstaking hand-iwork to bounce out the back of the wagon and slide down the bank into the river, but Sarah rolled her eyes and grumbled so only Faith could hear. "It's not like the men want to go into battle without muskets. Obviously, they tied them down."

Then her face softened as she studied Faith. "I am only a day or two behind you, and I will do everything in my power to visit you when I pass through Albany to join these miscreants."

Faith's vision went a little blurry. She blinked hard and gave Sarah an unladylike bear hug. "Please do," she said in Sarah's ear. But she didn't risk saying more. The men didn't need to hear her voice cracking when she was on her way back to Albany, where she had been nagging them to take her for two months. Crying now wouldn't very well do.

James came around to her side. "You're sure you can handle the horses?" He searched her eyes like he was looking for any signs of uncertainty.

"Your goods are safe in my hands."

Then he leaned in and pitched his voice low. "It's you I am most concerned about arriving safely."

Her heart jumped. The hard exterior he presented to the world hid such a tender soul. "Thank you." It was going to hurt to let him go.

James looked at the bench on the front of the wagon and tried to find a foothold for her so he could help her up.

"I have it." Giant Dieter came around, put one hand on either side of her waist, and lifted her up onto the bench like she was a child's doll. Then he handed her the reins.

She squared her shoulders and did her best to look the strong officer's daughter that she was. "Are we ready, gentlemen?"

They all nodded, and James gave her a little wink that made her heart jump.

At least she got to have one last adventure with him before returning to her real life.

She clucked her tongue and jiggled the reins over the horses' rumps, and they heaved the wagon into motion and walked out toward the gate in the palisade that led to the high road. Dieter walked next to them and smiled back at her. She seemed to have met his standards so far.

She turned and looked one last time at the great stone house, then set her eyes down the road toward Schenectady. They would not make it that far today, starting so late, with the laden wagon, and having to make recruiting stops. But Jaap and Leo had both told her they would lobby James hard to make a quick stop at their grandmother's house in Schenectady tomorrow.

All the other men agreed, saying no one should have to go off to war unless fortified by Oma Ten Eyck's baking.

They walked for hours, stopping at eleven different farms and cabins on the way to recruit. The men and the horses walked, at least. She sat on a hard wooden seat, and her tailbone throbbed, and each rut or bump magnified the effect.

Her stomach grumbled. And she desperately needed to step behind a bush. The men could simply step off the side of the road for a moment and then jog to catch them up. It wasn't fair. But their feet had to hurt. Hers did not. And she was not about to slow them down if she could help it.

James walked up next to the wagon. "How are you holding up?"

"I have the easy part, and I feel guilty. Wouldn't someone else like a chance to sit and drive? I can walk for a ways."

James smiled. "They are all used to walking long distances. They are fine."

David and Jaap were off to the left, each scanning the woods. They looked perfectly comfortable. Leo walked ahead, on point, making sure they weren't surprised around a bend.

Okwaho took the rear guard, so no one snuck up on them from behind. Dieter and Ben were off to the right, keeping an eye on the opposite bank of the river. Apart from the occasional glance over his shoulder to check on his horses, Dieter, too, looked perfectly at ease. Even Ben looked in good condition. Perhaps one had to do a lot of walking in Manhattan.

But they were moving so slowly with the laden wagon they had to be easy to track. Where had she landed herself that they couldn't just drive along the high road, but had to constantly scan for attackers?

"Satisfied?" He gave her a lopsided smile. Achy and hungry and anxious as she was, it still managed to set some sparks sizzling through her body.

Then the wagon hit a rut, and she winced and clamped her legs as tightly together as she ever had in her life.

James's brows knit together. "Are you sure you are all right?"

"I am absolutely fine. Onward." She gave him a big grin. Maybe he would believe it.

"Not much farther. We will stop and make camp for the night in about a mile."

Oh, thank the Lord. "You are the one in charge, and I shall follow your orders, Captain."

He grinned. The number of sparks going off under her skirts tripled.

James briefly laid his hand on her leg and then sped up to walk next to the horses, who were the most obvious target for anyone wanting to capture their muskets. Without the horses, they would have to abandon the guns or fight for them. Neither was a pleasant thought.

James scanned the woods continuously, which did not ease her nerves. But the view of him from behind might just help her survive one more mile. She watched each side of his rather glorious buttocks flex and relax in turn with each step, and let it hypnotize her.

There were worse ways a woman could spend a day.

She blinked hard when the men stopped, and it was the horses who stopped themselves because she didn't think to use the reins to ask them. Dieter came back and set the brake, then lifted his hands up to her.

He grabbed each side of her waist, and she gritted her teeth. If he squeezed her too firmly, she would wind up mortified.

He swung her off the wagon, and her feet touched earth for the first time since they left Fort Johnson. She hadn't gotten down off the wagon any of the many times they stopped along the way to chat up locals to convince them to join the ranger company. James had been too worried about her. When their attention was turned to recruiting, they were an easier target for anyone tracking them. He told her if she heard shooting, they would take care of the attackers and she should drive like the Devil was after her.

He appeared by her side and took her arm. "My legs always forget how to walk when I am in a wagon for too long."

She smiled at him through gritted teeth.

"What's wrong?" he asked.

Embarrassment burned her cheeks more than the sun already had today. "I just need to step behind a bush for a moment." There, she said it, and she hadn't died.

He led her to the edge of the road. Dieter swung himself up on the wagon and maneuvered the horses to park the vehicle.

"I can make it, thank you." She pulled her arm out of his.

He took it again. "I know you can, but we haven't scouted the area yet. I'm not letting you go wandering into the woods alone."

"James—"

"I promise I will avert my gaze, but I am not letting the French or Lydius take you while you are taking a piss alone."

Her heart pounded, but her bladder throbbed.

Chapter 40

James gritted his teeth. He was an ass not to have thought to stop earlier. The poor woman must have been ready to explode. He was an inconsiderate fool. Every one of the men had stopped at least twice on the road. She'd dutifully stayed in the wagon like he had told her to.

"Everything all right?" he asked as he scanned the woods around them.

"I'm perfectly fine. I don't need a nanny."

Her feet moved in the leaves behind him. Then a flap of fabric as she presumably let her skirts fall back into place. She was not happy with him, but mostly she was embarrassed. Pissing in the woods was second nature to him. It was anything but to her. He needed to get her back to her civilized life.

And they had been too easy to track today. The line of people looking to delay or just shoot them was getting too long.

She appeared next to him. "You may open your eyes now."

As if he would close his eyes in the woods with Lydius skulking about. "All right." He turned to her, and her cheeks were flaming red. How much of that was sunburn and how much was mortification was anyone's guess. Either way, this had been a rough day for her. "Why don't you sit in the wagon while we set up camp for the night?"

She snorted. "Most certainly not. You all have been walking the better part of the day, and I have been sitting. The very least I can do is to help make camp." She turned and stomped back toward the road where the rest of the men were unloading their gear.

James scanned the woods again, then followed her, listening for things out of place.

A stick snapped, and James swung his musket off his shoulder and stared in the direction of the sound. He studied the underbrush, muscles tense and ready.

A young deer stood and bounded off. James heaved a deep breath and swung his musket back onto his shoulder. The deer might be one of the few things out here that wasn't after them.

He caught up to Faith as she reached the road.

Dieter and Jaap had started pulling the crates of muskets off the wagon, and Faith came to a sudden halt. She turned to him, confusion clear on her face.

"We can't leave the muskets on the side of the road for anyone to take," he said.

She nodded. Standing to the side of the wagon, she watched them carry a crate down, then she grabbed two of the men's packs from the wagon and followed Dieter and Jaap.

Leo and Okwaho should have found a suitable spot to camp by now. James helped David slide the next crate off, and they followed the others, leaving Ben to guard the wagon.

Leo and Okwaho came toward them and gestured for them to follow the others, and then they, too, went to grab a load.

The damn muskets were heavy. And Leo had clearly picked a campsite far from the road, which was wise, but tiring.

A six-foot boulder blocked their way, so they skirted it, and found Dieter and Jaap had set the first crate down directly behind the boulder. He and David put theirs down on top of the first.

Faith was a little further on. After she set the packs under a tree, she followed Dieter and Jaap the quarter mile back to the road.

Dieter took the reins from Ben and backed the horses and wagon off the road and behind a small clump of tall bushes. Jaap had already gathered some branches to disguise it.

"Is there anything valuable in your trunk?" Dieter asked.

"Just a couple of gowns and my hair brushes." She smiled at the big man.

James asked, "Are they silver brushes or anything like that?"

She laughed. "Hardly. They can stay in the wagon, if that is why you are asking."

She seemed to be regaining her normal spirits. At least she was smiling and laughing again. She did reach in and grab her satchel.

"Does that have anything valuable?"

She put her arms protectively around it. "My books."

Of course. Well, she could always swing them at any attackers and knock them senseless.

Jaap and Okwaho finished hiding the wagon, and Dieter unhitched the horses. They were going to be the difficult part.

Dieter turned to him. "You can leave the wagon by the road, but they camp with us."

He was clearly not willing to have any debate about it, so that was one less decision to make.

Jaap went and took one horse from Dieter, since there was no room for the two horses to walk side-by-side.

Leo had some branches in hand, as did Okwaho.

"Cover our tracks?"

They nodded.

He gestured to Faith. "Shall we?"

He led her back to the boulder and around it.

Dieter tied the horses to a tree a bit further on from the muskets. He had let them graze at regular intervals, and he had insisted they be allowed to drink their fill every time they passed an easy access point to the river. Now he fed them some oats.

James looked around the campsite. Faith was going to have to sleep right in among them. It couldn't be helped. But at least she would be safe. The first man to look at her while she slept would not.

"Leo, Dieter, and Jaap, you take first watch." David, Okwaho, and James had barely slept in two days and needed to rest before they were any good on watch.

"I'll join them," said Ben.

"Good man." James slapped him on the back.

"Leo, you place everyone." Leo nodded, grabbed his musket and powder, and then led the others out beyond where James could see them.

The horses stood by the tree, occasionally tossing their heads or stomping a foot to rid themselves of flies, but they were otherwise quiet. Faith went to them and began scratching their necks up under their manes. Both horses leaned in and tried to scratch themselves against her just like they had before they left Fort Johnson. She braced herself so she could scratch them harder.

The horses grunted their appreciation, and she just laughed and scratched even more vigorously.

"Those horses sound like they are getting it on over there." Okwaho said to James.

"Seriously? This is not the time."

David leaned in. "Correct." He stared at James. "Not the time. I don't want to hear any grunting and moaning."

James smacked David on the back of the head, and David and Okwaho both laughed until they might bust a gut, which would serve them right.

Faith left the horses and came over. "What is so funny?"

"The village idiots have not had enough sleep and are getting as giddy as tipsy old ladies. Best to ignore them," James said.

David and Okwaho tried to regain control of themselves, but they continued to snort and chuckle like they were drunk. They would be useless until they got some sleep.

"Bed down." He said to them. "You need rest. We all do."

They chortled off to their bedrolls and spread them out near the musket crates.

James grabbed his bedroll, and Faith stood and watched.

He was an idiot. They had no bedroll for her.

Well, only half of them could sleep at one time anyway, so he grabbed Jaap's bedroll, then grabbed the other men's as well.

He unrolled the blankets and created a soft bed for her on the ground, then added his own blanket to the pile so she would have something to pull over herself. "You sleep here. I'll be right behind you."

Her eyes grew wide. "I can't sleep on that huge pile of blankets while you sleep on the ground."

"It won't be the first time I slept on the ground, and it won't be the last time. I'm so tired, I could sleep in a thicket." Which was pretty close to true. "Do you need to step behind a bush again before we sack out?"

She turned red and shook her head no.

"I know you hate this, but if you do need to, you wake me." No way was he letting her wander the woods at night. She could be abducted, or the men on watch would have too good a show. He wasn't letting either happen.

"Fine." She flopped down on the pile of blankets and turned her back to him.

He stretched out on the ground behind her and tucked his arm under his head as a pillow.

The woods and its inhabitants began to make their evening music as the sun finally set. Birds, frogs, the occasional wolf much farther off.

He watched the back of Faith's head as he listened to the symphony. Her hair shimmering in the light of the rising moon. Once they reached Schenectady, they would be able to procure tavern rooms on Johnson's tab. This might be his last chance to really study her.

A godawful snorting came from near the muskets.

Faith flinched in front of him, then she lay still as a stone.

The sound came again, and he inched up behind her. "Shhh, it's just me." He whispered.

Her head gave a tiny nod, making her hair bounce a little.

Now the sound was doubled. "They both snore like giant bears. I'm afraid it will go on until we wake them for their watch," he said.

Her shoulders sagged, then jiggled, and a tiny snort came from her. She rolled over to face him. "Don't they wake themselves up? Or each other?"

"If only."

Her eyes reflected the light from the moon. He reached out and stroked his fingers across her cheek, and she leaned into the pressure.

Then she turned and kissed the palm of his hand, which shot lighting directly to his privates.

He leaned in and kissed her. "We all need sleep. Good night, Faith."

Chapter 41

James was right. He hadn't slept in days, and he was going to have to be in constant motion once they reached Albany, as the men he was recruiting along the way gathered over the next week. There was nothing she could do to remove any of that burden for him. But it didn't stop her from wanting to.

She reached out and traced his cheek, just like he had done to hers. The stubble on his face tickled her fingers. He wasn't hers to keep once they reached Albany, but she wanted to be with him now.

David and Okwaho snored on behind her.

She traced her thumb along his lips. They were so soft for such a hard man. She slid her thumb back and forth, memorizing the feel of them. He lay completely still for a few moments. He might not even be breathing.

Then his tongue emerged and captured her thumb, sucking it into his mouth. The pull of the suction from his mouth made her breasts tingle and heat start to build in her core. His mouth was magic.

He reached a hand out and pulled her closer, then, still sucking on her thumb, he traced her breast through her clothing.

He should be settling in to sleep, and she shouldn't be distracting him. But she hadn't let herself believe she would feel his hands on her again, and now that she did, she didn't want him to stop.

She arched toward him and pressed into his hand. He released her breasts from her stays, and his fingers circled, insistent and pressing hard, then he pinched her nipple and she almost yelped from the shot of energy it sent straight down between her legs.

Her breathing came faster, and she couldn't just lie there any longer. It was as if she needed to touch him to reassure herself he wasn't a dream. And maybe if she could make him feel as good as he made her feel, that would be enough.

She reached out and slid her hand down his side, and muscles beneath his shirt jumped as she touched them. She slid her hand down further until it reached his manhood, which twitched and danced under fingers. He let her feel her way without telling her what to do.

He sucked harder on her thumb, and she grasped him through his breeches. He rocked his hips into her hand.

He was so strong, and he gave her so much power over him. Surely that meant something? He let her explore the length of him and run her thumb over the head of his manhood and circle it.

His hand slid under her skirt, and the muscles in her legs shivered with anticipation. She could at least share this with him.

He didn't linger. His fingers found their target and circled it with an urgency her own body matched.

Then he let her thumb slip out of his mouth and leaned in and kissed her hard. Before she could even respond, he had moved on to nibble at her neck, sucking and biting in the same rhythm his hand worked between her legs. But then he kissed his way down her chest, nipping at her breasts, which made her hips press harder into his hand. She had never felt so alive.

He kept going lower, nuzzling her belly, and bringing his other hand under her skirt, easing a finger inside her. His hands became the center of the universe. He became the center of her universe.

His head disappeared beneath her skirt, and she stiffened. This was too intimate, and she might not survive.

But his hands kept working, and his lips nibbled her inner thigh.

Oh, God.

He kissed her legs, alternating from one to the other, never letting his hands rest. She could barely breathe.

Then his tongue joined his hands, and she bucked against his face, unable to control her hips. She surrendered to the sensation of him at her very core, where he was leaving an indelible mark.

Before she could separate sensation from emotion, his tongue circled where his thumb had been, and then he sucked, and the muscles in her belly tightened.

His fingers thrust in and out and he alternated sucking and licking. The sensation was so intense it almost hurt, but her hips leaned into it like she would die if the pressure went away. If he went away.

He sucked harder and her entire body shattered into a million pieces that flew through the sky.

She bit her lips together to keep from crying out, but her body pulsed and pulsed, and his tongue kept sucking and licking, until the eruption subsided.

Her lungs heaved in and out like bellows, and her heart melted. All she wanted to do was hold him tight against her.

Gradually, he kissed his way back up her body, until his face was just a breath away from hers. She reached both arms around him and pulled him against her with every ounce of strength she could muster, and crushed her lips to his. His body rocked against her, and through their clothes, his cock hit places that made her shudder.

She needed to bring him to oblivion, just like he had for her. She had to make him know he was worthy of being worshipped, too. And the idea of him laid out in front of her, completely at her mercy, sent heat to every part of her body.

She rolled them over so she had him pinned on the blanket.

She reached for the buttons on his breeches, and her hands shook as she undid them. Not from fear, but from anticipation.

His hand reached to stay hers, but she pushed it away and released his manhood.

His breath got ragged, and she kissed him before he could say anything. She kissed around to his ear, where she whispered, "Shhhh." He was hers tonight.

He nodded slightly, and she kissed her way down his neck, lingering at the hollow just above his collarbone. The salt from his sweat tasted almost sweet.

Then she began moving down the front of him and found his nipple through his shirt. She kissed it through the fabric, and he sucked in a breath. Her teeth nibbled at the puckered flesh, and his cock jumped in her hand.

Feeling that surge of lust that he clearly couldn't control made her bold, and she kissed her way further down his body. She couldn't tell him what she felt with the others sleeping so close, she would have to show him with her body.

When she got to his belly, he was barely breathing at all, and the muscles under her lips flexed tight. With her free hand, she pulled his shirt up and ran her tongue around the contours of his navel, tasting more sweet salt.

His hand found her hair and began stroking it, like it couldn't lie still and had to find some movement it could make in rhythm with hers. Her tongue followed the lay of the hair on his belly as it coalesced into a line leading down toward her other hand.

She nibbled her way down until she reached a thicker thatch of hair that matched the one between her own legs. His cock felt even larger in her hand than it had the first time she held it, with his hand over hers, guiding her movement.

He continued to stroke her hair, not breathing at all, as best she could tell. She would have to breathe for both of them.

The head of his cock stood clear in the moonlight, her hand just below it, on his shaft, and her lips poised above it. He made no move but the stroking, which he continued with measured evenness in the place of breathing. She had never met a man who willingly let her take the lead in anything, let alone something intimate. He was so strong, yet so vulnerable.

She lifted her lips from his lower belly and placed them gently on the head of his shaft. It throbbed against them.

The tip of her tongue slid out between them and tasted his skin.

A huge exhale sounded from above her head.

She tried swirling her tongue around the tip that she held, and he exhaled more sharply. She had never felt more powerful.

Her fingers circled his shaft, and she pushed them down toward its base like he had shown her in the woods during the conference. His hips bucked up. He had consumed her with his mouth to drive her to oblivion, so she opened her mouth and slid it over him. His fingers tightened on her hair for a moment, then he resumed the stroking.

She ran her free hand down into his breeches and freed his ballocks. They were heavy in her hand as she caressed them gently in rhythm with the sliding of her hand down his shaft and her tongue on the head.

She opened her mouth further and pushed it down over as much of him as she could fit. Then she swirled her tongue around and slid him in and out of her mouth in the same rhythm as her hands slid up and down and squeezed and released his stones. Urgency drove her, and she was determined to make the most of the time she had with him.

He grew salty in her mouth, and she tried sucking on him. His hands froze again for a moment before resuming their movements on her hair, with a little less gentleness than before, like he felt the same urgency.

She sucked at him again, and then again. His breath was now irregular and raspy. She sucked harder, and his balls contracted in her hand. Then they convulsed, and his shaft convulsed, and his seed shot into her mouth faster than she could swallow. It leaked out and made his shaft slippery under her hand, which she kept working until at last the spurting stopped, and he grew softer in her hand.

A few months ago, she might have been embarrassed, but her heart pounded with something entirely different now. Gratitude? Maybe a little triumph?

His whole body was limp beneath hers. She had done that for him, just like he had done that for her. She kissed his belly, and up his chest to his neck, and his chin, then finally his lips. If she could have wrapped him up in her arms and protected him from all the evils of the world right now, she would.

His fingers still threaded through her hair, and he pulled her against him and kissed her so hard she could barely catch her breath. Then he ran one hand down her back and ground her hips against him. Then he rolled them on their sides, and turned her so her back was against his chest, and pulled her tight against him.

He nuzzled her neck, and her muscles melted.

He put his lips against her ear. "I will remember this until the day I die."

She snuggled against him, and his heart beat against her back. Her own heart softened and picked up the rhythm of his. So would she. She would have nothing else.

Chapter 42

Something jabbed into his ass and woke him up.

His arm was around Faith, his body curled around hers, and his cock hanging free of his breeches—all just as it had been when he had passed out.

Carefully, he removed his arm from Faith and stuffed his privates back in his breeches.

David's voice hovered just above his ear. "Don't bother—we heard it all. Get up. It's our watch."

Shit. Faith shifted in her sleep. He wanted to smooth her hair, but he wouldn't risk waking her. And the idiots were watching. Sweet Jesus, he had made a mess of this.

He rolled away from her and stood, made a rude gesture at Okwaho and David, and grabbed his musket. Then he motioned to the others to follow him.

They circled out in the direction Leo and the others had taken before they bedded down, and came upon the business end of Jaap's musket first. "Schenectady."

"Koekje." James said, and Jaap lowered his musket.

"You sound like you are still half asleep," said Jaap.

"Faith kept him up," said David. James jabbed him in the ribs with the butt of his musket. "Ouch."

"I would have thought you'd be in a better mood," said Okwaho.

"Let's get one thing clear right here and now. You heard nothing. You will not talk to each other about it in case she overhears you. Nothing happened."

"I need some of that nothing," said Okwaho.

The butt of James's musket found his ribs next.

"Bastard." Okwaho rubbed his side.

"You"—James shoved his finger into David's chest—"take this post." He poked Jaap. "You head back and make damn sure not to wake Faith. And I mean absolutely nothing."

James and Okwaho headed around to the right until they came face to face with Dieter's musket. "Schenectady."

"Koekje."

"We need a countersign that isn't food-related. I'm hungry," said Okwaho.

"You're always hungry," said James.

"I didn't eat—"

This time, James jammed the butt of his gun much harder.

"Fucker." Okwaho said. "I can't fight if you break my ribs."

"Then take this post and stop talking. To anyone." To Dieter, he said, "You can head back and get some sleep. Jaap has already gone back."

Dieter grunted and headed back toward the camp.

Leo had placed everyone well, which was no surprise. He had been living in the woods his entire adult life, and hunting and trapping meant defending his grounds.

James ran next into Ben's muzzle. Ben grunted when he could see James and began to lower his musket.

Leo's musket knocked Ben's back up, so it was aiming at James's chest again. "No countersign, no friend." Leo didn't just hunt and trap. He had fought in King George's War and knew his business there, too.

"Koekje," said James.

Ben lowered his musket again. "You are all obsessed."

"Obsessed or not, the countersign will save your life. I could have been French," James said, then he turned to Leo. "Anything I need to know?"

"All quiet." Leo turned and pointed at Ben. "Apart from the countersign, he did good."

Ben grumbled something in a language that sounded like German.

"Go get some sleep," said James.

They turned and headed back to the camp, leaving James with his thoughts and whatever might be out in the woods.

He scanned the surrounding ground and underbrush for anything out of place. Then at eye level. Then in the trees.

He listened. Birds, frogs, leaves fluttering in the breeze. Nothing out of order.

He didn't really expect the French to mess with them this close to Schenectady. If they were this close in, they would be scouting the town itself for intelligence. But he wasn't at all sure of what Lydius might be up to. And James wasn't one to take risks. Unless you counted putting his mouth and hands all over an officer's daughter, in ways that could get him stood up in front of an army firing squad.

He swept the area again, top to bottom, in case he missed anything the first time. During a change of watch is an easy time to get a jump on your enemy.

He rubbed his hand over his face and tried to rub the image of the men seeing Faith asleep and vulnerable from his mind.

The image that replaced it was his cock disappearing between her lips, and that created its own problem.

He would yank himself off to that image for many decades to come.

A bullfrog let out a giant frog-belch.

He watched for what had to be hours. His back started to ache from standing still.

He twisted it from side to side, and something caught the corner of his eye.

He turned and looked harder through the moon-dappled trees. The nighttime noises still sounded, and nothing moved.

But something had caught his eye.

He stepped away from the trunk of the tree that was his cover, careful to stay in shadow. The moon wasn't full, but with his eyes adjusted to the dark, he could see well enough, which meant anyone out there could also see him.

He moved almost silently thanks to the moccasins on his feet. Yet another thing he had learned from hunting with Leo. He kept low and didn't stray too far from his post, lest it was an effort to get him to do just that.

And he wasn't just guarding the sleeping men and muskets, but also Faith. She didn't belong out here, with people tracking them through the woods, waiting for a chance to do God knew what to them.

She belonged snug and safe in an elegant house in a fancy city.

And he didn't.

He shook off the thought and searched with renewed focus.

Then a small fox shifted in the undergrowth and glared at him, and then it got up and slunk off to find a more peaceful place to spend the rest of the night.

Was the fox his only company?

Hard to be sure. His presence might have disturbed the fox, or it might have been something else.

The sky to the east grew from black to a deep, dark blue, and then a slice of golden glow filtered through the trees.

Irrational as it was, he wanted to be the one to wake Faith. It would be his last opportunity. He shouldn't care as much as he did, but facts were facts. He did.

With one last visual sweep of the area, he relieved himself on the ground next to the tree, and then headed back to camp.

Dieter and Ben were hefting the first crate of muskets to take it back out to the wagon.

Faith was already awake.

His chest ached. He didn't even get to wake her up. And he would never have another chance.

And he needed to get over it.

She was scratching the horses and feeding them. She must have heard him because she looked up.

His heart gave an extra hard squeeze when her eyes met his. She smiled and then focused back on the horses. She combed their manes and forelocks with her fingers as they munched their oats and corn.

Jaap returned from a visit to the woods, buttoning his breeches.

David and Okwaho returned to camp together, noticed one of the crates was already off the stack, went and grabbed the next, and headed for the road with it.

Leo stared at something behind James, then got up and approached him.

"What do you see?" James asked in a low voice.

"Not sure. Could be nothing."

Jaap stopped on his way to the crates and grabbed his musket instead.

James looked to Faith.

She glanced at him and cocked her head as if to ask why everyone was acting funny suddenly. Then she glanced around quickly. Including her, there were only four of them left.

Chapter 43

Dieter and Ben hadn't returned. Neither had David and Okwaho. They had barely left, and it would take them time to get to the road and back. He couldn't risk calling for them and giving them away while they were all so spread apart and vulnerable.

James motioned Faith to stay where she was. She nodded.

Jaap mumbled something to Leo in Dutch, and Leo shrugged.

"What did you see while you were on watch?" Leo asked James, his voice barely audible.

"I thought I disturbed a fox, but something else could have."

Leo pondered for a moment.

"I'll show you. Maybe you'll see something I didn't."

Before they left, he turned to Jaap. "Guard her."

"I can help," she said. "At least give me a musket."

James looked at Leo, and then at Jaap, then back to her. "Have you ever fired a musket?"

"I'm better with pistols, but I fired a musket once." She poked her chin up, daring him to take her honesty and use it against her. Leo gestured to them to keep quiet.

If it was just the sleep-deprived fox, she would think he was a reactionary fool, jumping at shadows.

"We don't have a spare musket, anyway," said Jaap.

She glared at Jaap, and then at James. "Fine. Then Jaap and I can take the horses to Dieter, and if anyone comes for us, we ride over them on the horses."

"I don't need you coming up with military strategy right now." James kept his voice low, but it came out a little too close to a hiss.

Her nostrils flared. "I happen to be good at it."

Under other circumstances, her idea wouldn't be half bad, but he was not letting her risk herself that way. "Just be still for a moment so I can think."

James looked toward the road to see if there was any sign of the other four men. Nothing. And they would probably take time to uncover the wagon, so it would be a while before they returned.

He looked back at her. "Faith, you stay between the two horses." Their bodies would at least afford her some protection. He turned to Jaap. "You don't let anything touch a hair on her head."

Jaap made sure his musket was primed, and slung his powder horn over his shoulder. He tucked a second ball in his cheek, ready to spit it down the barrel for fast reloading. It was faster than using cartridges if you knew what you were doing.

Faith was frowning, but she went to the horses and slipped in between their bodies. They both looked at her for a moment, hoping she had more food, then went back to snacking on the leaves of the tree they were tethered to.

She glared at him over the back of the nearest horse.

He went to her. "This isn't where you belong, Faith. As soon as we check this out, we will get the horses hitched and head for Schenectady. You will be safe by tonight."

"I am neither foolish nor fragile. But I could be more useful with a weapon of some kind."

His hands gripped his musket tighter and about cracked the barrel. "I need to make sure you are safe."

"You won't even let me defend myself." Then she held up her hand. "Fine. Go. Leo is waiting."

He stared at her for a moment. It was his job to keep her safe, and she shouldn't need to defend herself. Then he turned to Leo, who still stared at the woods, and Jaap, who waited for them to move out. "Anything happens to her, and it will not go well for you."

Jaap acknowledged the order with a tip of his head, his expression serious.

He turned and went to stand by Leo.

"Show me where you saw the fox. We need to see if there are tracks, or we'll be sitting like ducks on a pond when we get back on the road," said Leo.

They both held their muskets in front of them as they stepped quietly into the woods.

Leo scanned to their right, and James scanned to the left. Jaap would have their backs for the first twenty yards or so, until he lost sight of them.

They made their way back to the tree where they had each stood their watch in turn. Leo crouched down and examined the ground.

James tapped him silently on the shoulder and pointed to where he had seen the fox.

Disturbing nothing, Leo searched the ground around the spot, and circled outward, looking for signs of anything that might have woken the fox besides James.

James kept guard, scanning for anyone watching them or anything out of place.

The woods were quiet. Even the bird calls were muted. The quieter it got, the more carefully James scanned. Leo signaled to him to come look at a patch of ground. A depression. Leo traced the edge of it and the shape of a foot materialized in front of James. Only Leo could have recognized it.

"Did you walk out here?" Leo asked.

James shook his head.

"Ben and I stayed over there." Leo gestured back toward the tree.

"Fresh?"

Leo stared at it. Then he scanned the area surrounding it. A small stone kicked over. The dirt where the stone had been was darker and more damp than the surrounding dirt. "Fresh."

"Shit." At least Faith wouldn't think he had been overreacting.

Leo kept searching now that he had tracks to follow. James followed behind him, scanning constantly, making sure no one snuck up on them.

The trail led away from the camp. Leo looked up. "Looks like they met up with at least two French." He pointed to a print with a patch near the heel. Only Leo could tell the difference between Abenaki moccasins and Canadian militia shoes. They were almost identical.

They looped to the left. Now that the tracks included multiple men, the trail was easier for James to see.

The prints continued to arc around until they were heading back toward the camp. They were about a quarter mile out now.

Leo looked up at him. "I'm guessing six or seven men."

It would've been a fair fight, if James's men had been all together. Which they were not.

And it was just Jaap protecting Faith.

"We need to get back," James said.

Leo nodded. They took stock of where they were leaving the trail in case they needed to pick it up again, then headed on a direct route back toward the camp at a jog.

The birds had gone completely silent.

He picked up the pace and passed Leo.

Then a sound like an angry bull moose split the air, followed by a gunshot, then another. It was Jaap.

James and Leo were both running flat out before the second shot fired, pounding through the underbrush, taking no care not to leave a trail.

Jaap had gone after someone with fury, which meant that someone was there to go after.

No feminine voice. No feminine scream. Maybe they didn't see her hiding between the two horses. Sweat stung James's eyes, and branches ripped at his face as he plunged forward where there was no trail.

Please let the others have gotten there by now. Jaap was brave to the point of recklessness, and he needed backup.

James and Leo both slowed slightly and swung their muskets around to a ready position in case they ran into any retreating enemy men. Running headlong into an ambush would be the height of stupidity.

They both crouched low.

He could hear the horses before they saw them. They were stomping and sounded panicky. If Faith was still between them, she could get crushed.

Trusting that two panicked horses were less dangerous than rushing in and drawing attention to her about killed him.

Leo made a hawk's call.

No answer.

James crawled forward and peered over an elderberry bush at the edge of the clearing.

Two Abenaki men lay on the ground.

Then a moan came from near the rock where they had stacked the crates last night.

Jaap lay on the ground.

James signaled to Leo to go to him, while James covered him from a few steps behind.

No one else was in sight. No Frenchmen, no Abenaki.

No Faith.

Chapter 44

Faith rubbed the withers of the horse that stood between her and Jaap.

She shouldn't have snapped at James. It wasn't his fault she wasn't well-trained with a musket. Even the one time she had fired one, the sergeant who had let her do it had gotten into serious trouble for it.

Standing between two horses in the woods, unarmed, when there might be a raiding party just beyond her view, made her want to scream. To let loose her frustration with everyone who had ever told her it was unladylike to want to learn how to protect herself, because her inability to wield a musket put her, and Jaap, in significantly greater danger right now.

The horse behind her nudged her shoulder with its muzzle, and she turned and gave it a scratch.

Then Jaap let out a scream that curdled the blood in her veins. He fired his musket and a native man fell dead at the edge of the camp.

Her heart slammed against her ribs, and the horses crowded together in alarm, almost smashing the breath from her body.

Jaap dumped powder down his musket on the run and spat a bullet down, and fired again. Another man fell face down on the ground. Thank God Jaap was a good shot. Then he dove into the woods, going after others, from the sound of the crashing around in the undergrowth. She had to find some way to help.

The horses slammed her body between them again, and she shoved her way out. She wasn't going to be trampled. Their eyes rolled, and they yanked their heads against their tethers.

No one else was there. Where were David and the others who had gone to the road?

One of the dead men had a musket lying next to him. She ran low toward him and grabbed hold of it. The strap caught on his arm, and she had to wrestle with his prone body to get it off.

She didn't know what group he was part of, but he was dressed differently from the Mohawk. She grabbed his shoulder and heaved his body onto its back, then froze for an instant. His eyes were open and staring at her. Jaap had shot the man right through the bridge of his nose.

She tore her eyes away from the gore and rummaged for his bullet pouch. She tugged at it, but couldn't get it to come free. Her stomach gave a lurch, but she hadn't eaten anything, so nothing came up.

The man had died clutching his knife. She reached for it and yanked her hand back. His skin was still warm.

Stupid—of course it was. He hadn't been dead but a moment. She grabbed his knife and cut the pouch from its string. Then she reached for his powder horn and tugged. The weight of the man's body trapped its strap, so she cut that, too.

Was the musket already loaded? She had watched troops load them often enough, and she knew how to load a pistol, but she didn't know how to tell if there was already shot in the barrel.

She scanned the woods. No one was visible, but footsteps sounded from somewhere out there.

Surely the man wouldn't have approached their camp with an unloaded musket. She stuffed a handful of shot in her pocket and tied the powder horn to her wrist, then swung the musket to her shoulder.

Just as she had it ready to fire, Jaap crashed through the trees at the edge of the camp, followed by a native man. She took aim at his pursuer and pulled the trigger.

The hammer fell, the flint sparked in the pan—and then nothing happened. A misfire. The man was almost on Jaap with his club swinging toward Jaap's head.

She rushed the man and swung the butt of the musket as hard as she could at his head.

She connected at almost the exact moment his club connected with Jaap's head. Jaap fell, and the man stumbled to his knees. Jaap turned and grabbed at the man's club, and another man emerged from the woods.

Faith swung the musket at him, but he dodged it and grabbed her around the waist, yanking her backward and almost folding her in half from the force of the movement. She clawed at his arm with her hands, but he didn't loosen his hold. Jaap was on the ground wrestling the man with the club. *No, no, no!* Her throat closed off her own breath.

Then her captor swung her up in the air and his shoulder slammed into her gut, forcing the air out again as her torso flopped down his back, and she could see only legs, feet, and the ground beneath them. He turned and ran, and Jaap's form, still wrestling, disappeared from her view as it was swallowed up by trees. She couldn't suck in enough breath to scream. Her head bounced off the man's back, and the blade of his axe jabbed her cheek as her head bounced too close to his belt.

She fought to keep her head away from it because one bad bounce, and she would lose her eye. Then she tried to brace her hand on the axe head to keep it between the blade and face, but the man reached back and smacked her arm away from it, yanking the powder horn from her wrist.

Another man joined them, running up behind them from the direction of the campsite. He was European and dressed in leggings, a loincloth, and hunting shirt, with a red cap on his head. French?

The shoulder of the man carrying her jammed her viscera with every step, and she fought to stay conscious. She had to try to keep track of where they went.

She had to escape. The further they took her, the harder it would be for anyone to find her. Panic choked her, but she swallowed it down.

Where was James? Where were the others?

They had to have heard the shots. James would come for her. She knew that in her soul, so she had to make it easier for them to track her or at least slow her abductors down so they could catch up.

The men didn't speak as they ran. Surely the one carrying her would get tired soon. She wasn't that light.

"*Où est l'homme?*"

A French voice. But the running barely slowed.

"*Mort,*" another native man answered.

No. They couldn't have killed Jaap.

When they had left the clearing, Jaap had still been wrestling a third man. She'd surely had the last view of him, and he was still alive. Unless that last man had rejoined them, and she couldn't see him as she hung upside down.

The man carrying her stumbled, and her head slammed into his back a fraction of an inch from the axe.

"Merde."

Faith hurtled backward, landed barely on her feet, and her momentum slammed her backward into someone. She couldn't see him, but he smelled of sweat and lavender, and her hair caught on something around his neck. He must have been the Frenchman who had spoken.

Lavender. Had he been what she had smelled in the woods by Johnson's house? Had he been the one behind the tree laughing at her?

The other native man was suddenly in front of her. His eyes burned with fury.

Before she could finish her thought, he bent down, rammed his shoulder into her middle, and stood. The world tilted and her backside rose toward the sky.

Her face slammed into a new back, and they were on the run again.

This time—thank heaven for small favors—her hipbones were against the man's shoulder, so she could breathe better. The bone kept his shoulder from rearranging her guts with every stride.

They reached a stream, entered it, and ran downstream through it for at least a quarter of a mile. Their pace barely slowed.

This was what her father and his men would be up against. She knew their training and could recite the drills in her sleep. Everything assumed open fields and massed men. There were no open fields and carefully cut roads to get to Fort Niagara. Men like James and the others, and the Iroquois warriors, were their only hope. They were used to these conditions. They could track.

They can track.

She had one simple ribbon in her hair. Her fingers fumbled as she bounced, but she got it loose. As long as she didn't struggle, no one paid her any attention. She tried to tear the ribbon in half, but it was too strong.

Then they slowed.

"Ici."

They left the creek bed, stepping carefully, not disturbing the ground. They were hiding where they had left the water to be harder to track.

The man carrying her ducked to avoid breaking a branch, and she reached out and shoved the ribbon into its leaves.

It fell. It fluttered back toward the water and settled half on a rock.

Did the men see it? They kept going. Then the current took the ribbon, and it rushed downstream. Gone.

She had nothing else to drop. She closed her eyes. She would not cry. Her head bounced on the man's back and her nose got slammed. That brought tears to her eyes, no matter how hard she fought them. They started running again, and her tears mixed with blood streaming from her nose.

How could they keep running? Her muscles screamed from the effort of breathing while upside down. Their legs must surely be more tired.

They crossed a patch of bare stone and started climbing. They rounded several boulders, then came to a sudden stop. She pushed her hands against the man's back to avoid slamming her already damaged nose again. One more hit and she would pass out from the pain.

The world rotated again, and she lost her bearings until her feet hit rock, and her legs collapsed from the sudden force of her weight, and she fell backward. Hard. She just managed to swing her arms back to brace herself and slow her fall so she didn't slam her head.

She looked up.

"Tu parles français, toi?" The man leered at her, and the jagged scar on his face throbbed red. From the ground, he looked ten feet tall. His toes were inches from her face.

She looked quickly around, and another Frenchman and two native men appeared.

Four sets of hostile eyes stared down at her.

Chapter 45

James covered Leo so he could go to Jaap, and then a crow called. David.

James returned the call, and then David, Okwaho, Dieter, and Ben rounded the boulder and rushed to Jaap.

"David, east. Okwaho, west."

They both nodded and went in opposite directions, muskets at the ready to try to make sure they didn't get surprised a second time. They didn't go far into the woods, or they would be too spread out.

Jaap moaned again. Leo probed the back of his head.

"Ow, you fucker." He was awake, and he reached up to feel his own head.

"You got lucky," Leo said. "Whoever it was didn't get a clean hit." James knelt down next to them.

Jaap slowly sat himself up. "Faith nailed him with a musket butt just as he hit me. She must have distracted him just enough."

Oh God, she had dived right into the fight. "Where is she?" James had him by the front of his shirt.

Leo pried his hands off Jaap. "Give him a moment."

One moment was about all James was willing to wait. He breathed through clenched teeth.

Jaap looked James in the eye. "They got her from behind. I got the first two, but then a third guy came at me with his club. That's when she tried to shoot the guy. She must have grabbed one of the dead Abenaki's muskets. It misfired, so she swung the butt at his head and stunned him."

"What happened to her?" If Jaap took one more breath without telling him, he was going to shake him.

"Another man grabbed her from behind. The bastard I was wrestling kneed me in the gut and knocked the wind out of me. By the time I could breath again, she was gone. And then I saw your ugly faces." His shoulders slumped, and his body couldn't match the bluster of his words.

James said, "Leo, find which way they went."

Leo took a last look at his cousin, who gave him a nod without puking or falling over. If he could move his head like that, he would probably be all right. Leo gave Jaap's shoulder a squeeze, grabbed his musket, and started looking around the edge of the camp for where they entered and where they left.

Leo would find the trail, and they would track them down and get her back. No one could track like Leo, and really, how fast could they be traveling? They would find her. They would.

"Dieter. Did you get the crates loaded?"

"Ya." He nodded. "We had to pull the wagon out of the scrub, or we would have been back sooner. Then we heard the firing from the woods, but didn't know if there were more coming after us, so we had to be careful."

They had to get those crates safely to Albany, no matter how much he wanted the extra men with him to help track down Faith.

"You and Jaap get the muskets to Albany."

Dieter nodded and stood and went to the horses. He soothed them and began checking their harnesses, tightening them and readying them to be hitched.

"I'm going after Faith with you, and you don't have time to argue. I am fine."

Shit. They didn't have time to argue—but if Jaap wasn't all right, he was going to slow them down and they might lose him, too.

"I tried, James." Jaap said quietly. "There were too many."

"I heard you going after them. I know."

"She did really good. If the damn musket hadn't misfired, we'd have had them."

She hadn't stayed put where he told her to. But Leo could track them. They had to get her back.

A succession of bird calls echoed through the trees. Soon Leo, David, and Okwaho all returned to the campsite from different directions.

"Teach your damn cousin to do more than a crow," James said to Okwaho.

"He likes crows. They're smart."

James glared at him.

"I'll teach him a chickadee," said Leo, looking at James.

David said, "Well, this should be brilliant for your career. Not sure if you should be more worried about her father or Johnson."

Richmond served under Shirley. Shirley was second in command to Braddock.

James was very much fucked.

He could dwell on that misery after they got her back. "What did you find, Leo?"

"One set of prints is deeper than the others. They must be carrying her."

That wouldn't last long. Once they were out of range, they would question her, and after that, either she could keep up on her own two feet, or they would kill her.

"Ben," James said. "Get word to Johnson. Tell him we are going after her."

Ben nodded in acknowledgment, then trotted after Dieter.

James grabbed his bedding, rolled it into a pack, tied his tumpline around it, and slung it over his shoulder. The others were doing the same. James ran his hand over his blanket. It was just a rough woolen blanket. But Faith had slept on it. She had given herself to him on it, and then she had turned the tables and taken him.

Oh God, he was a rash fool.

And now he might have gotten her killed. Should he not have checked out the tracks with Leo? Should he have sent Jaap? He replayed all of his options, but none of them would have changed a damn thing.

He had done what he needed to do, and she had been taken, anyway. *Fuck.*

He could fix it, though. He would get her back.

He stepped over to where the trail started. Now they knew where to look, the passage of their enemies was obvious. They all carried their muskets loaded and at the ready as they trotted along the tracks made by the raiding party.

They made good time until they got to a creek.

They stopped for a drink, and Leo scouted the opposite bank for what seemed like an eternity, and Jaap and Okwaho helped. David and James kept watch.

"We'll get her," David said quietly. "And maybe we'll get some intelligence that will even spare your ass with Johnson."

Leo crossed the creek back to them. "They didn't cross."

"Shit." James rubbed at the ache in his chest.

Leo turned and went right back to studying the creek bed, looking for signs of which direction they took.

James kept a careful eye in case they were lying in wait. They might not have wanted to carry Faith much further and decided to ambush them, so they didn't have to travel as quickly. They searched the creek for unending minutes.

"Nothing." Leo shook his head.

"What's your best take?" James asked.

"The obvious direction is upstream."

James rubbed his hand through his hair. Obvious was too obvious. The men had been clever.

James's head hurt.

"Downstream." James looked from one man to the next. None questioned his decision. If he had guessed wrong, it was all on him. "David, you go with Leo on that side of the creek. Jaap, Okwaho, you're with me on this side."

Okwaho was a solid tracker, and James wanted to keep an eye on Jaap to make sure he really was all right. Jaap had gotten his head good and scrambled this morning. And apparently it would have been even more scrambled if Faith hadn't tried to club the Abenaki.

His stomach lurched at the thought of her trying to shoot the man and the musket misfiring. And then she just ran at him and tried to crack his skull? She was almost as reckless as Jaap.

Which wasn't fair. Any of them would have done the same. What else was she supposed to do? Cower and wait to be abducted? That wasn't like her.

Jaap elbowed him and pointed to the ground.

He was supposed to be keeping an eye on Jaap, not the other way around. He wasn't very well going to find her if he couldn't focus on looking for tracks. Leo let out a low call.

Everyone stopped and looked his way.

He motioned them to cross to his side. "This looks like a good place to leave the creek without leaving tracks. Lots of rocks to step on."

Rocks littered the ground. If they stepped from rock to rock, they wouldn't leave prints, at least not once the water marks from their feet dried, which wouldn't take long on warm rocks in the middle of the summer.

Leo studied the low-hanging branches for signs of someone bumping them. They all fanned out and did the same. The further they went, the more they also looked down for prints, since the rocks thinned.

Nothing. The bastards had been careful, or they had chosen a different spot. James scanned the leaves and dirt at his feet.

No prints.

Then something different. He dropped to his knees and sniffed.

Leo appeared next to him.

James looked up. "Blood."

Chapter 46

Faith stared up at the four men surrounding her in the middle of the trail where they had deposited her.

Under other circumstances, they might be perfectly pleasant faces belonging to perfectly reasonable men she would be interested in conversing with. But not under these circumstances.

"*Écoute. Tu parles français, toi?*"

Of course she spoke French—every reasonably well-educated Englishwoman did—but maybe it would slow them down if they didn't know that.

"Excuse me? I don't understand." She tried to look perplexed. Which wasn't too difficult.

The smaller of the French men rolled his eyes at her. "Do you speak French?"

Ridiculous. If she had, she would have understood the question in French.

She put on her best London miss. "I am so sorry, but I am afraid I was a terrible student and I haven't a word of French."

They looked hard at her. She had exceeded the man's ability to translate.

"I do not speak French," she clarified.

This time, understanding shone in the man's eyes, alongside annoyance. He turned to his French companion. "*Non.*"

The man with the scar, who appeared to outrank the smaller one, spoke. "*Son père?*"

Oh heavens. If they were asking about her father, that meant they knew who she was, and she might have been their target from the start. She had been the one to put them in danger.

"Your father. Where he to go?"

"I really am so sorry. I am afraid I don't know his plans. Why would he tell a daughter? It isn't as if there is anything I could do."

The younger man thought hard for a moment, then hesitantly translated what she had said into French.

The other man looked at her like a schoolmaster. *"Non. Je ne tu crois pas."*

He didn't believe her.

"Tu es ici. Pourquoi?" The older man said directly to her, as if he knew she understood. She forced her eyes to the younger man as if she needed his translation.

"Why you are here?"

"I just want to get back to Albany." And she wanted to hear James and the others coming through the woods to rescue her. More than anything in the world.

She wiped her nose with her hand. It had stopped bleeding, but swiping at it got it running again, and she wiped her hand on the rock behind her. She must look a sight, but if it increased the odds of them being able to track her even one tiny bit, she would keep it bleeding all day.

The older man grabbed her by the front of her dress and pulled her to her feet. She wanted to break his hands. *"Ton père s'appelle Richmond?"*

Oh Lord, they did know who her father was. "Richmond?" She had better give them some reason to keep trying to talk with her. If they gave up and tossed her over their shoulder again, they would get that much farther ahead of James.

"Oui. Richmond." The older man stared into her eyes like he was trying to read the thoughts behind them.

"Colonel Richmond is my father."

The younger man translated and a smile spread across the face of the older man. *"Demande à elle si son père est avec Johnson ou Shirley."*

They knew the leaders of the two New York campaigns and they knew her father went with one of them. How did they know that?

"Your father, who is commander?" The younger man really needed to attend more closely to his lessons. Her own tutor would have wrapped her knuckles for such barbarism.

"I believe he goes to meet with someone named Braddock." At Fort Niagara with Shirley, but that was where Braddock was supposed to go after they wiped the French from the Ohio country, so it was truthful. And maybe if they thought he served directly under Braddock, they would back off.

The young man translated and the older man laughed. He looked at her with a snarl. *"Braddock est mort."*

Her heart stopped for a moment. Braddock couldn't be dead. He was the commander-in-chief of the entire British army in North America. The man had to be bluffing. She forced herself to look to the younger man for a translation.

"Braddock is dead."

She let her shock show now. What London miss wouldn't be horrified by that news?

But if Braddock was dead, then he couldn't meet up with Shirley at Fort Niagara and sweep on to Montreal. And Shirley would be commander-in-chief.

Her head throbbed. From the news, and from hanging upside down for so long. And her backside hurt. And she needed to relieve herself. If it weren't so humiliating, she should have just let go and peed on the man carrying her, but she hadn't been able to bring herself to.

"I need to relieve myself."

The young man stared at her. Good heavens. He didn't understand euphemisms.

"I need to piss."

His eyes widened in comprehension.

"Elle doit faire pipi."

The older man smirked at her and gestured to the ground beneath her.

"Here?" No. She would not.

The older man shrugged, but stared. *"Elle m'a frappé avec une roche pour qu'elle puisse pisser ici sur cette roche."*

The rock she had thrown in the woods had caused that scar. And now he wanted to humiliate her in return. Good God, what had she done?

But she needed to delay them. She needed to give James time. She could do this.

This man was going to die if she had anything to say about it.

Her face burned hot as she squatted down. She hiked her skirts up just enough to keep them from getting wet and let her bladder loose.

She was in the open with four strange men staring at her and watching the puddle grow beneath her. It was in the open. Easy to spot for anyone trying to track her. A cold wave washed through her heart. The son of a cur-dog would regret what he had just done.

The native men looked down and then looked at the French men in disgust. *"Allons-y. Maintentant."*

They scowled at him. They understood the Frenchman's error, and they weren't happy. It served the bastard right.

"Zut, alor, Capitain." Even the younger man knew the captain's desire to humiliate her had been foolish and could cost them.

"Ferme ta gueule." The captain told the younger man to shut up.

Then a rope passed across her vision, and before she could figure out what was going on, it tightened around her neck.

She turned to the native man behind her. *"Maintenant, tu cour avec nous,"* he said.

Oh God, she now had to run with them. How in heaven was she supposed to keep up in her skirts?

The captain sent the other native man to the front, then swung his musket around and motioned for the younger man to take up the rear. He motioned them forward.

"Excuse me?" She might as well try to delay the inevitable. "What is going on? What am I to do?"

The younger man jabbed her in the back. "Run."

They started along the trail at a jog, ducking beneath branches.

She dragged her feet when she could, but keeping up was already hard in her skirts and her lightweight shoes, and with a rope around her neck.

Her lungs burned within a few hundred yards, and her legs ached. One leg didn't want to work as effectively as the other. Her aching head didn't want her to run at all, but she forced herself.

They plunged on and the younger man's bayonet in her back inspired her to summon every ounce of strength to keep up.

They had to have run a mile by now.

Then the native man in the lead stopped short, with the others skidding to a halt behind him, herself included. In front of the man was a bear, blocking their way.

A *bear*.

She had survived this long to be killed by a goddam bear. Off to the side of the trail was a cub. She willed the cub to rejoin its mamma so mamma would leave them in peace.

A loud bang echoed through the trees, and something whistled past her ear.

The native man holding her rope dropped in a heap.

The others looked around and crouched low.

She dove for the dead man's musket. She yanked the strap off his shoulder before the younger Frenchman could stop her. She stayed low, and tried to crawl off to the side, but the younger man grabbed her ankle.

She swung the musket around and aimed for his head.

Chapter 47

James watched the man with the rope drop as he reloaded on the run.

She was there. They had caught up before the bastards could do anything irreparable to her. *Please dear God, let them not have hurt her.*

His feet pounded the trail, and the others followed close on his heels.

Faith was on the ground, and James stopped to take careful aim at the Frenchman in front of her. But she spun and grabbed a musket and she was blocking his shot now. He wanted to yell at her to get down, but that would warn the Frenchman.

She swung the butt end of it around and caught the man in the temple, and he fell back. She had learned from her misfire in the camp and didn't take the chance a second time. Smart woman.

James barreled down on them and pinned the man to the ground.

"That one," Faith yelled. He whipped his head around, expecting to see a muzzle facing him, but there was another Frenchman, scooting away behind a tree. "That one is the captain."

Which meant he knew more than the others and could provide more useful information to Johnson. She knew what was important in this moment.

James waved to David and Okwaho, who came up behind him. "Captain just headed for the trees. Get him."

He turned back to Faith. Blood dripped down her lip from her nose, her hair stuck out in every direction, and she was the most beautiful thing he had ever seen. But her nose was swelling like it might be broken.

"There is another," she said. "Not French. And a bear and her cub." She pointed up the trail.

"Jaap, Leo. Another Abenaki and a bear with a cub. Be careful. You're more important than the Abenaki."

He turned back to Faith. "Where are you hurt?"

She wiped her nose with the back of her hand. "I just got a bloody nose and my gut hurts from being tossed over their shoulders like a sack from the mill. I'm all right." She wiped her hand on her skirt and stood before he could offer her a hand. She was stiff, but steady. She looked around, like she was deciding which of the two parties to head out after.

"Let them take care of the captain and the other man." He reached for her arm, and she turned to him.

"They know who my father is." Her jaw was tight and her brows were low. "They were after me. I brought this on you all."

This was not her fault, but they weren't out of it yet, and he needed information to decide their next move. "How do you know they knew your father?"

"They asked me about him."

"They spoke English?"

She ran her fingers through her hair, ran into a leaf, and pulled it out. "This one speaks a little." She gestured down at the prone man under James's knee, then seemed to realize the dent on the side of his head was not something he would recover from. "Did speak a little," she corrected herself. "And I pretended I didn't speak French to make him take the time to translate. But the captain really wanted to know which campaign my father was going on. He knew about the campaigns to Fort Niagara and to the Crown Point. And who is leading them." She stopped fussing with her hair and looked him in the eye. "He said Braddock is dead."

James's gut dropped like a boulder. That couldn't be. And how was Faith so calm about having killed a man with the butt of a musket? She was far more concerned about news that the British army's commander-in-chief might be dead. Anyone else would be hysterical.

"They couldn't know that, could they?" she asked. Her face pleaded with him more than her words.

"We won't know until we can get to Albany and find out the latest dispatches. We will assume they were just trying to create stress until we know otherwise."

David and Okwaho emerged from the woods with the French captain bound between them.

Faith turned to James and grabbed his arm. "Should I still pretend I don't speak French, or do you want me to interrogate him?"

"For now, keep pretending, just in case he lets something slip, not realizing you understand. But you are the only one here who does speak French, so we may need to make use of that." She was amazing. She wasn't crying for them to take her back to Albany, and she wasn't distressed over the blood still trickling from her nose. She was trying to help. She *was* helping.

The captain struggled when he saw James and Faith. His glare would have melted a block of ice. *"Pétasse."*

Faith took a deep breath and looked away, but if he didn't already know she understood, he wouldn't have guessed. Once her face was turned from the man, her jaw set. He must have said something nasty.

David and Okwaho dragged him toward them.

Faith turned back to James with a pleasant smile set on her face. "This one doesn't seem to speak English."

The man looked from Faith to James and back again. He showed no flicker of understanding. Just raw anger. *"Connard, nous ne sommes pas seuls."*

James didn't need a translation to know whatever he said wasn't good. He looked too cocky. A cocky captive was usually one who didn't expect to be a captive for long.

Jaap and Leo returned empty-handed. They looked the captain over.

"Bear got the other one." Leo didn't look too upset by that. Neither did Jaap.

Faith, too, took that news in stride. But she looked like she wanted to say something.

The captain said, *"Leurs frères vont te foutre en l'air."*

Faith swayed slightly on her feet. James reached out and grabbed her arm, pulling her toward him. She collapsed into his arms.

"Faith, are you all right?" Was she hurt more than she let on? He was going to carry her back if need be.

She kept her voice low, whispering in his ear. "He says that their brothers are going to, um, fuck you, more or less. They aren't alone, and I think he means the brothers of the dead men are going to come after us. I didn't want to say it out loud in case he was just pretending he doesn't speak English."

James pulled his arms around her and held her tight. He had thought he wouldn't have another chance to do that. God, she was brilliant. He buried his face against hers and kissed her cheek.

Then he propped her back up on her feet. "Better now?"

She rubbed her forehead and blinked a few times for show. Then nodded. "I think so."

The captain smirked, and James's men looked concerned. "She'll be all right, and we need to get out of here. Now."

Leo turned his head toward the direction he and Jaap had just come from. Then he pointed at the sky. A flock of birds rose out of the trees, then another.

They all grabbed their muskets and David poked his knife into the captain's back. "You will move and move fast."

The captain snarled at him. *"Fils de pute."* Even if he didn't speak English, the knife was a pretty universal translation of David's meaning.

"Leo, take point, Jaap, rear guard." They both took up their positions, and everyone checked their muskets, horns, and bullet pouches.

Faith picked up the musket of the dead man where it had fallen, swung the strap over her head, then grabbed his belt and yanked it out from under him. She gathered his horn and bullet pouch and then buckled his belt around her waist and hiked up her skirts, stuffing them in the belt to keep them there. Holy hell, she was amazing, and they really needed her to be exactly that right now.

Leo led the way, and they all started to run back in the direction they had come. Even the captain understood the rules. Slow them down and get his throat slit.

But Faith didn't. The regular army had different ones, and her delaying tactics could have gotten her killed.

A shudder ran up James's spine. He had thrown her into a partisan war, and nowhere in the time they had all been at Fort Johnson had anyone bothered to explain the rules to her. They just assumed she wasn't part of it and wouldn't need to know.

They could have gotten her killed. They could still.

She ran ahead of him, following David and the French captain closely. Her feet would be a bloody mess in those delicate and utterly unsuitable shoes if they got out of this.

But she didn't slow, and for all that she had no training to know what to look for, she kept sweeping her gaze from side to side, looking out for anything that could pose a danger.

But on the run, even Leo could run them into an ambush without realizing it.

Chapter 48

Faith's lungs burned like someone had shoveled hot coals into them. They pumped in and out like bellows, but for how long? If lungs could simply explode, hers might do that at any moment.

But she pushed on. She had no choice.

When the French had her, she had thought if James and the others caught up and freed her, she would be safe. She knew better now. She was out of the hands of the French, but they were being pursued by a group of French allies, looking for revenge.

One foot in front of the other. Look for roots and for rocks. Don't trip. Keep going.

The French captain ahead of them ran hard. Why was he not trying to slow them down? What would they do if he did start to slow them down?

Puzzling out the tactics in play helped distract her from the pain in the bottom of her feet. Her shoes were for tea parties, not for running at top speed through the woods.

No wonder James and the others treated her like she was made for the drawing room rather than real life. She dressed the part. She acted the part all too often, as well.

Her breath tasted like blood. Her lungs must be bleeding from the effort. She absolutely would not drown in her own blood because that would be absurd.

The others ran so easily. Their bodies were used to this sort of exertion. That was why James had such a very fine backside and legs. Not a thought that belonged in her brain while she was running for her life. Then again, if she was going to die, his magnificent backside was not such a bad thing to think about for her final thoughts on this earth.

A musket shot ripped through the air.

They kept running. Faster.

Then Jaap screamed—that same scream he had made when he went after the men that attacked them in camp.

"Halt!" James yelled to them. Everyone skidded to a stop. As tired as her body was, her legs wanted to keep going. Instinct screamed to get away. But she whipped around and pulled her musket off her shoulder.

James sent David and Okwaho off the left, and Leo to the right.

He grabbed Faith's arm and dragged her and their prisoner behind a boulder. "Aim your musket at his ribs." James pointed at the captain.

Few things on earth could have made her happier at that moment. She jammed the muzzle hard between two of his ribs, cocked the hammer, and glared at the man.

"If he so much as twitches, shoot him."

The captain's eyes flicked from her to James. It didn't matter if he understood the words or not. He understood the actions. She pushed the muzzle of her musket harder into his flesh and stared at the son of a bitch until he looked away from her.

James was already gone to back up Jaap.

The woods were a hornet's nest of buzzing, biting bullets. It sounded like there had to be at least thirty men firing, but that couldn't be. They were only five, and how many Abenaki could there really be?

Regulars couldn't fire and reload so quickly. Jaap had spit bullets down the barrel to reload faster. They must all being doing the same. On both sides, because the firing kept going.

The captain shifted slightly to get a better view of the firefight. She jabbed the muzzle of her musket so hard into his side it ripped through the fabric of his shirt.

"Ta mère etait une pute." He glared at her but stopped moving. She almost gave up on pretending she didn't understand, so she could tell him it was his mother who was the whore.

The shots kept ringing out. It had to have been a quarter of an hour by now, but really, her sense of time was warped by all the chaos. It was definitely going on for too long. James and the others hadn't had time to gather as much shot and powder as they might need.

How much did the Abenaki have? Would they just keep firing until they ran out of ammunition? Then what?

Someone shrieked in agony. No way to know which side the shriek belonged to.

The shots were more spaced out now.

Feet crashed through the underbrush.

Grunts and sickening thuds reached her ears.

The captain shifted again, and she kicked him. He was the only person she could take her anxiety out on, and she had no qualms about doing it.

The aggressive screams and the agonized shrieks increased. None of the voices sounded familiar, but screams didn't always.

Suddenly James was next to her, dropping Jaap next to her. "Help him."

He turned just as an axe swung past his head. James ducked and shoved the man backward, and they disappeared behind the boulder.

Jaap moaned at her feet. She looked down. The captain was gone. *Shit.* But Jaap was more important. He had blood streaming from an ugly gash on his hip.

"Stitch. Need to get back out there." Jaap fumbled in a pouch and reached out a bloody hand with a needle and silk thread. "Sarah makes us carry it." He winced.

The blood was pooling under him. It was bleeding too much.

If Sarah had stitched her, Faith could stitch Jaap. Someone had to, and fast. The fabric of his breeches stuck to the wound.

No time to think. She unbuttoned his breeches and yanked them down, out of the way.

Jaap grunted in pain. "Don't let my cock distract you. It's bigger than James's." He tried to laugh, but it came out more like a cry.

She ignored his dangling privates and inspected the gash.

It wasn't so much deep as wide. The bone had kept whatever blade had done this from severing anything beyond repair.

What had Sarah done?

She had tied off each stitch individually.

Just do it.

She jabbed the needle into Jaap's flesh on one side of the gash, and he groaned. "Sorry."

"Stitch. Please."

She slid the needle across the open chasm that should not have existed and up through the flesh on the other side.

She pulled the thread tight and knotted it off.

She had no scissors to cut it.

"Where is your knife?" she asked Jaap.

"In"—he gasped for breath—"one of the bad guys." He gasped again.

No knife. She bent over and put her mouth next to his skin and bit the thread until it broke.

"Don't let," he sucked in a breath, "James see you get your mouth so close...." His voice trailed off.

Her heart broke. He was trying to make her laugh when he could barely remain conscious.

She had to go faster. She jabbed the needle in again, then across, then out the other side. Knot. Bite. Jab. Stitch. Knot. Bite. She was going to run out of thread if she wasn't careful.

She pulled each stitch tighter and bit each knot closer, using as little thread as she could.

His blood coated her hands to her wrists, and she could feel some of it caking on her cheek.

She bit off the next knot. Just a few more to go.

Jaap's breath was ragged, and he made no more effort to talk. That scared her more than anything. Jaap not wisecracking, was a very injured Jaap, indeed.

But the blood wasn't oozing out of the gash nearly as fast. She looked at her handiwork. It was about as even and tidy as her needlework samplers as a child had been, which was to say it was an ugly mess. But it was working.

This was what Sarah did. Sarah could teach her to do it better so she could help people, too. It was the first time a needle in her hand had ever felt productive.

Jaap was barely conscious now.

She reached down and yanked the points of her neckerchief from her gown's neckline and pulled it from her shoulders.

"Almost done." That was entirely for her own benefit, because Jaap was beyond sense.

She wrapped the delicately embroidered fabric around him, heaving his body up to tuck it under his hip. When she had the entire length of the gash covered, she tied off the ends.

James and the others were suddenly next to her.

"Help me do up his breeches to keep the bandage in place."

James lifted Jaap's hips, and David slid his breeches up and buttoned them. Leo smoothed his hand over his cousin's cheek.

"They've retreated for now, but they will be back," said James.

Leo stood and undid his blanket from his tumpline, and tossed the blanket to Okwaho. Then he heaved Jaap up on his back, and James slid the tumpline around Jaap's backside to make a kind of seat, and then wrapped the band around Leo's forehead. Leo grabbed Jaap's legs, and they all began trotting fast, back toward the south.

Jaap bounced slightly with each step, his muscles limp.

Chapter 49

David stopped for a moment in front of James. "What about the French captain?"

"Shit." James turned to Faith. "What does he know?" Her face was pale, but her jaw had a determined set to it.

"Nothing. I played dumb and delayed until you showed up."

"But he knows the French plans, presumably," said David.

James looked back the way they had come, and then at Jaap, limp on Leo's back as they receded through the trees. "No time. We need to get Jaap to a surgeon."

The men exchanged glances.

"Go," James ordered.

They all began hustling through the woods, trying to take a different route than the way they had come to avoid being easily ambushed if the Abenaki managed to get ahead of them. The French captain would tell them they were slowed by a wounded man.

That damn Frenchman. Bringing him to camp would have been a coup for James, or at least might have saved his hide from Johnson. And they all knew it.

They knew he was blowing his chance to make up for his rash decision to take Faith with them instead of handing her off to Lydius.

But getting Jaap back was more important. If Faith hadn't been with them, Jaap might already be gone.

They jogged as fast as they could. In another mile or so, he would have to take a turn carrying Jaap. He ducked under a branch. The less trail they left, the better.

Just ahead of him, Faith was stepping over a downed branch, careful not to jostle it. She had caught on quickly. And she was keeping up, which was going to take its toll on her. And Sarah would skin him alive for his stupidity in getting her into this situation. But that was a price he would willingly pay if he could get her back out.

Okwaho dropped back, scanning to their rear.

"Any sign of them?" James asked.

Okwaho shook his head. "But Jaap looks pale and Faith is pushing herself past exhaustion."

They were all pushing past what they were fit for, and they all needed food and water.

"You and Leo push forward with Jaap. Send me David back and we will stay with Faith. Carry her if need be."

Okwaho motioned David over and took off after Leo.

Faith was right next to him. "I do not need to be carried, and I will not slow us down." Faith's eyes were wild. "We stay with Jaap." She turned and followed Okwaho.

David looked at him, shrugged and picked up his run after Faith and the others.

Sweet Mary, mother of God.

James started running again, keeping a careful eye on Faith's gait, looking for a stumble or limp that would mean he would have to force the issue.

He could hear her labored breathing ahead of him, but she kept pushing forward.

She ran through the underbrush, and he watched for any signs of ambush. She stumbled over a rock, but caught herself and kept going.

James glanced back at David, who kept a constant check for signs of pursuit.

He turned back to see Faith's skirts snag on a bush. She kept going, but it pulled her a little off balance, and as she started to catch herself and yank the fabric free, he saw it.

A copperhead, just in front of her.

He launched himself at her and tackled her before she could plant her foot. He pinned her beneath him, and the snake rattled its tail and lunged for him instead. He shot his hand out and grabbed the snake a few inches behind its head and held on for dear, sweet life.

David's hatchet came down and cleaved the snake in two, and the half he held went limp in his hand.

James shook from the crown of his head to his clenched toes. His heart might explode out through his throat. It had almost gotten her. His brain ran through about five rosaries, but his mouth couldn't form the words.

David dropped his hatchet and pried James's hand open, and then tossed the dead fiend aside.

James lay on top of Faith, unable to make himself move. "Are you all right?" He had rescued her from the clutches of the raiding party and then almost lost her to a godforsaken snake, of all the infernal things.

The warmth of her body underneath his was the only thing he could focus on. She was safe. She was breathing. She was very much alive.

"I'm fine. Did its fang scratch your skin?"

He shook his head.

"Thank God," she said. Then she pushed him aside, scrambled to her feet, and hauled him up after her.

David still stared at him, wide-eyed. Then Faith gave his arm a tug and started running again, trying to catch up to Leo and Okwaho.

He and David sprinted after her. At least one of them had kept her head enough to remember that there was still an angry group of men after them, bent on revenge.

He was not going to lose her now.

She plunged on ahead of them.

They crossed the creek. That meant they were getting close to the camp. Lord only knew how many miles they had covered.

Once they got to the road, they still had to get at least to Schenectady before they could get transport to Albany to get Jaap seen to. And if the Abenaki were still after them, they would still have plenty of opportunities to ambush them.

Damn that blasted French officer.

A sharp whistle cut through the woods. Then a quick trill. Okwaho answered the call, since Leo was too winded from running with Jaap on his back. It was the call they had taught Dieter and Ben.

They all pressed harder. Even Faith somehow picked up her pace, sensing safety ahead. Another call, and they shifted their track slightly to the east.

Then around a tree, and they were facing the muzzle of Ben's musket. "Schenectady."

"Koekje," Leo gasped.

Dieter stood behind Ben. "What happened to Jaap?"

"Knife wound to his hip," James said. "Faith sewed him up, but he needs a surgeon. Badly."

James caught his breath as Dieter went to Leo and motioned him to set Jaap down. Leo started to shake his head, but he was spent, and carefully set Jaap down.

Dieter hiked Jaap up on his back like he was a mere pack, and they started back toward the camp. Ben joined James, covering their rear. They reached the remains of their campsite. Faith followed Dieter, keeping a close watch on Jaap. James spotted Faith's satchel with her books, among the other things they had left behind, and grabbed it. It was foolish, but they meant something to her.

They made their way out to the road. Dieter's wagon was there. Thank God.

"What did you do with the muskets?" If they did something stupid, his career was truly over before it had rightly started.

"They are safely in Jaap and Leo's oma's root cellar." Ben said. "Now I understand the countersign."

James chuffed out a little laugh. There was hope for the gunsmith from Manhattan.

Dieter carefully lay Jaap in the back of the wagon, and then lifted Faith in.

She bent over Jaap, checking for fever setting in and making sure his pulse was still strong. She smoothed his hair back from his face. James's heart swelled with gratitude.

"I borrowed fresh horses, and we don't have the crates anymore," Dieter said. "Everyone in."

James wanted to put out flankers, but it was getting dark and they needed speed. They were all too tired not to slow them down. He gestured for everyone to jump in, then turned to Dieter. "Go."

Dieter eased the horses into motion and urged them to a trot. This part of the road was smooth enough they could keep up a steady gait once the wagon was under way.

"David, Leo. You two watch the back corners."

They shifted around in the wagon until David and Leo were positioned at the back corners, looking outward for signs of pursuit.

"Ben, Okwaho, take the front corners."

They got themselves positioned, and his shoulders relaxed by a small fraction.

At the speed the horses could travel, they should be able to outrun the Abenaki party and the French captain, as long as their pursuers didn't anticipate which way they would go, and cut the angle. If they did get ahead of the wagon, they could pretty easily take out the horses, but James's little band would still have the wagon for a makeshift breastwork to shelter behind, so it wouldn't be prudent for the French and the Abenaki to attack them. Of course, pissed-off men intent on revenge weren't always prudent.

He scanned the woods to the north, but couldn't really see anything. If they had recaptured the captain, they would have a better sense of what was out there in the shifting shadows.

Behind him, Jaap groaned. That was good. Faith murmured soothing nonsense to him. She might not have Sarah's skills, but she kept a cool head and hadn't once panicked or backed away from the harsh realities of fighting in the woods. She was astounding, and his heart ached thinking about how scared she must have been.

The sky behind them gradually turned from rich purple to black. He turned and looked to the east for signs of Schenectady. It was dark. No stars. No moon.

When had it clouded up? They had been going flat out since they got up this morning and the weather had hardly factored into his perception.

He had been almost blinded with panic when they took Faith. He would never have forgiven himself if they had not gotten her back. Then he had just thrown Jaap at her and prayed she could stitch him up, and she did. She had been a key part of their successful escape.

And she thought to delay the French by pretending she didn't understand them, forcing them to take time to translate. And she had left a trail for them to track, even at the expense of her own humiliation. She was worth ten of her father for this type of campaign.

Once they got Jaap to a surgeon, they would take her to the colonel and he would marry her off to his lieutenant. A boulder settled on his chest.

She would make an excellent officer's wife.

He turned and looked over his shoulder. "Is he getting feverish?"

She felt Jaap's forehead. "Not yet." Then she adjusted her skirt to make a pillow under his head to keep him more comfortable.

His heart hurt.

He wanted to keep her.

When he got on the ship from Dublin, he promised himself he would let nothing distract him from his course to make a career for himself in the empire.

He hadn't imagined someone like Faith could even exist.

The wagon bounced in a rut, and Jaap moaned.

"Give me your bedroll, James." Faith reached her hand out without even looking up. Her focus was entirely on Jaap. He untied his tumpline and handed her the blanket. She tucked one end of it under Jaap's head and wrapped the rest around behind him so he wouldn't roll every time the wagon lurched.

Her father needed her. She had been trying to get back to Albany since the moment she woke up after her fall in order to help him.

He had to let her go.

Everything was dark now. So dark. His chest ached and felt hollow at the same time.

He sat and listened to the road roll past under their wheels.

Then the horses rounded a bend, and the first lights of Schenectady came into view. Civilization, such as it was.

Then he wanted the dark back.

Dieter slowed the horses as they approached the gate in the stockade.

They made a few turns and came to a stop before Oma Ten Eyck's small house. The men all jumped out of the wagon, and he dropped the tailgate. Faith held Jaap's head as Leo and David slid him off the back and carried him to the house.

Faith held Jaap's hand as they carried him in the front door, then she closed it behind them.

Chapter 50

Faith knelt and placed her hand over Jaap's warm forehead as he lay on a pile of soft blankets on the floor of his grandmother's tidy front room. The woman had insisted Faith call her Oma when they were introduced.

Oma pulled a worn, but elegant, silk cushion off of a chair and tucked it under Jaap's sweaty head, and then she caressed his cheek. Faith sat back on her sore heels to give her space.

Oma bent over and kissed Jaap's forehead. Then she looked at Faith. "Thank you for taking good care of my wild boy." She gave Faith a warm smile, stood up with surprising ease for someone her age, and retreated to her bedchamber for the night.

Leo followed her, carrying a lantern, doting on her as she doted on him. On all of them.

David and Okwaho were clearly comfortable in her house, and tossed their blankets down and stretched out on the floor. Dieter and Ben watched the cousins and followed suit. Oma Ten Eyck had already declared them part of the family when they carried Jaap in.

James came up behind Faith and spoke softly. "Why don't you rest?" He pointed to a comfortable-looking chair.

The smudges under his eyes looked even darker in the lamplight. He had slept maybe six hours total over the last two nights and had covered more miles on foot in the past three days than she could in a month.

"Johnson is going to be angry with you, isn't he?"

Johnson was his patron, and that relationship was in jeopardy because of her. And she couldn't undo that.

He gave her a weary smile and brushed his hand against her cheek. "At least you were able to find out that the French know our plans."

"That isn't much," she said.

He cupped her face in both hands. "We won't be bumbling along thinking they won't be prepared for us. That will save more lives than you can imagine. If we hadn't known, both campaigns could have been easily ambushed time and again along the march." He wavered a little on his feet. He was going to drop from exhaustion.

She grabbed his blanket and laid it out on the floor next to Jaap. Then she took James's arm and tugged until he finally consented to sit down on the makeshift bed she had made for him.

She pulled his moccasins off his feet and gently lay him down on his side.

He didn't resist. His eyes fell shut, and within a few breaths, he was snoring along with David and Okwaho.

She smoothed a loose lock of his hair off his cheek and brushed her lips over his. Lord, how she loved this man.

When the French had taken her, she had feared she might die, but she had never been more aware of being alive. She had fought back, and she had stayed alive and created a trail for James and the others to follow. She might not have been as useful as Sarah, but James said the information she got from the French was valuable. It made her feel valuable. So had stitching up Jaap.

And James had dropped Jaap at her feet and simply trusted that she could help as he went back to fight.

Tears gathered in the corners of her eyes. He hadn't questioned her ability, or over-explained what to do. He just...trusted her.

She wiped her nose with the back of her hand and winced. It would be sore for a while, but it didn't seem to be broken.

Leo came back into the sitting room, and she forced a smile.

"You must be exhausted. I'll watch Jaap," he said, his own voice gravelly with lack of sleep.

"Please, Leo, let me do it." She swiped at her nose again. "You all need sleep more than I do. You won't be able to rest for an instant once we reach Albany."

And she would have little else to do.

He nodded, then lay his hand lightly on Jaap's shoulder, the gold of his signet ring glinting in the light. "Thank you."

Then he stood and went to an unoccupied stretch of floor, laid out his own bedroll, and passed out.

She looked around the room at the sleeping men who had all risked themselves to rescue her. They had come for her as if she had been one of their own.

The least she could do was take her turn and watch over them tonight.

She didn't have Sarah's knowledge or skills. Maybe the women in Albany could teach her after everyone else had gone off on campaign.

She turned and gazed at James's sleeping face. He looked younger asleep, and she could imagine him as a ten-year-old boy. Her heart hurt for him.

How terrifying to be ten years old and have to sell himself to keep his family from starving?

She stroked his hair.

No wonder he wanted to make a name and place for himself. To not have to rely on Johnson for a roof over his head for the rest of his days. To earn a shred of comfort and stability that didn't depend on another man's whims.

She didn't care that James had nothing.

But he did.

She reached for his satchel to move it so it wouldn't be in his way if he got up in the dark. It was as heavy as hers. It *was* hers.

Her throat tightened. Jaap had been in such a state that she hadn't even thought to look for their things when they passed through their campsite. But he had, and the one thing he had grabbed was her books.

Her books were the least useful thing they had with them, and she was silly for having brought them from the wagon when they camped.

But exhausted as he was, he made sure she got them back. He could barely read, but he knew they were important to her, so he grabbed them instead of his own clothing. Clothing he probably couldn't afford to replace.

She reached for the lamp and lowered its wick so it barely glowed. Tears filled her eyes, and since everyone else was asleep, she just let them flow.

Chapter 51

James was bone-weary as he climbed the steps to Johnson's Albany house. He was about to find out just how angry Johnson was.

He quietly entered the front hall.

Jaap was on the floor in the front room, and Sarah was unbuttoning his breeches. His face was red, but it was likely from fever. Jaap didn't embarrass easily.

"I hadn't planned for such an audience," Jaap heaved a breath, "when I finally convinced you to get in my breeches."

"Shut up and roll to your side," Sarah said.

Johnson and his wife watched from the far end of the room. James stayed out of Johnson's direct line of sight. The others stood closer, ready to help. Good thing Sarah had arrived in Albany just before them. She hadn't taken as many detours as they had. Jaap was in better hands with her than with any of the doctors.

They all watched as she peeled Jaap's breeches down to reveal the makeshift bandage Faith had improvised.

David snorted. "Embroidered drawers suit you."

Jaap made a rude gesture, but he was already tiring. At least he was conscious. James stood behind Ben as Sarah began unwrapping the bandage.

Jaap sucked in air as the last layer of fabric peeled away from his skin.

Ben turned to James. "Shouldn't we get a surgeon?"

Sarah's jaw clenched, but she said nothing. Her dark skin got a reddish tinge, and she threw the bandage behind her without looking and hit Ben right in the crotch.

Then she bent over to inspect Faith's work. She motioned to Faith to join her on the floor.

James wanted to throw a napkin over Jaap's privates. Faith didn't need such an up close and personal view when they had the luxury of no one shooting at them.

"This section looks good." Sarah pointed to one end of the row of stitches, then she pointed at the other end of the row. "These are too tight."

Faith nodded. "I was running out of thread. Would it have been better to leave bigger gaps?"

He wanted to jump in and tell Sarah Faith didn't exactly have time to practice before he dumped Jaap in her lap, and to lay off her. But Faith didn't take it as criticism or get defensive.

Sarah puzzled over Jaap's hip. "If the bleeding is under control, yes, but if not, you might have needed to do just what you did."

Faith leaned over and inspected her work. "The stitches aren't very even, are they?"

"Were they still fighting?"

"Yes."

"Then they are as even as anyone could ask for." Sarah gave her a smile. "Slowing down to do pretty stitch work can get people dead." Sarah cleaned the caked blood from around the wound. The skin was an ugly red, but at least it didn't stink. That was a good sign.

Faith took a cloth and bathed Jaap's forehead with cool water to ease the heat of his fever.

"How long until he can march and fight?" Johnson asked. It was the first thing he had said since James entered the house.

"Give him a few weeks, and he will be ready to get shot at again. Or knifed, like this." She gestured to the wound he already had. "I am sure the line of volunteers to have at him will be long."

Johnson turned on James. His face was stern, like James had never seen it. James stood straighter and lifted his chin.

"If you had obeyed my orders and sent Lydius to take her, this would not have happened. Instead, you let him spend more time recruiting around Canajoharie, and now the Mohawks are only sending a handful of warriors and the western nations are sending hardly any at all. They think we don't have our house in order."

Which they clearly did not, if Shirley was telling the Mohawks that he could take away Johnson's command and position as Indian Commissioner at any time.

"Sir, even if Lydius didn't...hurt her, the French would have gotten her. One man couldn't have kept her from being abducted and carted off to New France."

Johnson's face colored, and James braced to get his head chewed off. Johnson didn't like his men to talk back to him.

"That would have been Lydius' problem to solve."

James's pulse throbbed in his temples, and he fought to keep his hands from balling into fists. "It would have been a serious problem for her, sir."

Faith searched his face. His cheeks burned. Everyone else could leave the room now, not that they would, if he was going to make a spectacle of himself.

"We don't need her. Her father does, which means Shirley does, too, and now you have delivered her to them," Johnson said.

"That's bullshit, sir."

The room went silent.

Faith's mouth dropped open. How dare Johnson say that right in front of her?

Johnson swept across the room and didn't stop until he was inches from James's face. "I trusted you, of all people, to stay focused on the job at hand."

"I did. We got her back." James could feel Johnson's breath on his skin.

"You were led by your cock, and you let one of my men get injured as a result."

Jaap spoke from the floor. "Sir—"

"Quiet," said Johnson, his eyes only glancing at Jaap before they returned to James's face. "And did you bring us a French hostage we could interrogate for intelligence?"

James swallowed again. Faith and Jaap had been more important.

"No." James kept looking Johnson squarely in the eye. If Johnson cut him loose, he would be alone in the world again. No hope of the means to support himself, let alone a family.

Faith cleared her throat. "We discovered they know about both the campaign to Fort Niagara and the campaign to Crown Point." She paused. "And they said that Braddock is dead."

Gratitude washed over James, and he could almost breathe for a moment.

Johnson cut his gaze to her, and then back to James. "We haven't heard any news of Braddock. We didn't need to lose a man for their misdirection."

Faith's face fell, and that sent a stabbing pain through his chest.

"We didn't lose a man, and the French know our plans, and we only know that because of Faith." She had been clever and brave to get that information, and it could save Johnson's campaign and the lives of God only knew how many men. "They know where we are headed. They know exactly which routes and forts to defend. Faith found that out. And she was clever enough to not let them know she understood them, so they don't know we can adapt our strategy based on what she learned."

Everyone's eyes were on him, and his stomach threatened to empty itself on the floor. He had already disobeyed and infuriated his patron. But he would not let Johnson send her away to her father with her thinking she had been anything but brilliant out there. Or thinking he regretted bringing her with them. Or anything about her at all.

Oh God, he couldn't let her go.

He had to, but he couldn't.

His vision got a little blotchy around the edges. He started to tremble worse than when he had grabbed at the copperhead.

Her father needed her. But her father would never see her value. Her courage. He would never see *her*. And she deserved better. And if she were married, her father would no longer have any legal sway over her. He could at least offer.

James said, "Faith, you were worth ten men out there. We need you."

His lungs wouldn't quite fill sufficiently, and his head got a little light.

She quickly glanced around the room, and no doubt saw everyone watching with inappropriate interest. But he couldn't tear his own eyes from her to confirm that. If he didn't say what he needed to say right now, he might pass out.

"Faith, I have nothing to offer, but *I* need you."

Chapter 52

"Faith!" her father bellowed from the hallway, his voice bouncing off the walls like a cannon shot. He barged into the room with Caleb trailing behind him.

Her head was spinning.

James just announced in front of Johnson and everyone that he needed her, and now her father was here?

She wanted to scream at them all.

She needed space to gather her wits. She looked at James. He stood like a stone pillar, glaring at her father.

"You have been absent far too long," her father said, bearing down on her. Sarah discreetly pulled her skirt over Jaap's exposed haunch, thank goodness. "I left you in the care of Mr. Johnson, and then I hear you were abducted by the French and their allies." He turned on Johnson. "Is this the care you took of my daughter?"

Johnson raised an eyebrow at her father. "The daughter you abandoned when she was injured?" He gestured to her. "She has healed well in my care, as you can see. And you may address me as *General* Johnson."

"Father. I'm here and I'm fine." She forced a smile at Johnson. "And I thank you, General Johnson, for the excellent care you and your people took of me."

She wanted Johnson and her father to go away. She wanted to go to James and ask what exactly he meant. He said he had nothing to offer. What did he mean?

Her father gestured at Jaap on the floor. "Why is there a half-clad man in the room in front of my daughter?"

James turned on him. "Sir, Faith stitched up Jaap's wound and probably saved his life." Again, he defended her at the risk of his career. He sacrificed too much. For her.

Her heart pounded so hard her entire body throbbed. She opened her mouth to speak, but her father cut her off.

"She has no business sewing up people. She never even mastered embroidery."

Her face grew hot. No matter what she did, she always fell short in his eyes.

James stepped up right in front of him. "She did a damn fine job sewing him up, and even Sarah has said she did exactly right." Then he turned to her. "Faith, don't listen to him."

Her father huffed, probably astonished that James would talk to him like that. But everyone who had been out in the woods, and Sarah, were nodding at what James said. Her heart swelled so large she could barely breathe around it.

They thought she had done well. James had risked his career to stand up for her. Again.

She turned to her father. "Stitching an injury has far greater utility and is significantly more helpful in an emergency." He should be proud of her, not insulting her. Jaap was a soldier, for heaven's sake.

Caleb looked from one of them to the other and then to the door and probably wanted to be anywhere else. He no doubt thought she wasn't worth this trouble.

"You need to do your duty to your family," her father said, his voice acidic.

Duty was all that mattered. Not her. But, dammit, she should matter to him. Her eyes stung, and her throat got tight. "I was doing my duty helping one of the king's soldiers stay alive to continue to fight. You need to do *your* duty and stop mortgaging my future on land you can't manage."

Her father's face turned stony. "How dare you lecture me on duty, girl?"

Girl? After all she had done taking care of his financial bungling, the only thing about her that still mattered to him was that she was born female? He couldn't even acknowledge that she was a full-grown woman? She felt like the air had been knocked out of her lungs.

After a silent moment, Mrs. Johnson said, "Sarah, perhaps it is time to get Jaap to a bed?"

"I can carry him." Dieter bent down and lifted Jaap like he was a rag doll, and Sarah removed her shawl and tossed it over Jaap's exposed flesh.

"This way." Mrs. Johnson led them from the room, and their parade of feet creaked up the stairs to the second floor.

The air in the room grew brittle. Jaap being there had somehow kept everyone at least slightly in check, since it would hardly seem decent to brawl directly over a wounded man's body. But now he was gone, as were the other two women.

James looked ready to take a swing at her father, and her father looked ready to egg him on. Johnson looked ready to let them go at each other. Caleb still looked like he wanted to crawl under the nearest piece of furniture.

She wanted to scream like an angry banshee. But she wouldn't. She, at least, could act like a civilized human being. "Please, everyone, sit. I am sure Mrs. Johnson will send some tea in as soon as she sees Jaap settled."

Johnson sat, and then her father. Slowly, everyone else's backsides found seats.

"Because *I* understand these things far better than you could," her father said, "or your mother in her day, despite her meddling, I have just purchased another parcel of land to secure your future. So you and Caleb must marry before we leave, in case of any unfortunate incidents."

"You did what?"

Caleb blanched. Had it only now occurred to him that a soldier could meet an unfortunate end during a war? Or was it that he realized he really was about to be stuck with her?

"I am sure a wedding won't delay the Niagara campaign too much," Johnson said. "Felicitations."

How dare her father speak of her—and her mother—that way? "Enough." Faith jumped to her feet and glared at her father. "I am not collateral on your loans so that you can overextend yourself. It is not my duty to free you from having to exercise a little bit of sense." She loomed over her him now. "I am not chattel!"

James stood and faced Johnson. "She is not a pawn in everyone else's war preparation and..." he waved his hand around in the air like he was searching for a word. "Gamesmanship."

Faith's mind whirled. He was going to get himself sacked and lose everything he had worked for. Standing up for her.

Her father gaped, open-mouthed. Looking from her to James.

"Father," Faith said, "I will not marry Caleb." The room swayed. He would disown her now, but she would not do his will for one moment longer. She would join Sarah and support herself by taking care of the army, if she had to. Sarah would teach her what she needed to know.

James still stood in the middle of the room, and he turned to her. "I...I have nothing to offer but poverty and more of what you just went through over that last two days. I would understand if you don't want any of that. But if you will have me, I will give you all I do have and lay down my life to protect you. I love you." He swallowed visibly and looked a little unsteady on his feet. "Please, marry me."

Faith's heart squeezed so tight she couldn't breathe. A few tears escaped and trickled their way down her cheek. He just stood there, face pale and heart hanging out for all to see. His hands trembled at his sides, and she wanted to reach out and caress him. Hold him.

She did have a duty here, and it was to protect the heart that James had just laid bare. The man who actually valued her.

The man she loved.

She took a deep breath, and her lungs quivered with the effort. She turned to her father. "Yes, a wedding before everyone marches out is exactly what is called for." She turned back to James and gazed into his beautiful eyes. "I accept James's offer."

James blinked, like he didn't quite trust his ears.

Her father's arm twitched as if he wanted to whip her like a mutinous soldier. "Are you with child by this Irish bastard?"

Her face burned. How could her father refer to James that way?

James stepped between them, like he could shield her from her father's words. "She most certainly is not, sir. What do you take her for?"

She was done with her father's abuse. "I will thank you not to refer to my future husband with such rude language. Ever."

James turned his face to look at her, brows raised, like she had caught him by surprise. Like he wasn't used to people standing up for him.

Her father's face was now a dangerous shade of red. "If this randy bog-trotter wasn't all over you like a rutting bull before now, it was only because he didn't want to be saddled with a woman who can't even darn a sock. And now his nether organs have overruled what little judgment he has." Then he turned on Johnson. "Is this the care you bloody Irish take of young women left in your household?"

General Johnson unfolded himself and stood to his full height. He towered over everyone since Dieter hadn't yet returned. "You may go now." He gestured to the door.

Her father only came up to Johnson's nose. That didn't stop him from tipping his head back so he could look down his own nose at Johnson.

Then he turned and left without a word.

Caleb stood and scuttled after him.

Faith swayed on her feet, and James wrapped an arm around her and pulled her in tight to his side, the heat of his body comforting her and giving her strength.

Johnson's brows lowered and his lips were pressed into a firm line as he stared at James. "You disobeyed my orders, let Shirley get the jump on us, risked our entire store of weapons, and got one of my men sliced open so you could go a'courting?"

Oh, no. He was going to sack James.

James just held her close to him and stared back at Johnson. "I recruited my full quota of men for the ranger company, sir, rescued the woman who helped tirelessly during the conference and who was under your protection, and with her help, I brought everyone back alive. And you now have all the information she got from the French." Then he looked pointedly down at her, and then back at Johnson. "I imagine you have something to say to Faith."

They stared at each other, neither speaking. She didn't dare breathe.

Then Johnson finally looked at her and gave her half a smile. "Thank you for stitching up Jaap, and for the intelligence you gathered. If we did not know our plans were no longer a surprise, it might have been catastrophic. Hopefully, they were lying about Braddock." He gave her a nod and left the room.

James pulled her against his body and held her. She pressed herself against him and wrapped her arms around him as tightly as she could. She had no idea what lay ahead of them, but nothing had ever felt so right in her life as being here in his embrace. His chest pressed against her with each breath. Her heart picked up the rhythm of his.

Chapter 53

The next evening, the chaplain attached to one of the New York militia regiments stood by the tavern's head table. Faith fussed with the stems of the daisies Sarah had grabbed from someone's dooryard right before the minster arrived. Her father hadn't spoken to her since she had agreed to marry James.

She wore her tattered gown, since Sarah hadn't had a chance to mend it, though she promised to do that before they left Albany tomorrow. Johnson would stand no further delays. If they were doing this, it was today.

Faith would travel with Sarah to learn more nursing skills and support Johnson's column, so she wasn't being left behind.

She turned her eyes to James, and her heart tripped. He looked eager and nauseated by turns. Most importantly, his eyes never left hers.

"Let's gather 'round and begin. I've got two more couples to marry this evening," the chaplain said from the front of the room.

They were marching off on a campaign against the French tomorrow, but she refused to let that rob her of the joy of this moment. All of their friends were crowded into the tavern, along with most of the rangers James had recruited along the way.

Sarah stood next to her and gave her a smile.

David stood on the far side of James, keeping a careful eye on him, and appeared ready to hold him up if he fainted. The men apparently had placed wagers.

She stroked James's hand, and he clutched hers so hard it almost hurt. Then his eyes glistened like glass.

He leaned in. "You know this means a life full of the sort of danger you just went through, right?" He smiled. "Last chance to back out and spend your life in the luxury you were intended for." He could joke about it now that she had finally convinced him he was everything she wanted.

"And die of boredom? I think not." She squeezed his hand, and her heart squeezed even harder. This man. He taught her her own value. What it meant to really live. Danger be damned.

He leaned in again and whispered in her ear. "I know I said it yesterday, but I love you." His cheeks grew a little pink.

She wasn't any more used to hearing that than he apparently was to saying it. But she was more than ready to get used to it. "You are the first, last, and only man I have ever loved."

He started to lean toward her again, then the minister tapped his Bible on the table like a magistrate with his gavel. "Dearly beloved," he said in a loud voice, cutting through the chatter and drawing everyone's attention to them. "We are gathered here to witness the marriage of Captain James Carroll and Miss Faith Richmond."

She grinned up at him. All those stops on the way had paid off. He had recruited his company, and angry though Johnson was with him, he had been good to his word and appointed him captain.

James had let her help him practice his signature last night, and he had signed the papers this morning.

The minster looked around. "If anyone has objections, speak now or forever hold your peace."

Johnson's voice boomed. "No one objects to anything but you dragging this out. Hurry up." He was angry with James, but he was here. That had to bode well for them.

The minister seemed to be in complete agreement with Johnson's urgency and looked over the crowd. "Who gives this woman in matrimony?"

Her heart gave a slow churn. No one did.

The room grew silent.

"I do," said Sarah.

"We do," chimed in David, Okwaho, and the others.

James squeezed her hand and looked around the room. A tear escaped the corner of his eye and he gave them a general nod.

Her own vision grew blurry. These people treated her with more care and consideration than her legal family ever had.

She sniffed. The minister had better get on with it before she started bawling.

"Do you, Faith, take James to be your lawfully wedded husband, to honor and obey, until death do you part?"

She gazed into James's eyes. "I do."

"And do you, James, take Faith to be your lawfully wedded wife, to honor and cherish, until death do you part?"

James stared deep into her soul. "I do." His voice rumbled low in her chest and the vibration made her whole body tingle.

"By the power vested in me by His Majesty, King George II, I now pronounce you man and wife." He snapped his Bible shut. "Go ahead and kiss her. I have to run."

James swept her into his arms. His lips crushed hers and one of his hands slid down and squeezed her backside.

She wrapped her arms around him and pulled him hard against her.

A whistle cut through the air, and Jaap—it could only be Jaap—let out a hoot from the chair where they had perched him. The entire tavern broke into applause.

James teased her lips with his tongue. A barrage of fireworks went off in her chest, and the sparkling trails quickly descended through her body, lighting up everything they touched and pooling heat as they settled between her legs. She pulled him tighter against herself.

"Save it for just a half hour so we can all eat," Sarah said, laughing as she spoke. "I'm famished."

James pulled his lips just slightly from Faith's, the tip of his nose resting against the tip of hers. "Don't forget where we left off."

An entire field of butterflies took flight in her lower belly. He was hers. "Let's eat fast, shall we?"

James gave a full-bodied laugh—the first she had heard him let loose since they were attacked. His whole body vibrated against hers. She grinned. After the horror of the woods, she was ready to grab life with both hands.

"Health and happiness to the newlyweds." Dieter raised a pint of ale.

"To the newlyweds!" said Leo, raising his pint.

Everyone joined in the general toasting.

Sarah pulled Faith out of James's arms. "You can have her back in a bit, but she needs to eat."

James loosened his grip enough to let her sit, even though his hand still rested on her shoulder.

David came up behind. "She needs her strength."

Faith's face lit on fire. But David had a point. Which made her face burn even hotter.

David laughed. "I trust you understand your duties to your wife, Captain?"

James smacked his arm. "Your turn will come, you pest."

"Not for a long time, my friend. I have other plans."

James looked right into Faith's eyes. "So did I."

Her heart slammed against her ribs. He was going to make her cry again. "Come, sit." She patted the chair next to her.

He sat, and she leaned against him, taking strength from the warmth of his body. Letting herself feel appreciated. Cared for.

The tavern keeper's wife swept up to the table with a giant tray of food. "Here you go, my loves." She set down a trencher of roasted meat for them to share. "Eat hearty." She gave them a big smile and waggled her eyebrows at them.

A laugh burbled up out of Faith's chest. Everyone knew what came next, so there was no point pretending otherwise.

Her eyes closed, and she imagined being joined so closely with him. Not sneaking off to be with him in the woods where no one would know, but legally, fully with him.

"Are you thinking about what I am thinking about?" he whispered in her ear.

She was growing damp between her legs. "Well, I can't very well read minds, so how would I know?"

He leaned in so his breath was tickling her ear. "I am thinking about laying you out on a proper bed—"

"Yes. Eat faster, for goodness' sake."

He laughed and shoved some food into his mouth. A little of the juice from the meat dribbled down his chin. Her eyes latched onto it, and licking it off him seemed like a splendid idea.

Then Jaap waved at her, gesturing her over to him. She glanced back at James, then gave him a quick kiss on the cheek and went to Jaap.

"Thank you, Faith." He glanced down at his feet. "Sarah says you probably saved my life."

Jaap looking contrite was downright unsettling. She reached her hand to his arm. "I hear you will go back and mend at your grandmother's, then join everyone in a few weeks."

He shrugged. "Oma's baking is medicinal. I'll be there in half the time."

"You will follow orders to recover." Sarah gave him a glare.

Jaap crossed his eyes at her, then turned to James, who had come up behind her. "You know you can't fight without me." And then he went back to eating.

Faith laughed, and James looked like he might be about to spit out a quick retort. She pulled him back to their seats and whispered in his ear. "He's feverish. Leave the delusional man be."

His face relaxed, and his eyes grew warm.

The tavern keeper came over, a full tray in his hands. "Compliments of the house." He placed a mug of ale in front of each of them, then bustled off.

She picked up the mug and started to raise it to her lips. Then James raised his and clinked it against hers. "To us."

A lump rose in her throat. She nodded to him, not trusting her voice, and then took a long drink of her ale.

He did the same.

Her heart could barely contain her love for him.

The tavern keeper's wife bustled out with a covered platter, interrupting her reverie. Leo followed, carrying plates. "Luckily, I baked this cake this morning. I must have had a premonition." She beamed at them, then turned to Leo. "You are a dear. Set those down on the table."

Leo set down the plates, and the tavern mistress began cutting the cake. First, she served Faith and James, then she started filling the other plates, and Leo began handing them around.

"Awfully domestic for a trapper," James said around a bite of cake. "He must be hoping if he helps, we won't ask him to pay the tab."

"Nonsense," said the tavern keeper's wife. "The dear man already paid for everything." Then she gave them each a motherly pat on the shoulder. "Including our best room for you for the night." She then went back to work.

Faith looked at Leo, still passing out plates of cake. He looked their way and gave them a smile and a nod. James nodded back and then pulled her close and fed her a little piece of cake.

She nibbled the tip of his finger.

His eyes flashed hot and with his free hand, he stuffed the rest of his slice in his mouth all at once.

She laughed.

James chewed quickly and swallowed a few times, then he stood. "I thank you all. I cherish you all. And I am now taking my wife and leaving you all for the evening."

He turned to her and lifted her right out of her chair as cheers filled the air.

Then he carried her to the stairs and up them.

His heart beat against her as she pressed herself to his chest. She tucked her head under his chin, and her body hummed with anticipation.

Chapter 54

The warmth of her body in his arms permeated his being. She filled every empty crevice in his soul.

He reached the top of the stairs. Theirs was the first room on the left. The door to the small room stood open and someone had turned down the covers on the bed. No blanket in the woods. A proper bed.

He crossed the threshold and pushed the door closed with his foot. He refused to give up his hold on Faith.

She turned her face up to his and kissed his chin. Her lips were soft on his freshly shaved skin.

He bent his head down and brushed his lips over hers. "Hello, wife."

She grinned at him and kicked her feet to be put down.

He set her down gently, and her eyes danced with heat. "Captain Carroll, I have never gotten to see your entire body, and I would like to finally get a good look at what I have just come into possession of." She raised one saucy eyebrow at him, and then her fingers made short work of the ties at his collar. Then she grabbed the hem of his shirt and tugged it up over his head.

His elegant English wife was bold. But he already knew that. He raised his arms to assist, and his skin turned to gooseflesh despite the July heat. She pulled the sleeves free of his wrists and tossed the shirt aside, then she gazed at his naked chest. After a moment, her finger began to trace its contours, and she leaned in and pressed her lips gently to the dip at the base of his neck.

He wanted to wrap his arms around her and throw her on the bed, but he forced himself to stay still and let her explore.

Her fingers traced down to the waist of his breeches and undid their buttons. He kicked off his shoes, then stood still again.

She shoved his breeches down over his hips, and her breathing came faster.

His cock jutted out toward her, hard and ready, but still he let her lead.

She bent and pushed his breeches all the way down to his ankles. He stepped out of them.

She ran her hands up the sides of his legs, making his skin tingle. Her hands paused briefly at his waist, then brushed up his chest to his shoulders. Then she pulled his arms out away from his body. His stones tightened as she continued her inspection.

Her eyes burned trails over his skin, and he could feel everywhere they looked.

She raised her face to him. Then she lifted her right hand and gestured for him to turn around. She was going to be the death of him.

He turned so that his back was to her.

The heat of her eyes ran from his shoulders, down over his ass, and all the way to his calves, then back up. That absolutely was not his imagination.

He concentrated on slow, even breaths.

"Turn."

He turned back to face her.

"Thank you for letting me stare. I've never had the opportunity before." She looked down, and didn't meet his eyes.

He put his hand under his chin and raised her face to his. He kissed her. "You looking at me is very arousing." His cock twitched on cue. He kissed her again. "May I undress you now?"

He'd had his mouth on her breast and on her sweet center, but he had never seen her naked. He suddenly wanted that even more than he wanted to plunge himself inside her.

Her cheeks got rosy, and she nodded to him.

He pulled the borrowed neckerchief from her shoulders, then fumbled with the pins at the front of her gown and undid them with trembling fingers. He peeled the gown up over her head and tossed it aside. Then he untied her petticoat and pockets and let them drop into a pool of fabric at her feet.

She stepped out of them, and her breasts heaved against her stays. Women wore far too much clothing.

He undid the laces of her stays and pulled them from her body, letting her breasts loose and unfettered as nature intended.

"May I remove your shift?"

She gave a quick nod.

He gathered the fabric with his hands and then lifted it carefully up and over her head.

She stood before him, perfectly naked. Absolutely perfectly naked.

And she didn't try to cover herself. She met his gaze, despite the color in her cheeks that was spreading down her neck.

He kissed her. He wanted to have her twirl around so he could gaze on every inch of her delicious body, but his cock throbbed, and they had their entire lives ahead of them for that.

His hands traced her sides and up under her breasts, his eyes never leaving hers. Her heart pounded against his palm. Her heart. His heart.

He kissed her again. "Wife, may I have permission to take you to bed?"

Her face broke into a smile. "You may."

He sat her down on the bed, just behind her, and swung her feet around so she was lying in front of him.

He almost never got to sleep in a real bed, and he was so very glad they had access to this one on the occasion of him making her his wife for true and all.

His wife. Oh god, he had never let himself think of having a wife of his own. And if he had, he would never have had the imagination to think of her. She was beyond all imagining.

"Please don't make me wait." Her voice was breathy.

He knelt on the bed and kissed her knees. Then he crawled up her body, kissing as he went.

He nuzzled at the curls where her legs joined her body, and she gasped. He kissed her and spread her open with his thumbs, giving him better access. Was it only three nights ago when he had first kissed her here?

She squirmed under him and her hips pressed forward. He kissed her again and began to suck and lick at the nub between her legs, and his fingers teased her opening.

Her hips bucked, and he slid a finger inside and stroked her in rhythm to his sucking. She moaned, and he sucked harder. He thrust in a second finger to stretch her a little and she rocked against him. He sucked harder.

"Oh, James." She arched and pulsed around his finger. She panted and moaned, and he kept up his thrusts until her body subsided.

Then he withdrew his fingers and crawled the rest of the way up her body and kissed her lips.

She devoured him.

He positioned his cock at her entrance and began to nudge his way in while her body was still relaxed from coming apart in his mouth.

Her hips began pushing against his with each gentle rock, then he met resistance.

"Keep going. I'm ready."

"Are you sure?" He nuzzled under her ear as he kept gently rocking against her.

"Yes."

He pushed. Gently, steadily. She gave a little gasp, and he stopped.

"Don't stop."

He pushed again, and the resistance was gone. Her heat surrounded him and he began to sweat in earnest from the effort of staying still as her body adapted to his.

This time, she pushed. A groan ripped from his throat.

She began rocking against him, and his hips took the hint and he began thrusting into her, his balls bumping against her and sending tremors up and down his spine.

He rocked harder, and she clutched her arms around his back, urging him on.

She was perfect.

His hips drove hard, and he grunted with the effort. She was right there with him.

"Oh god, oh James." Her legs came up around his waist and she dug her heels into his ass. "James!"

Her body started pulsing around him, and with a final thrust of his hips, his balls convulsed and he shot his seed deep into her body, and the pulsing went on and on until his vision got spotty. Then he collapsed on top of her.

Her arms wrapped tight around him, pulling him so tight, he could feel her heart pounding beneath his. Her legs still held their hips tightly together. Nothing could pry their bodies apart.

"I love you so much, James."

How had such a perfect woman chosen him? "I love you beyond words."

They lay like that so long he lost track of time. When he tried to take some of his weight off her, she pulled him back. Anchored him with her limbs. She wouldn't let him go.

Since he left Ireland as a boy, he had never had a home. Until now.

Passion's Return

Want to read more in this series for $0.00? *Passion's Return* is an action-filled, six-chapter romance in the *Romance and the American Ranger* series, and it includes a cameo appearance by Faith.

It is my gift to you when you join my Readers' List with the QR code below. Be on the lookout for other bonus content, as well!

Be sure to check your spam folder if you don't see the confirmation email. The system requires that you reply to that before it will actually sign you up. That is to keep pranksters from signing you up for random things you were not expecting.

And thank you for considering leaving a review of *Passion's Duty* wherever you purchased it or on Goodreads. It makes all the difference in the world in helping readers find books they will love, and it means everything to authors. Even a quick star rating helps a lot. Thank you!

Author's Note

I have always been fascinated by wars that preceded and set up better known wars. This naturally brought me to the Seven Years' War, as it is known in academic circles and in Europe, or the French and Indian War as many Americans know it, or the Great War for Empire, as the American historian, Lawrence Henry Gipson, suggested it might best be called.

This is the war that set the conditions for the American Revolution. In one sense, it was yet another in a long string of wars between the British and French that was played out, in part, in their North American colonies. But for all that the war spread over much of the globe, it was started in North America, by North Americans, over North American issues, and unlike in the previous conflicts, the British government realized it would be won or lost in North America.

It started in 1754, when the Virginia Militia and the French army came to blows in the Ohio River country, as each side maneuvered to have the better claim to that fertile land (which already belonged to the Native American nations that occupied it), and it ended in 1763. Indeed, nine years, not seven. But the academics and Europeans count from when war was officially declared in 1756, rather than when the fighting started.

This novel takes place in that space between when the first shots were fired and when first the major campaigns of the war began in the summer of 1755, a year before war was declared. One of the critical preparations for the war was gathering Native American allies on both sides.

For the British, this meant William Johnson, an adopted member of the Mohawk people, being put in charge of all interactions with Native Americans in the northern half of the British North American colonies. Most important among them was the Iroquois Confederacy, of which the Mohawks are a part.

The conference held at Johnson's home happened, and the words Johnson and Red Head spoke to the assembled 1000+ attendees in the novel
are the actual words the real Peter Wraxall wrote down at a frantic pace as
the historic conference took place. And Johnson's rivalry with Shirley is
well-documented and escalated precipitously over the following year.

Johnson was notorious in his own day for being of an amorous nature
and fathering many children. The estimates at the time ranged all the way
to almost 1000, though those high-end estimates were made by his detrac-
tors. Even his supporters generally acknowledged he had more children
than anyone was certain of.

There is much debate over whether he ever married his first wife,
Catherine Weisenberg, in the church, or if she was merely his common-law
wife. He had many long-term relationships, most famously with Molly
Brant, a politically powerful Mohawk woman. And most of these women,
including Catherine, began their relationship as his housekeeper. Hence
Sarah's refusal to even consider the position.

There were, indeed, free Black families in the region, and one hypothesis
about where Johnson met his first wife is that she was a German indentured
servant belonging to one of the local Black families. Germans made up a
large percentage of the population of the Mohawk Valley at the time, and
that specific group is known to this day as Palatine Germans, due to the
circumstances of their arrival, though most were not from the Palatine region of what is now Germany. Dutch families were also still a large portion
of the population in New York, which was formerly a Dutch colony.

The easternmost Mohawks had been in constant proximity to Europeans, and the English in particular, for over a century, and many, including Molly Brant's family, were Anglican and lived in English style
houses, and often wore English style clothing in certain settings. Therefore
the fictitious character of David would likely have been baptized at Fort
Hunter. The chapel there was the westernmost Anglican church in the
British Empire for decades. David would also not have been out of place
as one of the well-connected Native Americans to be sent east to New
England for an education.

Indentured servitude was the way most Irishmen made their way to New
York (or anywhere else in the British Empire) in that era. And while Biblical
injunctions about not holding Christians to service longer than seven years
meant that adults entering indentured servitude usually did so for from

four to seven years, that did not apply to children. They served until they reached twenty-one, so if James entered servitude at ten, he would have served eleven years with no one thinking twice about it.

By the 1750s, indentured servants did not receive land when their indenture was up. Clothes, seed, and maybe some farming implements were most likely to be their freedom dues, and men like James would not have had any capital to buy a farm, and so would likely have sold the seed or implements to survive. He would barely have owned the clothes on his back, and wanting to rise up was not a case of ego or blind ambition, it was merely wanting to have stability that did not depend on another's will.

That said, it is critical to understand that while indentured servitude was often brutal, and many died during their period of indenture, it was nothing like slavery in its long-term impacts. Indentured servants had legal rights, including the right to sue their masters. Of those who survived their indentures, which were limited in time, many successfully used their period of servitude to improve their lot in life, as James did. The same can not in any way be said of slavery.

And while many modern readers might think Faith was too timid for agreeing to her father's demands, she had very little legal choice. The laws of coverture meant women were not independent legal entities unless they were widows, and even then they would become the legal responsibility of their oldest adult son or stepson, if they had one. They were legally "covered" by their father or husband. Everything she might have considered "hers" was legally her father's. Any land or other property she brought to a marriage as a dowry became legally her husband's.

The social restrictions were not much easier to circumvent. Class was almost a physical barrier, and while frontier women, like Sarah and Louisa, would have had far more freedom to choose their husband and the skills to support themselves, Faith would not have had either. Had she been cast out by her father, she could have run afoul of vagrancy laws, and been incarcerated because she lacked the financial means to provide for herself. Unless her father allowed it, Faith would have had far less say in her own life than James, though James would likely not have known that.

In case you are interested in digging into any of this history further, here are some of the key sources I used researching this book.

- Anderson, Fred. *A People's Army: Massachusetts soldiers & society in the Seven Years' War.* Chapel Hill, NC: University of North

Carolina Press, 1984.

- Anderson, Fred. *Crucible of War: the Seven Years' War and the fate of empire in British North America, 1754-1766*. New York: Vintage Books, 2001.

- O'Toole, Fintan. *White Savage: William Johnson and the invention of America*. Albany, NY: State University of New York Press, Albany, 2009.

- Suranyi, Anna. *Indentured Servitude: unfree labor and citizenship in the British colonies*. Montreal: McGill-Queen's University Press, 2021.

- OldFortJohnson.org This is the non-profit historical organization that has preserved the home that William Johnson lived in during the Seven Years' War as a historic site. The staff were exceptionally gracious when I toured the site and even took us up into the attics so I could see the layout first-hand. I highly recommend a visit if you are in the area!

- FortTiconderoga.org This is the non-profit historical organization that has rebuilt Fort Ticonderoga (it was blown up at least three times while it was in service) and preserved its history. I spent two glorious days there grilling the incredibly patient and helpful staff about weaponry and clothing. Another fabulous place to visit, and very dog-friendly, too!

About the Author

Lizzie Jenks is an award winning author whose first book, *Devil in Our Hearts*, was a finalist for the Romance Writers of America Diamond Heart Award.

In her twenties, she fell so hard for the Daniel Day-Lewis version of Last of the Mohicans that she never recovered. To take up residence in that time and place, she spent years in grad school studying history, and then, to dive more deeply into the period, she began writing steamy romances set in early America.

Gritty stories about strong women and the men who earn their love have taken over Lizzie's existence, and she wouldn't have it any other way. You too? Connect with Lizzie on social media or, better yet, join her email list at LizzieJenks.com/newsletter/—that is the easiest way to get in touch.

Instagram: @LizzieJenksWriter
Twitter/X: @LizzieJenksBook
Facebook: Lizzie Jenks Author

www.ingramcontent.com/pod-product-compliance
Lightning Source LLC
Chambersburg PA
CBHW021043310726
48969CB00006B/1783